Praise for the *Sa*

"A heartwarming, emo[tional] story that I couldn't re[sist]. [Take a] trip to Sanctuary Island! I guarantee you won't want to leave."   —Bella Andre, *New York Times* bestselling author of the Sullivan series

"Well written and emotionally satisfying. I loved it! A rare find."
   —Lori Wilde, *New York Times* bestselling author

"Fall in love with Sanctuary Island. Lily Everett brings tears, laughter and a happy-ever-after smile to your face while you're experiencing her well-written, compassionate novel. I highly recommend this book, which hits home with true-to-life characters."   —*Romance Junkies*

"Redemption, reconciliation, and, of course, romance—Everett's novel has it all."   —*Booklist*

"Richly nuanced characters and able plotting . . . Everett's sweet contemporary debut illustrates the power of forgiveness and the strength of relationships that may falter but never fail."
   —*Publishers Weekly*

"Lily has a talent for metaphors that make me melt . . . and I love the way she ties the story together. I'm so looking forward to the next book in the series."
   —*USA Today's* Happily Ever After blog

St. Martin's Paperbacks Titles by Lily Everett

Heartbreak Cove

A Sanctuary Island Novel

LILY EVERETT

St. Martin's Paperbacks

NOTE: If you purchased this book without a cover you should be aware that this book is stolen property. It was reported as "unsold and destroyed" to the publisher, and neither the author nor the publisher has received any payment for this "stripped book."

This is a work of fiction. All of the characters, organizations, and events portrayed in this novel are either products of the author's imagination or are used fictitiously.

HEARTBREAK COVE

Copyright © 2015 by Lily Everett.

All rights reserved.

For information address St. Martin's Press, 175 Fifth Avenue, New York, NY 10010.

ISBN: 978-1-250-09617-3

Our books may be purchased in bulk for promotional, educational, or business use. Please contact your local bookseller or the Macmillan Corporate and Premium Sales Department at 1-800-221-7945, ext. 5442, or by e-mail at MacmillanSpecialMarkets@macmillan.com.

Printed in the United States of America

St. Martin's Paperbacks edition / March 2015

St. Martin's Paperbacks are published by St. Martin's Press, 175 Fifth Avenue, New York, NY 10010.

10 9 8 7 6 5 4 3 2

For Georgia, Jeff, and my new baby nephew, Sam.
Congratulations on your beautiful family!

Acknowledgments

A lot of writers these days say they don't need an agent, and only need an editor to check their spelling and grammar—but that is not how I work. I couldn't do what I do without the support, encouragement, advice, and savvy of my agent, Deidre Knight. And my books would be nowhere near as good without my editor, Rose Hilliard, and her intuitive understanding of character, pacing, and ramping up emotional intensity.

Any writer would be lucky to have a team behind them like the one at St. Martin's Press, especially Lizzie Poteet, Elsie Lyons, Erin Cox, Mitali Dave, Angela Craft, Anne Marie Tallberg, Jen Enderlin, the entire production and sales teams, and too many wonderful, talented people to name! There's a reason I've been at SMP for my entire publishing career.

As a social person in a solitary job, I feel so lucky to have a fabulous group of writing friends to laugh, whine, party, and brainstorm with. Huge thanks to Roxanne St. Claire, Kristen Painter,

Sarah MacLean, Tracie Stewart, Ana Farish, Julie Ann Walker, Kristen Callihan, Amanda Carlson, Amanda Bonilla, Gena Showalter, Kresley Cole, Julie James, Beth Kery, and everyone on my various author loops. You know who you are! I love y'all.

Last but certainly not least, I have to thank my family. I dedicated this book to my sister, whose early reading of the manuscript helped me catch some horse-related mistakes, and who (completely coincidentally) named her brand-new baby boy after my hero, Sam! I also owe my mom and dad for forcing me to get out of the house to swim laps and walk our dogs together. And to my husband, Nick, who believes that every character in every one of my books is based on him in some way . . . all I can say is you're right. Andie has your dedication to community, your loyalty, and your straightforward honesty. Sam has your secretly soft heart, your strength, and your devastating effect on a woman's senses. Thank you for being my inspiration!

Prologue

October 2013

Sheriff Andie Shepard leaned into the smooth bark of a tulip poplar and let the tree trunk do the work of propping up her tired body.

All around her, couples danced on the patch of cleared grass surrounded by long picnic tables laden with potluck dishes, pitchers of lemonade and sweet tea, and bowls of punch. Andie smiled at the exuberant happiness buzzing through the crisp evening air, making the town square glow as bright as the white twinkle lights strung from the gazebo and the tall oak trees.

Standing on the edges of the crowd, Andie got a wistful sense of what it must feel like to truly belong here on Sanctuary Island. It made her all the more determined to find her place in this town, amongst these people.

A whirling couple narrowly missed tripping over a folding chair at the end of Andie's table, their laughter loud enough to scare away the fireflies.

Some people were having just a little bit too much fun, courtesy of one particular bowl of punch. The groom had doctored that bowl with a generous pour from a silver flask, making sure everyone knew which punch was now adults-only. Andie had been standing guard ever since.

Which she likely would be for another few hours yet. She smothered a yawn. Her shift started before dawn today, and it wouldn't be over until the last wedding guest stumbled home and tumbled into bed, safe and sound.

She blinked to clear the exhaustion from her vision, and when she forced her eyes open, her heart slammed into her throat.

It was him.

Sam Brennan loomed across the picnic table, his tall, muscular form haloed in the golden glow of the twinkle lights. His face was cast in shadow, but even when she'd had him under the direct glare of the sheriff's office fluorescent lights, Andie hadn't been able to get a good read on him.

Because of the beard, she told herself, straightening automatically as she studied the close-cropped brown bristles darkening his jaw—but deep inside, Andie knew it was something more.

"You should go home, Sheriff," he said abruptly, the low rumble of his voice vibrating through her like the roll of distant thunder. "You look like hell."

Better than a zap of lightning to the seat of the pants. Andie braced her feet and pulled herself upright, gritting her teeth against the urge to snap back at him. She schooled her features to cool, composed professionalism and crossed her arms over her chest. "I'm not here in a decorative capacity, Mr. Brennan."

Sam lifted one of the folding chairs as if it were

made of construction paper, and turned it so he could straddle it backwards and prop his folded arms on the backrest. He smoldered up at her through unfairly long lashes. The flickering light of the votive candles clustered on the picnic tables somehow accentuated his rough, masculine charm.

"Don't tell me," he rumbled, "you came to make sure Ben and Merry had a wedding license, signed in triplicate. Or no—I bet Jo needed a permit to host a party like this in a public park."

"Good thing Jo got her permit in a week ago." Andie stared him down, unwilling to apologize for the fact that she cared about her job.

Trust the rules, her father used to say. *They'll keep you on the right path when your emotions try to send you off in the wrong direction. Hearts can be misled, but the law is constant.*

Sam Brennan shook his shaggy head and squinted into the distance as if he couldn't imagine following such a silly, pointless regulation—and there it was. The reason Andie had a hard time getting a read on him.

He met her gaze squarely, an odd light glinting in the depths of eyes the color of bittersweet chocolate. "Waste of paper, if you ask me. If people want to get together to celebrate a wedding, they ought to be able to. No regulations, no restrictions."

Sam Brennan was a throwback to another time, when the rule of law held no sway and a man had to come up with his own personal moral code to guide his actions.

The thrill that ran across her nerves the moment she met him, the jumpy, unsettled twitchiness she battled every time their stares clashed, was because she recognized the essential danger of Sam Brennan.

He had the heart of an outlaw.

"I don't make the regulations," Andie said, her voice sharper than she wished. "I just enforce them."

She was used to the way most people kept her at arms' length—the khaki sheriff's uniform tended to make civilians nervous, even the ones who'd never committ a crime. Andie accepted that distance, even though it was lonely at times, and she had real hopes of one day being accepted by this crazy little town as one of its own.

But when Sam's mouth flattened into a tight line, nearly hidden by the beard, Andie caught her breath at the intensity of his expression.

I'm more than the badge, she thought with an ache, but even the idea of saying it aloud flipped her stomach and singed the tips of her ears with embarrassed heat. Would such a sentiment ever even have occurred to her father, or his father, or any of the long line of law-enforcement officers she'd sprung from? No way.

Pulling herself together, Andie kept her voice calm and firm. "In this case, what I'm enforcing is the law about not driving while intoxicated. Some of these folks are going to need a ride home, and I don't know if you've noticed, but Sanctuary Island is a little too small to support a cab company."

Sam's brows winged up, as if she'd surprised him again. Blowing out a breath and shaking his head, he plastered on what looked like a very determined smile. "Believe it or not, I didn't come over here to pick a fight with you."

No, you came over here to tell me I look like hell, Andie's wounded vanity grumbled, but out loud, all she said was, "What can I do for you, Mr. Brennan?"

A muscle ticked in his rough jaw. "You can accept my apology, and my thanks," he gritted out, the words grinding over each other like gravel under truck tires. "My cousin told me the judge decided to sentence the kids to community service, nothing on their permanent record."

"That was the judge's decision," Andie pointed out cautiously. "You should thank her."

Sam grimaced, palming the back of his neck. "I did. She told me you called her up and argued for Matt and Taylor, since it was a first offense for Matt and both of them are minors . . . I mean, it's ridiculous they were charged with trespassing at all, but you didn't have to speak up for them. So thank you."

"Don't strain yourself," Andie said sharply, causing Sam's gaze to fly to hers, surprised. "I didn't do it as a favor to you."

His eyes narrowed. "I never thought you did."

"I only put in a good word," Andie insisted, leaning in to make her point. And it was true. After Sam's nephew had been caught trespassing and drinking underage with the bank manager's daughter, Andie felt for the kids. The boy wasn't a troublemaker, and the girl had worked hard to turn over a new leaf. There was nothing to be gained by saddling either of them with a criminal record.

"You've actually got a heart underneath that uniform, don't you?" Sam said slowly, his deep brown eyes studying her face with disconcerting sharpness.

"Of course I do," Andie said over the thud of her heart in her ears. "I'm a firm believer that people need other people. That's one reason I take this job so seriously—we all need each other's help sometimes."

"Unless you're used to going it alone." The darkness in his gaze expanded like a black hole, sucking in all the light and air around them.

Andie's heart rate crested on a tidal wave of need, the need to know more, to find out what turned Sam Brennan into a loner who believed in nothing and no one, the need to make him leave Sanctuary Island before she did something really crazy . . . like kiss him to see if that would make him smile.

Sam blinked and shook his head like a big, shaggy dog. The tension between them splintered, changed, as he met her eyes once more. Only this time, his gaze was shuttered, the black fire there banked and smoldering.

"The look on your face," he said, sardonic amusement quirking his lips. "Don't worry, Sheriff Shepard, remember I'm not a permanent member of your flock. Just passing through, looking after Matt while his mom bangs around Europe on her honeymoon. She'll be back in a couple of days, so I won't be here long enough to cause any trouble on Sanctuary Island, I promise."

Thank God for that, was all Andie could think. She wasn't sure she could deal with the disruption and chaos Sam Brennan caused in her psyche for longer than a few days.

"While you're here, I'd appreciate it if you'd at least pretend to respect the laws of the island," she said stiffly.

Slapping both big hands on his denim-clad thighs, Sam swung up from the chair and replaced it neatly under the table. "Sure thing, Sheriff. As a special favor to you."

"Not breaking the law is not a favor."

He held up his hands in surrender. "No, of course. You're right. Just a little joke. Or is it against the rules to even joke about breaking the law?"

Now that he was standing, Andie was uncomfortably aware that she had to lift her chin to meet his gaze. At just shy of six feet in her beloved cowboy boots, Andie was used to towering over people, but Sam Brennan still had at least five inches on her.

A warm breeze stirred the flames of the votive candles and made the twinkle lights dance in the branches. Staring up into Sam's watchful brown eyes, Andie became abruptly aware that their table had been abandoned as the other guests crowded around the impromptu dance floor. No one was nearby or even looking their way, everyone apparently having too much fun to glance back toward the edge of the party.

Adrenaline poured through her, slowing time to a crawl even as her own movements got sharper, stronger, more deliberate. Andie stepped around the table, going toe-to-toe with Sam Brennan without ever dropping her stare.

"It's not against the law to joke," she answered. "But that doesn't make it funny."

His low laugh was a husky growl on the breeze. "Haven't you ever heard of doing the wrong thing for the right reason?"

Andie firmed her jaw and shook her head at the infuriating man, and Sam shocked her by reaching out one of his huge hands to glance along her cheek. For such a giant guy, his touch was surprisingly gentle, almost tender.

"Never mind," he said softly, his melting chocolate gaze holding her captive in this oddly private, silent moment. "I hope you never have to make a choice like that, Sheriff."

Andie blinked, momentarily spellbound by the

wistful twist to Sam's lips as he continued. "That's part of what I love about visiting this place. Everything seems simpler here, clearer. People say what they mean and mean what they say. Out there in the real world . . . well."

"You could stay," Andie heard herself saying. She blinked again, the twinkle lights dazzling at the edges of her vision.

For a moment, Andie glimpsed the unguarded truth of Sam's reaction, the raw regret that crossed his handsome face in a spasm. "I wish I could. But I can't."

Andie ducked her head, appalled at the disappointment shafting through her. It was for the best, she lectured herself severely. Sam Brennan got to her in a way she'd never experienced. A way that felt dangerous.

That shiver of danger squeezed her chest again as Sam dropped his hand, curling it into a big fist at his side.

"I have responsibilities of my own," he said, as if he were reminding himself. "I can't afford to get distracted."

Andie jerked her head up, tilting her chin. "Who's distracting you? I'm only trying to be hospitable."

"Sheriff Andrea Shepard," Sam breathed, his gravelly voice thick with an emotion she was afraid to examine. "You have no idea how distracting you are, do you?"

The feeling is mutual, mister. "My friends call me Andie."

Sam smiled, brief and almost tender. "Andie."

Tension filled the space between them again, but this time it felt warm and enveloping, like stepping out of the air conditioning and into the humid heat of a summer afternoon. The moment spun out for the length of a breath, a heartbeat, and then the song that had been playing ended and the couples on the dance floor applauded, sending up a loud cheer.

Stepping back, Sam tucked his hands into the front pockets of his jeans. His green flannel shirt-sleeves, rolled to the elbow, exposed the corded strength of his tanned forearms. "Sounds like the party's over. If I take a load in my truck and you take the rest in your SUV, I bet we can get all these partygoers home in one trip."

Andie nodded. "Good idea. I'll start rounding people up."

She was proud of how steady her voice was, considering she had no idea what the hell just happened.

"Send your overflow to me—I'm parked in front of Hackley's Hardware." Sam jerked a thumb over his shoulder and gave her a half smile. "See you around, Sheriff."

"Sheriff" again, not "Andie," she noted with a pang. She didn't let it show, though. Instead, she nodded and held out her hand, saying, "Thanks for the help. I appreciate it."

"I owed you." Before she could shake her head in denial, he said, "Oh, don't worry. We're not even yet. But it's a start."

He clasped her hand for a single heartbeat before dropping it and striding away, leaving Andie's palm burning with the brief contact. She closed her fingers around the tingle, keeping it safe, and watched Sam Brennan walk out of her life. The image of his mile-wide shoulders and muscular back tapering to his trim waist and endless legs carved itself into her brain, and Andie didn't even try to stop it.

"It's for the best," Andie murmured to herself.

Sam Brennan was too much of a threat to her hard-won peace and serenity.

Thank goodness he was leaving Sanctuary Island. She could only hope he wouldn't be back anytime soon.

Chapter One

Six months later . . .

Sam Brennan pressed a soothing hand to the door of the mare's travel stall and wished he were on the top deck to catch the first glimpse of Sanctuary Island on the horizon. It had been too long since he saw the place.

Hurry the hell up, he silently coaxed the ferry. *The rusty old clunker used to go faster than this.*

After a terrible storm the year before incapacitated the ferry that used to shuttle between Sanctuary Island and Winter Harbor, Virginia, the town council had voted to retire the old girl and put a special measure on the ballot to fund a brand-new ferry. When his cousin happened to mention last week that the shiny new ferry sported a travel stall for large animals, the plan dropped fully formed into Sam's head like a gift.

Sanctuary Island was the perfect hideout, for a ton of reasons. It didn't hurt that the only members of his family that Sam still talked to lived there, and his cousin Penny had been kind enough—or crazy enough—to extend a blanket invitation to stay with her anytime. Even better, she'd wound up marrying the guy that owned the house where she was caretaker, so there was plenty of room for the new couple, Penny's teenage son Matt, and a spare cousin who traveled as light as a single leather duffel and a well-worn, hand-tooled saddle.

But by far the biggest benefit to making his getaway to Sanctuary Island was that he was known to travel there once or twice a year, often bringing a horse with him. So this particular trip shouldn't raise any eyebrows. Not even the sleek, dark chestnut brows of the prettiest lady sheriff imaginable . . .

Another muffled thud against the stall door reminded Sam to guard against distractions, no matter how perfectly curved and sweet smelling. The miserable, frightened mare in the stall was the main reason he'd steered his course to Sanctuary Island.

"Just a little longer," he promised softly, heart squeezing like a fist. "And you'll be settled nice and cozy in your new digs at Windy Corner Stables. All we have to do is wait for the cars to get off the ferry when we dock, then walk down the gangplank and straight into the trailer Jo Ellen is sending for us. Easy as pie."

The mare's distressed breathing was audible even through the metal of the ferry's reinforced stall door, and Sam sighed.

Something told him his fantasy of making a quick, no-muss-no-fuss transfer from ferry to trailer wasn't going to come true. Still, no matter what happened when he finally got this godforsaken animal off this boat, it was a damn sight better than the fate that awaited the poor horse back on the mainland.

Sam could only close his eyes and pray that the dangerous risk he'd taken wouldn't land his newly acquired horse—and himself—in even worse trouble. Silently vowing to keep his head down and make as few waves as possible, Sam ignored the banked fires of want in his belly.

He'd avoid Sheriff Andie Shepard on this trip because he had to. No matter how much he wanted to touch her, kiss her, claim her . . . he couldn't. Not yet.

Some risks were too dangerous to take, even for a man like Sam Brennan.

There were only so many places a fifty-pound bulldog could hide.

Holding her breath, Andie unhooked the flashlight from her utility belt and crouched to shine it through the small hole in the old stable door. She squinted around at what she could see of the broken-down, abandoned stalls, but she saw no movement other than the dance of dust motes in the sunlight filtering through the partially caved-in roof. Andie made a hopeful kissing noise. "Come on, Pippin. Are you in there? Your daddy's pretty worried about you. Come on out."

He had to be there. She'd already checked the pine copse behind Mr. Leeds's big plantation-style house, the overgrown kitchen garden where the dog liked to dig up vegetables, and the crawl space under the wraparound porch—which explained the red clay dirt streaking her khaki uniform where it clung to her sticky, sweaty skin in damp patches.

Sighing, Andie contemplated the ragged hole in the stable door. Was it even big enough for a dog of Pippin's considerable bulk to squeeze through? She had zero desire to step foot in a building that ought to have been condemned years ago if there wasn't a chance the missing dog might actually be inside.

What alternative did she have, though? She couldn't go back up to the house and tell Dabney Leeds—the wealthiest full-time resident of Sanctuary Island, leading member of Sanctuary's town council, and a major contributor to local political campaigns—that she hadn't been able to find his beloved bulldog.

But there was a limit to what Andie was willing to do, even in an election year. Risking her life in a derelict outbuilding just to be able to tell Mr. Leeds she'd searched everywhere—was it really worth it? Especially when she was running unopposed. Her time would be better spent going through the pinewood again, this time with a pocketful of dog treats.

Decision made, Andie wiped her hands on her thighs and prepared to stand up—when her gaze snagged on a wisp of blue fabric clinging to one of the torn slats in the stable door.

Her heart sank. She'd seen that shade of blue before . . . on a certain depressed bulldog who'd been crammed into a sailor costume.

She was going to have to go in.

The spring breeze kicked up, sending a chill through Andie's bones when the dilapidated stable building creaked ominously. Standing, she put a hand to the pocked, rotting wood of the door and felt the tremor as the wind shook the entire structure. She was so focused on tracking the building's rasping groans that she almost missed the faint whimper from inside.

Pippin. He was in trouble. Maybe he'd gotten trapped in there, or injured, and that's why he hadn't come when she called. The world went sharp and clear as determination filled Andie's chest. She didn't pause to ponder the fact that her body was having the same response to rescuing a runaway bulldog as she used to get from tactical raids on drug dealers' hideouts back in Louisville.

She pulled in a deep, bracing breath and grasped the rusted iron handle of the sliding barn door. It stuck, of course, but Andie kept the pressure slow and steady until the door finally yielded with a piercing shriek. When the opening was wide enough to slip through, Andie shone the flashlight around the dim interior.

The stable clearly hadn't been used in years, maybe decades. Piles of dried green hay had drifted down from the sagging loft, filling the still air with the smell of mildew and decay. Wind whistled through the cracks in the walls, and when Andie narrowed her gaze up at the sharp, uneven slope of the roof, she got a clear view of clouds moving quickly across the pale April sky. It was really blowing out there.

In here, it wasn't much better. Andie's pulse sped at the knowledge that this old place could come down around her ears at any moment. She reminded herself that the building had managed to stay standing for a long time, even through last spring's terrible storms. There was no reason that today should be the day it collapsed.

Except for the fact that today was the day Andie

had to go poking through it, moving fallen beams and generally disturbing whatever structural integrity it had left, in her search for a wayward bulldog.

She whistled softly. "Hey, boy. I know you're in here someplace. Come on, puppy."

The low whine from deep in the gloom sounded so human, Andie almost fumbled her flashlight. There, in the furthest corner of the stables under the droopy overhang of the loft, Pippin squatted, looking miserable. Or maybe that was just his face.

"Hey there!" Andie moved closer, careful about it in case Pippin got spooked and ran off before she could get her hands on him. But after a single, morose glance, Pippin twisted his stocky body and started licking at his left haunch, below the ripped hem of his mud-streaked sailor suit. Andie squinted—was that blood?

Concerned, she picked up the pace as the wind buffeted the building again. In the corner, Pippin switched from licking the scratch on his hindquarters to giving his undercarriage a good tongue bath. Andie snorted. Trust a male creature to get distracted from an injury by a little attention to his manly parts.

Hoping that indicated his wound wasn't serious, Andie reached the dog just as a particularly loud creak sounded through the structure. Her gaze shot to the loft, which shuddered as she stared up at it as if it were about to come tumbling down. There was no time to coax Pippin out on his own, even if he could still walk.

Instead, Andie bent her knees and got her arms around his squirming bulk, and lifted him against her chest. Thank the sweet Lord she'd kept up with PT since she took this job or she'd never be able to heft a reluctant, wriggling bulldog and hustle them both to safety. Pippin was fifty pounds of muscle, fat, and heavy bone—and he apparently hadn't had a pedicure in a while, judging by the pain raking across her skin wherever he flailed those scrabbling paws.

The next few minutes were a blur of huffing, puffing, barking, and whimpering, but Andie got them out of the stable more or less intact. However, when she tried to put the struggling bulldog down, he refused to stand on his own feet. Groaning, Andie heaved him back up and staggered toward the main house. As soon as they were within view of it, Andie had to bite back another groan.

Mr. Dabney Leeds was standing on the porch, banging his brass-topped cane impatiently against the floorboards. "Finally! Took you long enough. Where was he?"

Reminding herself that Mr. Leeds's querulous tone was most likely a cover for how worried he'd been about his furry friend, Andie gasped out, "In the old stable out back."

"Is he hurt?" Mr. Leeds's anxious gaze roamed over Pippin, who'd given up wiggling, at least. The bulldog had gone absolutely limp in Andie's arms, turning his bulky body into a dead weight.

"I think it's just a scratch," Andie said, concentrating on hauling herself up the porch steps.

Mr. Leeds scowled. "My poor baby! Hurry on now, get up here and put him in his bed so you can call Dr. Fairfax for me."

A perfect miniature replica of the cushioned wicker porch furniture sat beside the gliding loveseat. Andie deposited her burden on the pink-rosetted pillow and straightened with a hand to her back. Mr. Leeds fussed over Pippin, who closed his eyes in resignation, apparently having given up on his bid for freedom. At least for today.

Andie pulled out her cell phone to dial the local veterinarian just as the radio receiver clipped to her utility belt crackled to life.

"Disturbance in progress down at the dock," the dispatcher's staticky voice said.

"What are you waiting for?" Mr. Leeds's angry demand shocked Andie into looking up. "Call Dr. Fairfax, girl! I won't have my dog contracting an infection because of your incompetence."

"Sheriff? Come in?" Ivy Dawson, Andie's brand-new dispatcher, sounded impatient and annoyed, a combination Andie already recognized as an indication of actual worry.

"I'm sorry, Mr. Leeds. I have to take this call," Andie said, unhooking the radio from her belt. "Feel free to step inside and call the vet yourself—I'll keep an eye on Pippin."

Her finger hovered over the "talk" button but before she could press it, Mr. Leeds banged his cane against the porch railing, making Andie and Pippin both jump. "No! Now I've sat here all morning waiting on you to do your job. I'm not waiting another second. I'm a Town Councilman! The council directs the Sheriff's office, so you'd better do what I say, girl. Quick now!"

"Mr. Leeds, I understand you're upset," Andie said, holding onto her patience with both hands, "but I have a duty to all the citizens of Sanctuary Island, to keep people safe and be responsive to their needs. I can't ignore a call like this."

Mr. Leeds narrowed his watery eyes. Despite his stooped bearing and the tremor in his thin muscles,

Andie felt a chill rush through her at the sheer force of will in the man's eyes. She must never make the mistake of underestimating him. Dabney Leeds was used to getting his own way.

"You can't ignore a call. Not even for the biggest campaign contributor on the island?"

Andie's stomach knotted at the unsubtle threat. She could survive without Dabney Leeds and his bags of money, so long as no one else entered the race. But the deadline for a candidate to throw his hat in the ring hadn't passed yet, so she couldn't be sure.

Still . . . what kind of sheriff would she be if she caved to the demands of a single wealthy, entitled old man? "I'm very sorry, Mr. Leeds." Andie kept her tone as firm and no-nonsense as she could. "But I'm going to have to go. You have a nice day, now."

She didn't have time to appreciate the dawning rage on Leeds's pinched face as she turned and strode back to her county-issued SUV. "Sheriff Shepard," she said into the radio as she got behind the wheel. "What's the disturbance, Ivy?"

"Oh, thank the sweet heavens," Ivy said. "I was starting to worry I'd have to leave the station to go check it out myself, and I do not do wildlife. Especially not the actually wild kind."

They were really going to have to work on Ivy's radio communication skills. "Give me the rundown," Andie said calmly, throwing the truck into gear and heading up the winding driveway back toward Shoreline Drive.

"It came from down at the harbor. Buddy called it in, something about a horse going crazy and trying to kill someone? Although I don't know what a horse would be doing down by the harbor where the ferry captain could see one. Don't the wild herds usually stick to the other end of the island?"

"They're called bands, not herds. And yes, they do." Andie pressed down the gas and hustled through the center of town toward Summer Harbor. "The wild horses aren't domesticated, and we strictly enforce the rules about not feeding them or trying to touch them, so they mostly keep to the uninhabited northern tip of the island. But sometimes one of them will get separated from his or her band and become disoriented."

"And try to kill people?" The alarm in Ivy's tone made Andie bite down on a grin. Ivy was a recent transplant from Atlanta, and as she'd put it in her phone interview, she was not a "nature girl."

"That would be highly unusual," Andie said soothingly.

Ivy hmphed. "I notice you didn't flat out deny the possibility."

"Maybe you haven't been here long enough to notice, but big cities have nothing on small towns when it comes to the variety of creative ways people can find to get into trouble."

"You know that's right," Ivy agreed. "How many big city cops spend their morning tracking down a runaway bulldog dressed like the villain from a James Bond movie?"

"No monocle today," Andie replied, laughing. "It was the sailor outfit."

"That poor animal! Can't we arrest Mr. Leeds for pet abuse or something?"

Resolutely not thinking about how many problems that would solve, Andie sighed. "I don't think it's actually against the law to spend thousands of dollars on toys, treats, and fancy costumes for your dog."

"Well, it should be. It's a fashion crime, at the very least." Ivy paused. "You sure you're okay to check out the harbor call? I know dealing with Mr. Leeds is pretty stressful."

"I'm fine," Andie insisted. "And I'm almost there anyway. I'll keep you posted."

"Don't get trampled by a stampeding stallion," Ivy advised. "Over and out."

Grinning and thankful, once again, that she'd ignored Ivy's lack of experience and followed her gut about hiring someone who could make her laugh, Andie replaced the handheld radio on her dash as she crested the sandy hill above the harbor. The Atlantic Ocean rolled out in front of her like a deep blue carpet, the mainland an indistinct smudge of gray along the horizon.

The sight sank into her bones and lifted her up, the way it had ever since she first stepped foot on this tiny, undeveloped gem of an island. Without even a causeway to connect it to the mainland, the only link between Sanctuary Island and the closest town of Winter Harbor, Virginia, was a two-hour ferry ride.

At least they'd finally retired that rusted-out old hulk of a ferry after it sprang a leak during a storm last spring. The town council had taken up a collection to help defray the cost of upgrading, and it had been worth Andie's time approving the permits for every pancake breakfast and spaghetti social to see the brand-new, shiny red of the five-car, high-speed ferry pulling away from the dock for the return trip to Winter Harbor.

An inhuman scream of fury ripped through the

air and raised every hair on Andie's body. Shading her eyes against the sharp glint of the sun off the ferry's polished chrome railings, Andie blinked down at the scene below on the pier.

The angriest horse she'd ever seen stood at the foot of the ferry ramp, swinging a great black head and pawing at the ground. A tall, broad-shouldered man had hold of the taut lead rope attached to the horse's halter, and as Andie watched, he took a slow step closer to the horse.

Are you insane? Andie wanted to yell at the man who'd been crazy enough to try to put a halter on a wild beast. But even as she grabbed for the tranquilizer dart gun stowed under the passenger seat and tumbled out of her SUV, the horse reared up on its hind legs, front legs flashing out in a lethal kick that had Andie sucking in a breath. Without hesitating, she brought the dart gun up to her shoulder and sighted down the barrel.

But instead of taking a forceful hoof to the chest, the man sidestepped calmly, as smoothly as if he and the horse had choreographed the move ahead of time. The step put the big man's wide back between Andie and the horse, and before she could warn him out of the way, he did something she could hardly believe.

He dropped the lead rope, his only hope of controlling the black horse, and lifted his arms slowly. Holding his arms out from his sides as if to prove he was unarmed, the tall man sidled up to the nervous, trembling animal.

Cursing under her breath, Andie moved as smoothly as she could down the hill, trying to get into a better position to be able to tranq the dangerous animal. She circled around to the right and as she got closer, a thrill of recognition stiffened her limbs and nearly had her dropping the dart gun.

The tall man whose intense attention was all for the horse—deep brown human gaze locked with fathomless black equine—was Sam Brennan.

Chapter Two

Andie's heart swam up into her throat then dived down to the pit of her stomach. Sam was back on Sanctuary.

He'd been back on the island for all of ten minutes, she guessed from the ferry schedule—and Andie was already getting called in. No doubt about it, Sam Brennan was a trouble magnet.

Sam didn't look especially troubled, she noted as she crept closer, careful to stay downwind of the horse's powerful sense of smell. He certainly didn't look like a man facing down messy death in the form of a thousand-pound wild animal that felt threatened and trapped.

No, the line of Sam's muscular shoulders was relaxed, his stance as easy as if he were ordering a strawberry cone at Miss Ruth's ice cream stand. His chiseled lips moved behind his close-cropped beard. She couldn't hear what he was saying at first, but as she drew nearer, she started to make it out.

"You're safe, I'm here, no one's gonna hurt you, sweetheart, you're safe . . ."

The endless litany rolled off of Sam's tongue like honey over gravel, rumbly and reassuring. Andie felt her own jumping pulse begin to calm. And as she stared in disbelief, the horse stopped pawing the ground and dropped its big head to stand still with legs splayed and sides heaving.

Sam took a final step that brought him to the horse's side. Andie clenched her finger on the dart gun's trigger, but when Sam brought one thickly muscled arm up over the mare's black neck, the horse only heaved out a shuddering snort and submitted quietly to the touch.

Andie's attention snagged on the gentle confidence of Sam's hands running over the horse's quivering coat as though checking for unseen injuries. And now that the situation seemed more under control, Andie's brain went off high alert and finally took in the details of the horse.

The sleek muscle and short-trimmed mane told Andie this wasn't one of Sanctuary's wild horses. And if that weren't enough, the tight navy blue bandages that wrapped the horse's forelegs from above the knee to the top of the hoof would've made it clear this horse belonged to someone.

Owned or not, this horse was still pretty wild.

As she stepped up behind Sam, the horse jerked its head, prompting Sam to tighten his grip on the halter and lean in to whisper more soothing words into the horse's long, twitching ear.

Andie lowered the dart gun, carefully pointing it at the ground while Sam talked that crazed animal into a calm so deep, it almost seemed drugged.

"Whoever you are," Sam continued in that same reassuring tone, "stay the hell back. I've just about gotten her unwound, and I don't need any more so-called help."

Stiffening, Andie held her ground. She wasn't stupid enough to go barging into a situation that was already on its way to being handled, but she'd been called in for a reason.

"I'm not here to get in your way," she told him quietly, making sure to keep her tone smooth and free of threat. The mare swiveled an ear toward her, eyes rolling until the white showed, but she stood still beneath Sam's palms. "I'm here to make sure no one gets hurt, including that horse."

That got him to look at her, finally. In a single swift glance over his shoulder, Sam took her in from head to toe. Andie felt the heat of his gaze passing over her skin, and she felt the moment his gaze caught on the dart gun in her hand because the dawning light in his eyes snuffed out.

Sam's lip curled into a silent snarl, but his voice never rose above a husky whisper that sent shivers down Andie's spine. "You shoot this horse, you and me are gonna have a big problem, Sheriff."

"We already have a big problem, Mr. Brennan." Andie didn't lift the gun, but she didn't relax her battle-ready stance either. "That animal is clearly dangerous, not just to others but to itself. And if I have to tranq your horse to stop it from breaking its own leg in a fury or lashing out at someone, you can bet I will."

A glimmer of respect shone from the bitter chocolate depths of Sam's eyes, but the tense line of his mouth never softened. "This mare has a heart murmur. Too large a dose from that tranq gun could kill her."

Andie sucked in a breath and sent up a prayer of thanksgiving that she hadn't had to shoot. "I'm sorry."

"What for? Almost putting my horse down without so much as a by your leave?" A low growl rumbled through Sam's words, making the horse dance nervously in place.

"No," Andie said, gritting her teeth to keep things civil. "If you're unable to control that animal, you have to take the consequences. I won't have her breaking loose and rampaging around my island, injuring innocent people. What I'm sorry for is the heart murmur—I don't know much about horses, but I understand that condition can make it hard to sell them."

With another soothing stroke, Sam gentled the animal down and deliberately neutralized his tone. "I'm not trying to sell Queenie. I only recently acquired her, myself."

"You bought a horse with a heart condition? I thought most horse owners got vet checks before buying, to avoid doing that."

"I'm not most horse owners." A half smile twisted Sam's lips but never reached as far as his eyes. "I don't buy horses for my own personal use, or to put out to stud or race—I take problem horses, ones who've been abused or neglected, and I rehabilitate them. Give them a chance at a new life."

Andie felt a surge of admiration tighten her stomach and swallowed hard. A Sam Brennan who flouted the rules and bucked authority was dangerous enough to her sanity . . . but a Sam Brennan who'd dedicated his life to rescuing mistreated horses? She was in serious trouble if he planned to stick around Sanctuary for long.

"And Queenie is one of your rescues?" Andie asked softly.

Sam ducked his head in a slow nod. "She's got spirit, and a long life ahead of her doing something useful, if I can get her to trust people again."

"Well, Sanctuary Island is a good place for that." Andie glanced across the water churning into white froth in the wake of the retreating ferry. "I bet you were the first person to use the stall on the new ferry."

"Yeah, I was going to ask," Sam said. "Not a lot of ferries sport a state-of-the-art way to transport horses."

Andie smiled, pride in her adopted home filling her belly with warmth like sunshine. "Not a lot of tiny islands are home to one of the world's few bands of free-roaming wild horses. That stall was a big plus when the town council managed to pass the ballot measure to get a new ferry. Our local veterinarian made the argument that if he ever needed to get one of the wild horses some serious medical help, he'd need a way to transport them to the mainland. The people of Sanctuary are pretty protective of the wild horses, so that was all it took."

"I know Ben Fairfax, I've brought horses to him before." Sam glanced up. A dangerous gleam flickered in his eyes. "In fact, as I recall, you and I almost danced at Ben's wedding the last time I was here."

Cursing herself for the hot flush she felt creeping up her neck, Andie shrugged as nonchalantly as she could. "You have a very different recollection of that night than I do. What I mainly remember is hauling drunk party guests home in the middle of the night."

"Believe me, Sheriff Shepard," Sam murmured, "I remember everything about that night."

The earth shifted slightly, as if Andie were standing at the edge of the ocean with the tide rushing out to steal the sand from beneath her feet. If she hadn't locked her knees, she would have swayed toward Sam, drawn by the intensity of his focused attention and heavy-lidded eyes.

Pulling in a breath that smelled like clean sweat, sweet hay, and the complicated leather-and-sandalwood scent of Sam, Andie clumsily changed the subject. "Is that why you brought Queenie here now? To see Dr. Fairfax? I would have thought there'd be plenty of qualified veterinarians back where you live, in . . . where was it?"

Sam arched one brow to let her know he hadn't missed her tactical retreat, but he let her get away with it. "Ben's a great vet, really good with the skittish ones. I'll be glad to have him examine Queenie."

"So this will probably be a quick visit, then," Andie surmised, unwilling to examine the bolt of disappointment that shot through her. She should be relieved Sam wouldn't be sticking around to unbalance her and make her question her life choices! She had enough on her plate already without this inconvenient attraction to an unrepentant bad boy . . . who appeared to have a heart of gold under that air of danger and mystery.

"That depends," Sam said, his gaze sliding away to land on Queenie. Quiet now, the horse stood with her head lowered miserably, as if she'd given up. "As much as I admire Ben's medical opinion, I actually brought Queenie here hoping to rehabilitate her for work as a therapy horse. No telling how long it'll take me to retrain her and get her safe enough to be around kids, but that's what I'm aiming for."

No telling how long. A wave of anticipation shivered across Andie's skin, undeniable and unwelcome. She dredged up a professional smile from somewhere. "Well, sounds like you've got it under control! Is someone coming with a trailer?"

"Jo Ellen," Sam supplied. "She texted me she's running behind, but she should be here any minute."

That made sense. Jo Ellen Hollister owned Windy Corner Stables, the only commercial horse barn on the island, and Dr. Fairfax was married to Jo Ellen's younger daughter, Merry. Convenient. So what was bugging her?

Andie went over the conversation in her head. Being suspicious—some might say paranoid—was an occupational hazard. Most of the time, nothing came of it. But every now and then, Andie's gut knew better than her brain, and she'd learned the hard way to listen to it . . . especially when it came to damnably attractive men.

Something told her she'd better keep an eye on Sam Brennan. "Okay then, I'll leave you to it. Good luck with your rehab efforts."

"Thanks, Sheriff. I'm sure we'll see you around."

Andie shrugged, trying to ignore the slow smile Sam gave her, hot enough to leave scorch marks. "Not necessarily. Unless you're planning to get on the wrong side of the law while you're here."

"Aw, I'm not much of a planner." Sam turned up the heat on that grin to eleven, and Andie felt her breath catch in her throat. "I hope you and I will always be on the same side, Sheriff."

Andie felt her instincts kick into high gear. What was it about this man that roused her suspicions as quickly as he aroused the rest of her?

Sam held his breath as Sheriff Andie Shepard's ocean blue eyes sharpened. Why the hell couldn't he stop himself from taunting her? The last thing he needed was the law poking around, asking questions and giving him—and his mare—suspicious glances.

Even if the law on Sanctuary Island came in a tall, slim, lightly freckled, redheaded package. And even if the universe saw fit to test Sam's resolve to keep to himself by outlining every subtle line and curve of the sheriff's body in mud-streaked khaki.

It wasn't his fault. There was no way he could stop himself from reaching out and pulling a piece of straw from the chestnut braid lying over her shoulder. The satiny rub of her dark red hair across his callused fingertips made everything low in Sam's body tighten in a rush. "Why, Sheriff. You took a roll in the hay and didn't invite me? I'm crushed. Who's the special guy?"

He loved how fierce she looked when she frowned. "A roll in the . . . oh. His name is Pippin, actually."

But somehow, she was even sexier when she smiled. The dimple that winked to life in her right cheek was almost enough to distract Sam from how much he suddenly wanted to hunt down this Pippin and knock out his front teeth.

"What the hell kind of name is that? Sounds like an orphan kid in a Dickens novel."

Andie smothered a laugh. "I'd be careful talking like that, if I were you!"

"I think I can take some loser named Pippin," Sam huffed, flexing his shoulders.

"I don't know," Andie said, eyeing Sam's arms and chest doubtfully. "Pippin is a pretty hefty guy with a lot of pent-up rage."

It didn't matter how competent he knew Andie was, or that she could likely take care of herself. Sam's protective instincts rushed to the fore. "Has he threatened you?"

The low, dangerous tone of his voice set poor Queenie on edge. Andie's eyes widened as the horse spooked sideways and Sam cursed himself silently. Turning all his focus back to the mare, he let all traces of aggression flow out of him and into the weathered boards of the pier.

"I'm sorry," Andie said quietly. "That's really not something to joke about. No one has threatened me. Pippin is a bulldog, his owner is one of my most frequent callers."

Sam stared straight ahead at his own hands gentling the skittish horse. "Okay, now I feel like an idiot."

"Don't, please. I shouldn't have teased you. I just didn't realize your rescue service extended to humans."

When he chanced a glance over his shoulder, the small, guilty smile that quirked her lips went a long way toward making Sam feel better.

His heart squeezed strangely when he and Andie locked stares. All he wanted to do was stretch out his fingers and skim the warm silk of her skin, to trace the outline of her ribcage down to the lean curve of her waist. But he couldn't, even if the breathless moment of crackling electricity arcing between them said she might not mind.

He didn't need to draw any more attention to himself and Queenie than he already had. If Sam were smart, he'd be pushing her away, not reaching out to pull her closer.

On the other hand, no one had ever accused Sam Brennan of being smart.

"I'm glad to see you again," he said, hearing the rasp of hunger in his own voice.

Drifting closer, almost as if against her will, Andie looked up at him. "Me, too."

It sounded like a confession dragged out of her after hours of interrogation. Sam couldn't blame her for not wanting to be attracted to him. He knew it was a bad idea for both of them—but as he lifted his hand from Queenie's neck to take Andie's chilled fingers in his, he couldn't care.

Tugging her gently closer, Sam raised their joined hands until the backs of Andie's knuckles skimmed along Queenie's glossy coat. The mare quivered but held still, her head low and her sides heaving as she calmed under their combined touch.

"That's amazing," Andie breathed. "When I first drove up, I thought she was going to kill someone. But you . . . all you did was talk to her."

Sam shrugged, hiding the way her words warmed him from the inside out. "I've got a way with the broken ones."

"You put them back together." She smiled to herself, like she'd learned a secret about him.

This was wrong. He had to stop this—for her sake, as much as for his and Queenie's. Stepping back, he disengaged their hands, leaving Andie petting Queenie with a surprised look on her face.

"I try." Sam shrugged again, feeling the stiff

tension in his shoulders. "It's not always possible. Some things, some people, are too broken to save."

Andie's clear blue eyes, the same color as the ocean behind her, watched him. Sam scowled, hating the feeling that she could see right through him.

"I don't believe that," she said quietly, her fingers gentle as they tangled in Queenie's mane. "No one is too broken to save."

From bitter experience, Sam knew exactly how wrong she was. Memories gave a raw edge to his voice. "Lady, don't ever leave Sanctuary Island. You'd never make it as a cop anywhere else with that soft heart."

Chapter Three

The flash of pain in her ocean eyes brought him up short. Regret pulsed through him, making him want to haul her into his arms and bury his face in her neck, apologize for being a jerk. Then Andie's gaze shuttered, locking him out, and Sam knew he'd pushed her away for good.

It was better this way. Better that she hated him than that she start liking a guy who could never give her anything but trouble.

A cloud of dust and the crunch of the parking lot's gravel under heavy tires broke their staring contest. Andie turned to watch as Jo Ellen wheeled her pick-up truck and the attached forest-green trailer past the guardhouse and down the hill with practiced ease.

"Looks like our ride is here," Sam said, finally reaching down to gather Queenie's loose lead rope and saying a quick prayer that the horse would stay calm through the process of loading into the trailer.

"Hey, Jo Ellen," Andie called out in a friendly

voice, as if she hadn't just been half a heartbeat away from either kissing Sam or punching him in the face.

"Sheriff!" Jo swung down from the cab of her pick-up and landed lightly on her booted heels. "And Sam. How are y'all doing?"

Strands of silver shot though Jo's dark brown ponytail and there were laugh lines radiating out from her eyes. When she smiled and held out her hand to the sheriff, Sam couldn't help but contrast the easy, comfortable-in-her-own-skin woman with the strung-out alcoholic he'd first met more than a decade ago.

Having witnessed her struggle with addiction and recovery up close and personal, Sam respected the hell out of Jo Ellen Hollister. If his own parents had been half as gutsy and determined to get clean—but there was no point in thinking about that.

Behind Jo, a teenaged girl climbed down from the passenger side of the truck and gave him a quick smile. Trying to hide her obvious nerves with a toss of her dirty blonde hair, she called out, "Hey, Matt's Uncle Sam."

Sam blinked, recognizing her as Taylor Mc-Namara, the kid who'd convinced his cousin's son, Matt, to sneak out to a protected piece of beach with a bottle of rum, and nearly got them both arrested for trespassing. "Technically, I'm Matt's cousin Sam," he told her, trying to keep the growly disapproval out of his voice. No need to go upsetting Queenie again when he'd just about gotten her calmed down. "How are you, Taylor?"

"Okay," she said vaguely, her attention zooming in on the horse at the end of Sam's lead rope. "She's gorgeous. Steeplechase?"

Every nerve in Sam's body prickled to high alert

at her casual mention of one of the main classifications of horse racing. "Nah, this girl's not from the tracks. She is a Thoroughbred though. Good eye."

Taylor frowned, staring at the stallion, and Sam caught the sheriff watching the exchange with interest out of the corner of his eye. As if sensing the rising tension, Jo Ellen clapped Taylor on the back and said, "Come on, kiddo, help me get the trailer open and ready for him."

Grumbling, the sixteen-year-old stomped around to the back of the trailer and Sheriff Shepard watched her go, an enigmatic blankness settling over her pretty features.

Not for the first time, the enormity of what he was attempting here, the absolute nightmare of a mess he'd gotten himself into, crashed over Sam's head. How the hell did he think he was going to pull this off?

The same way you've gotten by this far in life, he reminded himself firmly. *By trusting yourself—and no one else.*

"Is it safe to have a violent horse out at Windy Corner?" Andie asked abruptly. "Now that you're about to get the therapeutic riding center up and running, I'd think you'd only want the gentlest, most predictable horses at your barn."

"Queenie isn't normally violent," Sam stated, working hard to keep the growl out of his voice.

Andie shot him a raised brow.

"She's got some issues," Sam allowed. "But traveling is stressful for most horses—today was the exception, not the rule."

"If anyone can get this mare smoothed out and happy again, it's Sam," Jo promised, huffing as she bent to attach the heavy metal ramp to the back of the trailer. Sam shifted his weight, aching to get over there and help with the heavy lifting, but even that minute change in his stance had Queenie snorting nervously and swiveling her ears to check for threats.

"Anyway," Jo continued, "I've got ulterior motives for offering up Windy Corner as a foster home for Queenie. I'm planning to ruthlessly use his knowledge and experience to help out with the first few therapy sessions. He's going to make a great side walker."

Sam tried to wipe his face clean of whatever confused expression he'd sported to make Jo grin at him like that.

"A side walker? I don't know." The way Andie hooked her thumbs in her gun belt shot heat straight to Sam's groin. "Sounds like something we might have a law against. I'll have to check the books."

"No matter what it is, I'm game," Sam promised Jo. "Anything I can do to help out, to thank you for taking Queenie in—just name it, and it's yours."

"You may be sorry you said that," Jo muttered as she slapped her hands on her denim-clad thighs to shake off the sawdust from the floor of the trailer. "A side walker—different from a streetwalker, Sheriff!—is a volunteer who walks beside the mounted client to provide steady support through the session. Depending on the client's needs, he or she could have both a side walker and someone else to lead the horse through the exercises . . ."

Pausing, Jo went a little red around the neck. "Listen to me carry on! Y'all weren't asking for a lecture on the ins and outs of therapeutic riding. We're all so caught up in it at the barn, I tend to forget it's not the main focus of life for everyone on the island!"

"Don't apologize, this is fascinating," Andie said. "Can anyone volunteer, or are you only looking for people with horse experience, like Mr. Brennan?"

Uh-oh. Was the sheriff about to volunteer her time to the center? Sam saw the way Jo perked up. Looked like he might be spending even more time with Sheriff Andie Shepard. His smart head said, "No, no, no," but the stupid head? The one in his pants? That head was all for it.

"No experience required!" Jo looked as if she wanted to sweep Andie up in a bear hug. "We'll teach you everything you need to know before you ever have to go into a session. Are you interested, Sheriff? We'd sure love to have you."

The last gasp of Sam's rational brain coughed out, "Hey Jo, ease up. I'm sure Sheriff Shepard has better things to do with her time off . . ."

Andie raised her cinnamon-colored brows. "What better way could I spend my time than helping people in this community?"

"That's already your day job," Sam argued. "You don't need to make a hobby out of it, too."

"I may not need to, but I intend to. I've been looking for a way to get more involved in the community ever since I moved here three years ago. It's high time I took the plunge. Jo, count me in."

Jo, who'd been watching the volley of back and forth like it was a match at Wimbledon, smiled slowly. It wasn't a comforting expression. "I'm so happy to hear it, Sheriff. It's always great when two volunteers start at the same time—saves us a heap of trouble when it comes to training."

"What do you mean?"

Now it was Andie's turn to sound nervous, but Sam had no time to enjoy it before Jo said, "Because we can pair the two of you up and train you as a team."

Sam locked his jaw on the protest that wanted to escape. The last thing he needed was to spend more time with the sexy, too-competent sheriff and her penetrating gaze . . . but part of him—three guesses which part—liked the idea. A lot.

Taylor braced one booted foot against the side of the trailer to keep the tack trunk she was sitting on from sliding when Jo took a wide, slow turn, and considered her options.

She could jump on the chance to text Matt that his favorite uncle—or cousin, whatever, Sam was uncle aged—was in town . . . or she could play it cool, and wait to see if Matt showed up at the barn on his own, looking for Sam. Playing it cool would obviously be . . . cooler. But impatience itched at her fingertips, urging her to tap out a quick message to her best friend.

Okay, Matty was pretty much her only friend. But didn't that make him the best, by definition? Taylor's best friend, the hottest guy in school. The guy she'd totally had a chance with last year before she screwed it up completely and lost Matt to happy coupledom when he started dating Dakota Coles. Now Matt and Dakota were everyone's favorite couple—they were that sickening high school duo that seemed destined to be the king and queen of both homecoming and prom. They'd probably get voted Most Likely to Stay Together Forever.

Taylor McNamara, on the other hand? Most Likely to Pine and Wallow in Regret.

Two more months, she reminded herself. Then school would be out and she wouldn't have to see

Dakota's smug smile as she pranced through the halls hanging off of Matt's (sinewy, muscled) arm.

In fact, after graduation, chances were good that she wouldn't have to see Dakota Coles for a long time. That was enough to bring a smile to Taylor's face, although the smile faded at the reminder that she wouldn't be seeing as much of Matt, either.

That decided it. Playing cool was for people with time to dick around. Taylor had goals, and her deadline for achieving them was fast approaching.

When she couldn't get through more than a couple texts without embarrassing typos caused by the rough ride in the trailer along with Sam's horse, Taylor gave up on texting and called Matt instead.

"Is Sam really here?" he demanded as soon as he picked up the call.

Taylor laughed. "I have no motive for lying."

"I can't believe my mom didn't tell me he was coming!"

"Well, what were you going to do about it? Clean the house and make up his room? I thought you had people for that."

Matt made a scoffing noise that didn't quite hide his discomfort with the fact that Taylor's teasing was only the truth.

"Oh come on," Taylor said, annoyed that she felt bad for bringing it up. "Your mom married a billionaire—for love!—and now you're set for life. I know it was a little freaky at first, but aren't you used to it by now?"

The breath he huffed into the phone was mostly a laugh. "That's what I love about you, Tay. You don't sugarcoat things."

As much as she wanted to thrill to the sound of the 'L' word and Matt's nickname for her mingling together in a single sentence, the rest of the sentiment made her grimace. "Sorry. I know it was weird for you."

"No," Matt protested unconvincingly. "I mean, I'm happy for my mom, and I like Dylan a lot. And obviously it's great she doesn't have to work two jobs anymore and all that. I just . . . for a long time, it was me and Mom against the world. And I'm glad she has Dylan, but everything is different now."

Taylor thought about her dad and how sad he'd been after her mom died, and how much happier he was now that he and Jo were together. "I know. Something special happens when you've just got one parent, and all you have is each other. Letting other people into that is hard, but it's the right thing to do."

"Especially since we're going to college soon," Matt mused. "I would've hated leaving Mom alone. Now at least I know she'll be taken care of when I'm not around."

Taylor's eyes burned the way they always did when she thought about leaving home. Leaving Sanctuary Island, leaving her dad and Jo and the horses at Windy Corner . . . leaving Matthew Little. "Man, this conversation got heavy in a hurry," she said gruffly.

"My bad," Matt apologized with a quiet laugh. "I know you hate all this sappy emotional stuff."

If only he knew. Taylor had gotten friendly with plenty of emotions this past year.

A year of watching Matt laugh, hold hands, and cuddle with someone who wasn't Taylor. A year of knowing that even if Tomboy Taylor could compete with perfect, pretty, girly girl Dakota Coles, Matt would never, ever cheat.

"I don't hate the emotional stuff," Taylor insisted, wincing at the fierce seriousness in her tone but unable to soften it. "You can tell me anything, no matter what, and I won't judge you or make fun of you. I hope you know that."

"I do." Matt sounded touched, as if he knew that hadn't been easy for Taylor to say. "Nobody gets me like you do, Tay. That's why you're my best friend. Man, I'm going to miss you next year."

Taylor leaned her head against the metal wall of the trailer and tried to tell herself her eyes were watering because of the hay dust in the air. "Me too, Matty. Me too."

"Best friends forever," Matt declared, and this time he was the one who sounded fierce.

Taylor echoed him. All she could think was that if Matt's friendship was what she could have, she'd take it—but if she didn't at least try for something more, she'd regret it for the rest of her life.

Less than two months until graduation, then three months of summer. That was her window. Time to jump out of it and see where she landed.

Chapter Four

By the time Andie closed her front door behind her, it was hours after her shift was supposed to be over. In those hours, she'd mediated a dispute between neighbors involving a wandering goat and an unfortunate clothesline, reprimanded a teenager for speeding down Island Road, filed a mass of paperwork before it could completely cover the surface of her desk, and fended off Ivy's far-too-interested questions about Sanctuary Island's newest arrival.

"I'm just saying, Corinne Larkin, down at the market, well she said she saw him driving past in Jo Ellen's truck, and Corinne said he she could tell even from a distance that he's a stone cold fox," Ivy had eagerly related.

"More like a wolf," Andie told her, doing her best to be firm. "Seriously, I've got a feeling about him."

Ivy gave a catlike stretch and curled her red mouth into a smile. "If what Corinne said is true, I'm curious what feelings he could give me. Unless, of course, you're calling dibs."

Andie had told her dispatcher not to be ridiculous, but deep inside, she was uncomfortably aware that she hadn't warned Ivy off of Sam for purely altruistic reasons. He might be volatile, but there was something magnetic about him, something that drew Andie's attention and turned her blood to warm honey.

Determined to put Sam Brennan out of her mind, at least long enough to get a good night's sleep, Andie unbuckled her heavy utility belt and hung it on the hat rack by the door. She was already fantasizing about a long, hot shower, her fingers on the buttons of her uniform shirt, when her phone rang.

"Oh, no," she moaned, squeezing her eyes shut. Andie took the space of a breath to wish she were the kind of person who could ignore the phone call, but there was no point wishing for impossible things. It could be work. It could be important. It could be life or death. She plucked her vibrating phone out of the jacket she'd tossed over the back of her sofa.

The unknown Maryland number on the screen froze her in place, every ache and pain forgotten as her mind went blank for the space of a heartbeat.

That was either a telemarketer or . . . her brother.

When he was on active duty, stationed somewhere out there in the world, his only way of phoning the states was a prepaid calling card, which showed up on caller ID as an unknown number. Andie's heart raced. Even knowing the telemarketer was more likely, seeing as how she hadn't had more than a brief email from Owen in almost five years, Andie's finger still hovered over the "talk" button, paralyzed by fear.

What if it wasn't Owen, but his commanding officer, calling to let Owen's next of kin know that he'd been wounded or, God forbid, killed in action?

If that was the truth, she needed to hear it. No matter how much it hurt. Andie hit "talk" and kept her voice firm.

"Sheriff Shepard," she said, taking strength from her official title and sending up a quick prayer for good news.

The rush of relief that hit her system at the sound of her brother's voice in her ear weakened her knees. He sounded good. Scratchy and rough, yes, and there was as much background noise as if he were calling her from inside a blender, but it was Owen.

"So you're a sheriff now? Dad must be over the moon, even if it's not the Louisville PD."

Andie made her way to the couch on unsteady legs. "Are you okay?" she demanded, ignoring the reference to their father. There was no way she was wasting this precious chance to talk to her baby brother by getting into the same old argument.

Owen's stubborn defiance of their father's wishes—and Andie's doomed attempts to step into that gap and follow in their father's footsteps—had caused enough distance between them already.

"I don't have to be wounded or dying to call my big sister," Owen protested. There was a short pause where they both considered that. "Okay. Maybe that's fair, and I'm sorry I haven't kept in touch better."

"It's been years, Owen." Andie wished she could keep the hurt out of her tone, but she'd never been a very good actress.

"Crap. Has it? Sorry. I just . . ."

He sighed and Andie could picture him palming the back of his neck, the way he'd done as a kid when he was feeling guilty. Completely against her will, her heart softened. She let him off the hook, like she always did—because someone in their dysfunctional little family had to do it, and it certainly was never going to be Dad.

"I know. You've been busy. How's the army?"

"I made the Rangers, Andie."

She caught her breath and put out a hand to steady herself against the back of the sofa. "Wow. Owen, I'm so proud of you. That's an amazing accomplishment and I know you worked incredibly hard for it."

"You have no idea." He huffed out a laugh she could barely hear over the clatter and static of noise in the background of the call.

"Where are you calling from?" she asked. "If you're allowed to say."

"I'm not," he told her grimly, "and I wish I could tell you I called to catch up, but the fact is, we're going wheels up in about seven minutes and I have a favor to ask."

Andie didn't even hesitate. "Anything."

He paused for a breath as if she'd surprised him. When his voice sounded in her ear again, it was lower, strained. Owen never did like to let on that he had a heart. "You might regret that when you hear what it is."

Andie's chest hurt with how much she loved him. Maybe if they'd grown up with a mother's tender guidance, they'd be better at saying it out loud. But Andie did the best she could—she showed how much she loved and worried for him through her actions. "Whatever you need. I mean it."

"I have a kid."

The world reeled beneath Andie's feet for a dizzying second. "You got married? When? Who is she? And I have a baby niece or nephew already? Owen!"

"I'm not married," he interrupted forcefully. "And you have a niece, but not a baby. She's eight years old."

Andie swallowed around a huge, painful lump of emotions. Had they really become so disconnected, so estranged, that her youngest brother had been in a serious relationship for almost a decade without telling her? "Owen, what on earth . . ."

"I didn't know about the baby." The words ground out of him, stark and uncompromising. "She never told me."

Andie took a deep breath. She'd trained to handle crisis situations calmly and efficiently. "Who is 'she'? The mother?"

"Someone I dated briefly right before I enlisted. I was way out of the picture by the time she figured out she was pregnant . . . and the thing between us—it hadn't ended well. I don't know how hard she tried to contact me or not, and I can't ask her because she died in a car accident two weeks ago. It took them this long to locate me from what she'd told the kid—I guess she didn't keep great records."

"Oh no, Owen . . ." Andie wobbled around the corner of the sofa and let her knees go, sinking back against the couch cushions to stare up at the swirled plaster of her living room ceiling. The mother, dead. And the father? About to head out on a classified mission with his elite special ops strike force. Basically as unavailable as it was possible to be. "Where is your daughter? Right now?"

"That's where the favor comes in." Owen lowered his voice, his desperation seeping through the phone line to raise every hair on Andie's body. "She's on her way to Sanctuary Island."

"I need to sit down," Andie said faintly. She

blinked. "Oh. I'm already sitting down. Maybe I need a drink. Owen, what?"

"Her name is Caitlin, she's got no other living family, and the army has rules about soldiers who can't make arrangements for their dependents. I can't come home right now—I can't leave my team in the lurch, right before an op—but I have to be able to show I've set my kid up somewhere stable and safe. Please, Andie. I need you. Caitlin needs you."

Working to slow her quick, shallow breaths, Andie tightened her grip on the phone until the plastic bit into her hand. "I don't know anything about taking care of a little girl."

"You know more than I do," Owen argued. "You were one!"

"No, I wasn't. Not really."

Andie didn't exactly mean to say it, but the quiet words dropped into the sudden silence like rocks into a lake. She could almost hear Owen remembering what it had been like to grow up in their spotless row house in Louisville, with no mother and a father so embittered by her loss that he'd dedicated himself to discipline and rules. It was a house without softness of any kind.

Those memories were the current that ran through every conversation she and Owen ever had, no matter how brief.

"I know," Owen replied, regret heavy in his voice. "And I wouldn't ask, I've got no right to expect help from you, but Andie—if you don't take her in, they're going to send her to Dad."

Andie's heart stuttered in her chest. Even though she was normally the one defending their father to Owen, the idea of sending another motherless little

girl to live in that cold, strict, regimented house . . .
"Oh. Owen, no. Of course Caitlin can come here.
I'll do my best, and it's only temporary, right?"

"Right! Once this mission is over, I've got some
leave coming to me. We'll figure it out in a month
or so."

"A month. Okay. There's a limit to how badly I
can screw a kid up in four weeks," Andie said, trying to sound sure. Because, priorities. Whatever her
worries and fears, however much she wanted to lecture Owen on responsibility and slap him silly for
getting some girl pregnant and not even knowing
about the baby . . . they couldn't deal with all of that
now. "Seriously, Owen, don't worry about a thing.
Keep your mind on your mission. All I want you
concentrating on is coming home safely."

"Yeah." His voice and the background noise faded
for a second, as if he'd muffled the phone against
his chest. When he came back, he said, "Sorry, my
CO is giving me the high sign. I've got to go. Thank
you for this, sis, from the bottom of my heart. I'll
make it up to you, I swear."

"Be safe," Andie rushed to say, but Owen had already disconnected the call.

Great. She hadn't even managed to find out when
the girl—her niece—Caitlin—might be showing up,
or who'd be bringing her. She'd made sure to email
Owen her new address and phone number when she
moved to Sanctuary Island; she knew that she, not
their father, was listed as Owen's next of kin. Surely
that meant they'd be able to find her.

Nervous energy propelled her off the couch. She
still needed a shower, and the guest bedroom needed
to be made up, her side arm locked in the safe un-

der her nightstand, and what did eight-year-old kids like to eat, anyway? Was the frozen pizza she'd planned to defrost for her supper okay? It had vegetables on it. Green peppers and tomato . . . and olives counted as vegetables, too, right?

Andie glanced down at her watch. 7:03. But that was useless knowledge. There was no way to gauge how much time she had when she didn't know where the girl was. But the distant blast of the ferry's horn, down at the harbor, went through Andie like a gunshot.

The ferry was the only way on or off the island. It ran between Sanctuary Island and Winter Harbor, Virginia, in the morning and evening. Every resident of Sanctuary had the ferry schedule memorized. Seven in the morning and seven at night.

Was it possible Caitlin could be arriving on that very ferry?

Stripping frantically, Andie pitched her dirty uniform into the hamper and leaped into the shower for the fastest scrubdown of her life. She wasn't going to meet her niece for the first time smelling like an escaped bulldog. Once she was clean and dressed in jeans and a thick navy cable-knit sweater against the chill spring evening, she felt more in control of the situation.

At least until her doorbell chimed. Andie tugged the spare toothbrush from her last trip to the dentist from its wrapping and dropped it into the cup next to her own. Taking a deep breath and rubbing her damp palms along her thighs, she made her way across the living room to open the front door.

On her doorstep stood an older woman in Army Dress Blues with gold stripes on the shoulders and a small cross pinned to her collar. And standing slightly behind her, as if taking cover behind her legs, was Caitlin.

Andie's throat squeezed tight. She'd never seen this child before, but she would have known her for family instantly. The similarity to the little brother who lived in Andie's memories was unmistakable. Caitlin had Owen's serious mouth and way of tilting his head, the freckles he'd lost over the years, and the carroty orange-red hair that had been the bane of Andie's existence growing up.

When Caitlin ducked a glance from beneath her pale lashes, Andie's heart expanded like a balloon, filling with helpless, overwhelming love. Connection. Family. Belonging.

This was going to be amazing. Andie imagined herself holding out her arms, imagined her niece running into them, imagined picking her up and twirling them around in the sunshine . . .

But as Caitlin met Andie's eyes, the girl shrank back, hunching her shoulders as if trying to make herself invisible. Andie bit her lip and cautioned herself to slow down. She really knew nothing about Caitlin or what her life had been like up until now.

"Sheriff Shepard?" the woman inquired, reminding Andie that she and Caitlin weren't alone.

"That's me," she said, tearing her gaze from her niece to smile at her caretaker.

"I'm Lieutenant Loretta Phelps, Chaplain at Fort Benning. Your brother was there for Airborne School last year, part of his Ranger training. When Sergeant Shepard found out what had happened," the chaplain said delicately, with a glance down at her silent charge, "he asked me to bring her to you."

Lt. Phelps was in her thirties, with a sensible

brown bob and the sort of plain, kind features that made Andie want to trust her immediately. "And we're very grateful, Lieutenant. I know Owen would want me to thank you for going well above and beyond the call of duty. Please sit down and be comfortable—I hope you'll stay the night with us."

"Thank you, but I can't," Lt. Phelps said, with a small, regretful smile. "I'm on leave right now, but I need to report back to base by oh six hundred tomorrow."

"So soon." Then all three of them stood there awkwardly on Andie's carpet, unsure where to look or what to do. She realized she'd been counting on the buffer of another adult's presence, at least for the first night, but apparently she and Caitlin were soon to be on their own.

And after that one swift glance, Caitlin hadn't met Andie's eyes again. Instead, she'd opted to stare down at the scruffy pink backpack at her feet. Andie crouched down to put herself on Caitlin's level. "Hey there, I'm your Aunt Andie. It's nice to meet you."

That familiar blue gaze flicked up to Andie's face, almost unreadable. Dread fluttered down Andie's spine at the thought of what kind of life could train such a young girl to blank her expression. No kid should have this much self-control, this ability to hold herself still like a mouse hiding from a hawk. Remembering herself at age eight, and how grown-up she'd thought she was, Andie mustered up a smile and held her hand out. Caitlin glanced at the chaplain before stepping forward to shake Andie's hand. Like the strangers they were . . . for now.

Pushing out a shaky breath, Andie felt her smile widen into something real and hopeful. They had time. She could push gently at Caitlin's boundaries, make her feel safe enough to let down the walls. It would take time and patience, but Andie had that in spades.

"I'm sorry, but I should really get going now if I want to make tonight's return ferry," Lt. Phelps was saying, and Andie mustered up an understanding smile as she stood.

"Of course. Can I give you a ride?"

"I have my car." The chaplain turned her gentle face down to the girl at her side. "Caitlin, it was wonderful to meet you. I know you'll be very happy here on this beautiful island, with your aunt."

Caitlin shrugged one skinny shoulder and said nothing, and Andie experienced an odd moment of embarrassment, as if Caitlin's stiff silence reflected on Andie somehow. She simultaneously wanted to urge Caitlin to politely thank the chaplain—and also to step in front of Caitlin and defend her from anyone who might criticize her for rudeness. Was this what being a parent felt like?

Lt. Phelps didn't appear offended or judgmental. Instead she laid a sympathetic hand on Caitlin's shoulder as a silent good-bye, and walked to the door. With one hand on the knob, she said, "Sheriff, if I could have a moment?"

"Uh sure." Andie looked uncertainly at the motionless child in her living room. "I'll be right back, Caitlin, and we'll get you settled in. Okay?"

Another shrug. Squaring her own shoulders, Andie followed the chaplain out into the cool April night. She crossed her arms over her chest and waited for Lt. Phelps to find the words she was obviously searching for.

"I didn't spend much more than a day with Caitlin," she said finally, "but on the trip here, I couldn't help but notice that she's struggling."

"Hardly surprising," Andie pointed out, keeping her voice low. "Considering her mother just passed away, and all the big changes that have come flying at her. Anyone would be struggling, much less an eight-year-old."

Lt. Phelps nodded. "I didn't get a lot of information from the Child Protective Services rep who was assigned to Caitlin's case, but . . . I got the impression that the mother's death wasn't the reason for the assignment. The rep seemed to know Caitlin better than the couple of weeks it took for them to track down your brother."

Andie crossed her arms over her chest to ward off a sudden chill. "You mean, CPS had gotten involved with Caitlin and her mother before? As in . . . Caitlin was abused?"

"I'm not privy to the details of her file. As her temporary guardian, you might be able to get more information if you apply for it, but generally, the involvement of CPS can mean several things. Abuse and neglect, certainly, but that covers a range of situations. I just thought you should be aware, so you could follow up with the CPS rep and get Caitlin any outside help that might be appropriate, like therapy."

"Do you really think that's going to be necessary?" Andie asked, heart aching in her chest.

"I can't say," Lt. Phelps told her softly. "From my observations, Caitlin is deeply troubled, withdrawn and unresponsive to most adults, especially women."

"And now she's been dumped on an adult woman she's never met," Andie finished painfully, staring over her shoulder at the closed door. "Maybe this was a bad idea. I don't want to make things harder for her than they already are."

"You're her family. No one in the world can make it easy, what she's got to go through now . . . but you can help. If you're anything like your brother, you'll be fine."

The slight smile lit the chaplain's plain features with a warmth and happiness that transformed her face. The light pink blush that suffused her cheeks didn't hurt, either, and Andie bit her lips against a smile.

That was Owen, all right. Her baby brother, making friends and breaking hearts wherever he went.

"Owen and I are both in your debt," Andie said, holding out her hand. "I don't know how we can ever repay you for taking your own personal time to bring Caitlin all the way here, but if you ever need anything, I hope you'll call. And that you'll at least let me pay your expenses for the trip."

Lt. Phelps waved away any thought of payment and shook Andie's hand. "I was glad to do it. Your brother is a good man, even if he doesn't always believe it himself. Good luck, Sheriff Shepard."

With that last, perfect insight, the chaplain walked briskly down the slate paving stone walkway to climb into her little gray car. Andie watched her go, her mind a whirl of new information, worries, and aching empathy for the child who had nowhere to go and no one to count on but an aunt she'd never met.

Andie braced herself to chisel away at Caitlin's walls, but when she went back inside, the girl was no longer standing in the middle of the living room. Instead, she'd curled up on the sofa with her head on her ratty backpack and her sneakers dangling off the edge like she'd been trying to keep her feet off the cushions. Andie's neck hurt just looking at the weird angle of Caitlin's thin body, but the girl was fast asleep.

"Tomorrow is a new day," Andie promised herself in a whisper as a spasm of love shuddered through her. "And everything is going to be all right."

As she lifted the too-light burden of her sleeping niece into her arms and carried her down the hall to tuck her into the guest bed, Andie did her best to believe her own words.

Chapter Five

Sam liked his room at Harrington House. The Victorian mansion where his cousin, Penny, used to be the caretaker and now was the mistress, was one of the oldest homes on Sanctuary Island. Sam's window looked out over the town square across Island Road, an expanse of bright spring green grass and tender saplings sheltered by big, old oaks.

He was shoving his feet into his boots when Matt rapped his knuckles on the open door frame. Sam gave the kid a quick grin. "Up already? I thought you were supposed to be a teenager."

"I was sure you'd be the one sleeping in, old man," Matt countered, smirking. "You said last night we were up way past your bedtime."

"It takes more than a Scrabble grudge match to wear me out. Unlike your wimpy mother."

Penny had pleaded exhaustion by nine o'clock, heading for bed with a sweet kiss to Matt's forehead and a squeeze of Sam's shoulders. Her new husband, Dylan, had made his excuses not long after. It had been more than a year, but those two still acted like newlyweds.

"Mom's never been a night owl." Matt shrugged, but a hint of a frown darkened his hazel eyes.

"Y'all are doing all right here, aren't you?" Sam got to his feet, keeping a weather eye on his young cousin.

"I think so. I mean, yeah. Things are good."

Sam tucked his tongue into his cheek. "Real convincing, kid. I hope you're not considering a career in politics."

Slugging Sam half-heartedly in the shoulder, Matt made a face. "Lay off."

After Penny grabbed Matt and left her jackwagon of a first husband, Sam had been the only man Matty had to look up to for a long time. And maybe Sam wasn't exactly cut out to be anyone's hero, but he'd done his best. And even now that Dylan was in the picture and apparently in the running for Stepfather of the Year, from what Sam had seen, it was a tough habit to break. "Hey, y'all are putting me up in your house, least I can do is play armchair family counselor."

"We don't need a family counselor!" Matt insisted, twitchy as all hell.

Sam spread his hands and dropped his voice to the tone he used on nervous horses. "Seriously, Matty. You in trouble? Maybe it's not family stuff. Maybe girl trouble?"

Bull's-eye. Matt's cheeks went red and splotchy, his gaze dropped to the floor, and he shifted his weight from foot to foot like the awkward, shy, overweight kid he'd been up until his growth spurt hit last year. "No," Matt muttered. "I've got a girlfriend. The most popular girl in school, actually."

Sam had spent most of his school career hiding out in wood shop, because Mr. Farley was the only teacher who didn't bat an eye at a kid who showed up with bruises. Sam had been thinking about other stuff back then, consumed with getting big enough to fight back or run away, not dating and social status. His understanding of what it meant to be dating the "popular girl" was mostly based on movies and TV at this point. "That sounds good. So what's the problem?"

"There's no problem." Matt threw his hands in the air then turned and stomped down the stairs.

Sam followed him more slowly, turning the conversation over in his mind. "Does this have anything to do with Taylor McNamara?"

Matt stopped so suddenly, Sam almost crashed into him and sent them both diving face-first down the steep wood staircase. "I'm not cheating on Dakota!"

"Nobody said you were," Sam pointed out reasonably, with a gentle nudge between the kid's shoulder blades to get him moving again. The scent of fresh-brewed coffee and sizzling bacon rose warmly up to greet them, making Sam's mouth water. "All I'm saying is, watch out for Taylor. She's a live wire."

Matt gripped the elaborate newel post at the bottom of the banister and tilted his chin up to look Sam in the eye. "You think she's a bad influence, but you've got the wrong idea about her."

"I was there when she convinced you it was a good idea to swipe a bottle of rum and sneak out to the protected part of the wild horse preserve," Sam reminded him, arching a brow.

"But you weren't there when we did the community service with Sheriff Shepard," Matt said earnestly. "The sheriff had us hauling fertilizer and paving stones, digging flower beds and edging pathways for the rose garden Dylan and his brothers donated to the town."

Sam's idiot imagination flashed on an image of Andie Shepard surrounded by rosebuds and green leaves, wearing nothing but sunlight, freckles, and a seductive smile. It took him a second to tune back in to Matt's recitation of Taylor's many fine qualities.

". . . and even though she had to be at the barn early to help coordinate the therapy riding volunteers, she got up at five every morning last summer to do her part. And after the first few days, I realized she was doing way more than her part, so I started showing up at the crack of dawn to make sure we pulled equal weight. And we just . . . talked. While we worked, we talked about all kinds of stuff, and we became friends. Good friends. Taylor's a good person, Sam. Better than anyone realizes, including her."

Sam smoothed a hand down his close-trimmed beard to hide his smile. "Sounds like Taylor's really been there for you this past year."

"She has." Matt glanced down the hall to the kitchen, where they could hear the murmur of Dylan's deep voice and Penny's soft, contented laughter. "You'll see for yourself—she's out at the barn almost every day. Just promise me you'll give Taylor a chance."

Sam was beginning to get an inkling of what Matt's girl problem might be, but instead of pointing it out, he slung an arm around the kid's wide shoulders and steered him into the kitchen. "I promise, I'll give Taylor a clean slate and get to know her."

Sam nodded gravely through Matt's thanks and

a few additions to the list of Taylor's Virtues, and kept his insights about Matt's girl troubles to himself. At least until he had a chance to judge whether Taylor really was this amazing, perfect paragon, Sam didn't intend to stick his oar in and get Matt to realize that of the two girls in his life, he'd spent five times longer rhapsodizing about his best bud than he had about his popular girlfriend.

When Sam finally escaped his cousin Penny's attempts to "feed him up" by heaping every breakfast food she could think of onto his plate, he was more than ready to work off all the biscuits and gravy with a long day at the barn. He didn't just love the horses and the satisfaction of helping them learn to trust humans again—he loved the physicality of the work. He liked to push his body hard, to feel the work he'd done in the ache of sore muscles at the end of the day.

Unfortunately, no one at Windy Corner appeared to want to get any work done that morning. Instead, they were all gossiping about the strangers who'd ridden over on the ferry the night before.

Sam shook his head and went back to sorting through his tack and his training kit. Something about a female army officer and a kid, blah blah. He tuned it out fairly successfully until someone mentioned Sheriff Shepard. At which point, Sam perked up like a stallion scenting danger on the wind.

"I wonder if this means the sheriff won't show up for her volunteer session this afternoon," Jo Ellen mused.

"She better." Taylor made an indignant face without looking up from texting on her phone. "The volunteer schedule is perfect this week and I hate having to reschedule people. It throws everything out of whack and all the other volunteers whine and complain. It sucks."

"I think the sheriff gets a pass on this one," Jo said mildly. "I know better than most how disrupting it can be to suddenly find yourself in a position to mother someone."

"You know, a while back, I might have taken that personally." Taylor tapped a contemplative finger against her chin, but the crinkle at the corners of her brown eyes was all mischief. And beyond a squawk, she didn't resist when Jo grabbed her in a headlock and ruffled her short blonde hair.

"But now that you're all grown up," Jo Ellen laughed, "and have realized that the entire world doesn't revolve around you . . ."

"Says who?" Taylor demanded, tugging free with a toss of her carelessly tousled head. "My life is tuned to the Taylor Channel. It's All Taylor, All the Time, from where I'm standing."

She held the snotty pose, hands on hips, for a handful of seconds before rolling her eyes, giving a full-body shake and going back to her phone with a snort. Sam resisted a smile. He was starting to see why Matt liked this girl. He watched her fingers fly over the face of her phone and wondered if she was texting Matt. She'd been basically glued to that thing since Sam arrived that morning.

"How are Ella and Merry doing, anyway?" Sam asked, doing the polite thing to get the conversation back on track. And if that meant eventually circling it around to find out more about what was up with Andie, then so be it. Good manners dictated the whole thing.

"All three of my girls are doing well," Jo Ellen said with a fond glance at her soon-to-be stepdaughter.

"Ella's talking about moving here full time after the wedding. Merry is giving her the hard sell, of course. She'd love to have another back-up babysitter for Alex, when she and Ben want some time alone."

Sam's head swam a little bit. It was either from the leather polish fumes or from the idea of having so much family, so many interlocking relationships, so many people to deal with. "Sounds like you've been busy."

"That's life." Jo shrugged one plaid-flannel-clad shoulder. "I'd rather be busy and surrounded by family than completely relaxed and alone."

Sam, who'd been alone in all the ways that mattered for most of his life, felt a strange pang in his chest. Ignoring it, he arched a brow in Jo's direction. "Let's talk again in a few months, after the therapy center is up and running and a big success, and you're trying to plan another wedding and help your daughter move and get this one off to college. You might change your tune."

"Fair enough." Kicking her brown paddock boots up onto the metal desk and folding her hands over her stomach, Jo didn't seem especially concerned.

Until Taylor piped up with, "Who says I'm going to college?"

Jo's boots hit the ground with a thud just as a car door slammed out front and a voice called, "Hello? Anyone here?"

Every cell in Sam's body lit up like the first fireflies on a summer's night. It was Andie. He'd know that sweet, husky voice anywhere.

Dropping his half-cleaned halter back into his tack trunk, Sam stood and glanced at Jo and Taylor. They were locked in some kind of silent stare down that looked likely to explode at any moment.

Figuring he'd best get clear of the blast radius, Sam pointed at the office door. "I'll go see what the sheriff wants."

Sam edged out the door with a sigh of relief that almost choked him when he saw Andie Shepard's tall, slim figure silhouetted between the open barn doors. At her side, a careful foot of distance between them, was a little kid.

Curiosity simmered alongside the ever-present attraction that flared to life whenever Sam was close enough to Andie to see the subtle cinnamon flecks of her freckles. He tucked his hands in his pockets to keep from touching her when he walked a few steps closer—and by now, he could see the banked desperation in her deep-sea eyes and the downturned corners of her wide, pink mouth.

"What's up, Sheriff?" he asked, keeping it light and easy while he got the lay of the land.

She ran a hand through her hair—loose waves of dark red-gold today, the first time Sam had ever seen it down, and suddenly all he could think about was plunging his fingers into the silken strands and fisting his hands to hold her still as he plundered that mouth. Andie caught her bottom lip between her teeth for a split second and Sam's blood went hot and thick.

Down boy, he told himself. *Not the time or the place or the audience you want for something like that.*

"Something . . . unexpected has come up," Andie said, more uncertain than he'd ever seen her. "I'm going to be looking after my niece, Caitlin, for a little while. Until my brother can come home."

Sam watched as Andie put a tentative hand on Caitlin's shoulder, only to see the girl twitch out of her grasp like a colt shaking off flies. The way Andie's face fell into resigned lines told him this wasn't the first time she'd reached out and been rejected, and the blank, closed-off look on Caitlin's young face made Sam's heart ache. His protective instincts, never far from the surface, bloomed into a need to help these two find their way to each other.

A soft whicker from the integration stall behind him was all it took to remind Sam of why he couldn't get caught up in the sheriff's problems. He had enough of his own to deal with.

Still, he couldn't help asking, "You bowing out of the volunteer gig? I'm sure Jo Ellen will understand."

"I don't want to quit on them before we even get started." Frustration clipped Andie's words short and brisk. "But I don't see how I can manage it. I've got to go on duty this morning, and I guess Caitlin's going to have to hang out at the office until I can get her into school and figure out day care, and I'm not sure how long Owen is going to be away—"

She broke off when Sam put his hands on her shoulders, and she stared up into his face with the blankness of real panic. "Breathe," Sam told her softly, sliding one hand to cup the back of her long, pale neck.

Andie squeezed her eyes shut and ground her back teeth—Sam could feel the pressure where he held her—and when she opened her eyes again, the panic had dissipated. That was a good coping mechanism, right there, Sam noted . . . and not something a person developed unless panic attacks were a frequent occurrence. The beautiful lady sheriff got more interesting every time he saw her.

Which was a problem.

"I'm fine," Andie said, mostly steadily. "You can let go of me now, I'm not going to pass out or anything."

Sam realized he'd been staring into Andie's fathomless blue-green eyes for way too long. He ought to step back, let them both reclaim their personal space, but he couldn't quite bear to stop touching her now that he'd gotten his hands on her. His right hand flexed gently against the nape of her neck, dragging the pads of his fingers through the delicate tendrils of hair there, and Andie rewarded him with a shiver.

"Maybe you're the one keeping me on my feet," Sam said roughly. There was something gut-wrenchingly sexy about a woman who was tall enough to look him in the eye.

The tension between them crystallized, fragile and sharp and unbearably sweet. Sam breathed her warm breath and savored the firm curves of her body mere inches away. His heart kicked against his ribcage. He officially didn't care that this was a terrible idea. He was going to kiss her.

Except Andie planted her hand in the center of his chest and stopped him. "Wait a second," she said, looking around frantically. "Where's Caitlin?"

Chapter Six

Andie had never been so grateful for the training that allowed her to leap from Unwillingly Yet Undeniably Aroused to Crisis Mode.

"She can't have gone far," Sam pointed out, striding over to the barn doors to peer out at the front paddocks.

"Caitlin?" Andie called. She jogged down the wide barn hall to the opposite set of doors, but there was no sign of her niece on the sloped hill leading down to the training rings. "Are you hiding? Come on out, sweetie, I promise I'm not mad."

She and Sam met back in the middle of the barn. He shook his head, mouth a thin line. Andie wondered if he was really that worried about Caitlin or if he was just annoyed that her disappearance had interrupted their little . . . whatever it was, back there.

His next words made Andie feel bad that she'd ever questioned Sam's motives. "She's not out front, unless she's climbed a tree or something. Let me check with Jo and Taylor in the office—maybe they saw something."

"I can't believe I lost her," Andie said, her throat tight. "I haven't even had her for a full twenty-four hours."

Sam paused at the office door. "You haven't lost her," he said firmly. "She's just . . . misplaced at the moment. Don't worry, we'll get her back if we have to take this barn apart, board by board, and comb through every haystack. Caitlin's a little bigger than a needle—we'll find her."

Before Andie could do more than register the kindness lighting his deep brown eyes, a soft noise from the stall behind her had her whirling in place.

Most of Windy Corner's horse stalls were generously sized boxes, enclosed on all sides and with a heavy sliding door onto the main barn hall. But the stall Sam strode toward was more of a pen situated between two stalls, closed off from the hall with only a couple of vertical bars. To enter it, he had to lift the top bar and step over the bottom, which he did with the smooth grace of practice.

Andie's heart jumped into her throat at the realization that all Caitlin would've had to do to get into the stall was to duck between the bars. Rushing to peer over the chest-high wall, Andie saw her worst fears confirmed.

Caitlin crouched in the far back corner of the stall, staring up at Queenie, the half-wild black horse Sam had brought to the island the day before.

The horse that had been so unruly and threatening, someone had called the sheriff for help.

And that horse was between Sam and Caitlin.

Every muscle in Sam's body wanted to tense, but he forced himself to relax. Queenie was already worked up enough, with the rescue and the ferry ride and a new barn. Sam couldn't afford to add any more stress to the situation.

From the corner of the stall, the little girl piped up. "The horse isn't hurting me. I'm not afraid."

Sam's heart rate slowed. "That's good. Caitlin, right? You're doing great."

"The horse likes me," the kid said, like she was trying to convince herself.

Her high, clear voice was a new sensory input for Queenie, who'd never spent a lot of time around kids. That could've made the mare nervous—but instead, she seemed intrigued. Every word out of Caitlin's mouth had her cocking long, sensitive ears in the kid's direction.

"Caitlin, honey," Andie said, strained. "Come on out of there. Just edge around the side of the stall toward Sam, he'll help you."

"No. Don't want to." Caitlin planted her sneakers into the sawdust bedding that covered the floor of the stall.

Sam couldn't tell if Caitlin was afraid to move or just being stubborn, but either way, he said, "That's fine. You're good right there, sweetheart. Stay put."

Sam held up a warning hand to Andie before she could argue. He shook his head at her, keeping one eye on the tense mare. Andie's fingers clenched on the stall barrier like she wanted to vault over it and sweep Caitlin out of harm's way by force, but she gave Sam a reluctant nod.

Grateful that she at least trusted that he knew more about horses and barn safety than she did, Sam reached a slow, calm hand and settled it on the horse's black rump. Queenie sidestepped jerkily, craning her neck back to see Sam.

"Queenie is okay, for the moment," Sam told

Andie quietly, "but if anything happens to spook her, we could be in real trouble."

"If anything happens—like a door slamming or a car backfiring?" Andie asked.

"Or sudden movements close by her head," Sam told her. He heard Andie suck in a breath and gave in to the urge to comfort her. "Don't worry, I'll get Caitlin."

"Be careful." Andie was so intent, so worried, that Sam risked a glance in her direction. His gaze snagged on hers and an electric current arced between them, sharp and hot. Andie's cheeks washed with red and she lifted her chin. "I mean, be careful with Caitlin. And thanks."

"Don't thank me yet." Sam ran his hand firmly and gently along Queenie's quivering side as he walked slowly up to the horse's head. Combing his fingers up the tangled crest of Queenie's coarse, black mane, Sam murmured subvocal reassurances to the traumatized animal. And all the time, he inched closer to the skinny redheaded girl in the corner of the big stall.

Caitlin watched him coming, standing unnaturally still. Sam couldn't remember ever seeing a kid her age who wasn't in constant motion, energy practically exploding from every pore. But Andie's niece was like a little statue. She kept giving Sam wary glances, but most of her attention was on the horse standing over her. From her vantage point of four-feet-and-change, Queenie must look gigantic. Caitlin didn't seem afraid of the mare, though. In fact, the kid seemed more nervous about the human adult approaching her than she did about the very real possibility of getting trampled by a rampaging horse.

Sam thought he recognized the type. He was one

himself. Keeping his right hand working on untangling Queenie's mane with slow, careful tugs, Sam grinned down at Caitlin. "So, you like horses, huh?"

Caitlin shrugged but never took her eyes off Queenie's soft nose as the mare lowered her head and shuddered in appreciation of Sam's scratching fingers. He ran his hands up Queenie's ears, paying particular attention to the pressure points at the tips, and watched as Caitlin's gaze followed his petting movements as if she were imagining her own hands running over Queenie's inky dark coat.

"I can tell you've got horse fever," Sam said, teasing a little. "It's not usually dangerous but it can result in the patient having an uncontrollable desire to get close to any horse in the vicinity."

"Not just any horse." Caitlin immediately pressed her lips together like she regretted speaking up, but Sam gave her an encouraging smile.

"Queenie is special," he agreed.

"She's perfect." Intense and fierce, in that moment Caitlin sounded exactly like her aunt.

"She will be," Sam told her. "But we'll have some work to do, to get her there."

She frowned. "What do you mean?"

"See, she's been treated badly by the people who were supposed to take care of her, and it's made her jumpy around people. But with time and patience, I guarantee, she'll be your best friend if you let her."

Caitlin's eyes lit up and for the first time, Sam realized they were the exact same ocean blue as Andie's. "Can I pet her?"

"It's good that you asked," Sam said, letting his approval show loud and clear. The girl blossomed under it like a sunflower lifting its heavy head to the sky. "Smart. And since you're smart enough to ask, and smart enough to see how special Queenie is . . ."

Sam reached out his left hand and, after a short hesitation, Caitlin put her much smaller hand in his and let him guide her to stroke slowly over the white star on Queenie's forehead. Her forelock feathered down over their fingers, making Caitlin's bright smile appear for a brief instant, like the flicker of light on a fish's tail as it turned to swim into deeper waters.

Queenie snorted, her warm breath and whiskery muzzle nosing equally at Sam's belly and Caitlin's shoulder. The little girl turned big eyes up to Sam, wonder and joy illuminating her pale face; Sam couldn't help smiling back. "You ready to get out of here now?"

Caitlin pulled free of his grasp with a scowl. She shook her head, mouth going tight and stubborn, but Sam had her number now. He knew what to bribe her with.

"How about if I promise you can help me with Queenie's training? And when she's ready, you'll be the first one to ride her."

Caitlin's face shuttered, wary skepticism arching her brows in an expression far too mature for her young face. "I've never been on a horse before, ever."

"Then I guess we'll have to train you at the same time as we train Queenie, so you'll be ready for each other. What do you say?"

She didn't say anything, just watched him with narrowed eyes. Sam didn't waste his breath trying to convince her that he was on the level. He waited patiently to see if she'd come to him on her own.

But when she finally spoke, Sam wasn't prepared for her question.

"Are you a friend of my dad's?"

Sam blinked. "Uh, no. Sorry, I've never met the man. But I'm a friend of your aunt's."

The word "friend" might not be the best way to describe Sam and Andie's situation, but he wasn't about to explain the complicated layers of interest, attraction, suspicion, and deception that truly characterized the connection between them. Especially since Sam barely understood it himself.

Caitlin sighed, apparently not all that reassured. Seemed weird to Sam, but maybe they hadn't spent much time together, or maybe that was normal. How would he know? His experiences of family life had been pretty sporadic and, for the most part, bad. At least that had been true of the family he'd been born into. It was funny how those earliest lessons stuck with a person.

From outside of the barn came the growl of an engine and the crunch of tires coming up the gravel driveway. Queenie went stiff, every sinew straining, her ears swiveling to take in any sound that might spell a threat.

They were out of time. Sam couldn't take the chance that whoever it was would slam their door and send Queenie into a spinning, kicking frenzy. One blow of her flailing hooves, and Caitlin could be seriously injured.

"Time's up," he told her. "You gonna take my deal or not?"

"I guess." Caitlin shrugged, more tense than he'd seen her yet. It was as if she felt that by agreeing to Sam's terms, she'd given him some kind of power over her—and to minimize the danger, she was determined to pretend she didn't care whether or not he came through.

Which told Sam that someone in Caitlin's young life had made promises they couldn't deliver on. More than once. And now Caitlin would literally rather get trampled by a wild animal than admit she'd gotten her hopes up.

Sam closed his eyes against the memories sucking at him like quicksand, but he didn't struggle under their weight. Struggling would only sink him faster. Instead, he faced the images that surged to the front of his mind calmly, without fear, and let them pass away back into the darkness where they belonged.

He blinked his eyes open and held out his hand once more. "You've got no reason to trust me. I can't force you to believe in my promise, and I know what it's like to feel like you can't trust anyone. Like you're on your own. But if you want to learn to ride—if you want to ride this horse, you're going to have to work with me. You're going to have to trust me at least enough to do what I say. And here's your first test."

She stared at him steadily, giving nothing away, and Sam had to admire her poise. "What do I have to do?"

"Follow me out of this stall. Step where I step, don't wave your arms around, and don't dawdle. Got it?"

Caitlin gave a short nod, her reddish-orange brows furrowing in concentration. Sam turned back toward the stall door, moving smoothly and quickly, keeping his ears open for the sound of her light footsteps behind him.

There. Caitlin was following him. Sam felt a slow smile break across his face just as he looked up and saw Andie's worried face. Her eyes were bright with unshed tears, her lips almost colorless, and freckles standing out on her milky skin like flecks of cinnamon.

Andie mouthed "Thank you" at Sam, and his heart swelled. He guided Caitlin forward to squeeze between the horizontal bars of the stall barrier, keeping his body between her and the twitchy mare. In seconds, they were both out of the stall safely.

Turning back from making sure the bars were securely in place, Sam saw the awkward, aborted gesture Andie made toward hugging her niece, and the way Caitlin stepped aside. Andie caught him looking and her mouth twisted in bleak recognition. "So not only are you a horse whisperer—you're a kid whisperer too?"

"Caitlin and I reached an understanding," Sam told her. "She stays safe—which means, she stays out of Queenie's stall, or any horse's stall when there's no adult around—and I'll teach her to ride."

"Oh!" Andie glanced swiftly back and forth between Sam and her niece. "I couldn't ask you to take the time to do that."

"You didn't ask. I'm offering. And anyway, this deal has nothing to do with you, it's between me and my new student. Right, Caitlin?"

"Shake on it." Caitlin stuck out her hand, all defiant and serious, as if she didn't really believe Sam would.

When Sam gripped her cold, thin fingers and shook once, firmly, Caitlin's eyes went wide. Sam grinned down at her, then used the hand he was holding to tow her across the hall to the tack room.

The smell of worn leather was thick in the air, and Caitlin stared openmouthed at the racks of saddles lining three walls. Sam tugged her past them and over to the back wall where a dusty full-length mirror leaned in the corner.

Standing her in front of the mirror, Sam twisted to heft a green plastic trunk over to Caitlin. He flipped the lid, releasing a puff of dirt, and showed her the pile of black velvet riding helmets inside.

"There oughta be one that fits you. Root around till you find it, I'm going to go talk to your aunt for a second."

Caitlin shot him a suspicious glance out of the corner of her eyes, as if she knew very well he wanted a few minutes alone with Andie and she was ninety-nine percent sure he wouldn't be coming back.

Figuring the only way to prove her wrong was to, well, prove her wrong, Sam shooed her toward the trunk of helmets and backed out of the tack room. He caught Andie just as she was about to stick her head into the office, probably to tell Jo and Taylor she wouldn't be able to volunteer.

"Wait!" Sam called, jogging down the hall to pull her away from the office. His long fingers circled her wrist easily, her slender bones feeling somehow sturdy and capable against his palm.

Andie paused, glancing down at where they touched, but she didn't pull away. Her shoulders were slumped and tired, the angle of her head exposing the vulnerable nape of her neck. "I've got to talk to Jo, then get down to the sheriff's office. Is Caitlin okay in there?"

"There are no untamed animals in the tack room," Sam assured her. "Although if she's determined to get into trouble, I imagine she'll find a way. Is she always so stubborn?"

To his surprise, red bloomed up Andie's pale neck

and into her cheeks. That creamy redhead's complexion sure didn't let her hide a thing. "I wouldn't know. I met Caitlin for the first time last night. Before that, I didn't even know she existed."

A few things clicked into place for Sam. "That actually explains a lot."

Andie bristled, challenge lifting her chin. "Like what?"

"Like the way neither of you seems to know what to do with the other," Sam said bluntly.

The momentary defiance seeped out of Andie like helium from a balloon. "Oh, that," she said glumly. "Yeah. I don't know how common it is for kids to decide they hate you on first sight, but . . ."

"She doesn't hate you," Sam protested. When Andie only shook her head despairingly, he dropped her wrist to grab her by the shoulders and make her meet his serious stare.

"Caitlin does not hate you," he insisted. "She just doesn't trust you. Which makes sense—she's in a strange situation and she doesn't feel safe yet. It'll take time, but she'll come around. So long as you show her you care, and I know you do."

"You seem to know an awful lot about it," Andie muttered. "What makes you such an expert?"

Why did Caitlin immediately respond to you, and not to me?

Sam heard the question Andie truly wanted to ask, but he didn't know how to answer it without giving away far too much about his own ugly past. Instead of admitting how much of himself he'd instantly recognized in Caitlin's haunted eyes, he shrugged and let go of Andie's shoulders to stick his hands in his pockets. "Sometimes it's easier to see what's going on from the outside. Anyway, the point is—just stick with her. She'll come around. And in the meantime, I have a proposition for you."

"What's that?" Andie gave him a wary look.

Sam didn't give himself time to weigh the pros and cons—the potential benefit of having the sheriff owe him one versus the dangers of getting closer to her—because when he looked into her tired, worried, unhappy eyes, there was only one thing he could say.

"Here's the deal. I'll watch Caitlin for you while you're at work, teach her to ride, make sure she doesn't get kicked in the head by any horses—and in return, you come back this evening and volunteer with me."

Chapter Seven

Andie blinked. Whatever she'd expected, it wasn't this. "I can't let you do that," she repeated automatically. "It's too much to ask."

"Haven't we been over this? I want to do it." Sam rocked back on his heels, loose and easy in his big, muscular frame. When he gave her that half smile, white against the dark silk of his short beard, it was hard for Andie to remember all the reasons she'd had for wanting to stay away from this man.

But there were reasons. Good reasons, like the fact that the last time she fell for a smooth-talking man with an air of danger, he turned out to be truly dangerous—in more ways than one. Given that the pull she felt toward Sam was a hundred times stronger, Andie knew she had to keep her wits about her this time.

She shook her head with a smile that was hopefully cool and polite. "Thank you, really. But I'll figure something else out."

"Why can't I stay here?" Caitlin's high, angry voice demanded from behind her. Andie squeezed her eyes shut for a heartbeat. When she opened them, Sam had the decency to look apologetic.

Hating how helpless she felt, Andie turned to face Caitlin's accusing expression. "It's just . . . not a good idea. Mr. Brennan has a lot of work to do, I can't expect him to look after you. Besides, don't you want to come see where I work?"

"No," Caitlin said, with the heartless honesty of the very young. "Let me stay here with the horses."

With Sam, she didn't say, but Andie could tell it was what Caitlin meant. Andie hadn't known her niece for very long, granted, but she'd seen enough of the girl being silent and shut down to recognize how different she was with Sam. He had a way of getting through to her—something Andie had yet to figure out.

"It's really no trouble," Sam offered mildly. "In fact, I'll put her to work. I could use the help mucking stalls and feeding the horses."

"I don't know." Andie fisted her hands tight on her hips as she studied the sod floor of the barn like she'd find the answers she sought in the swirls of red clay dust and broken pieces of hay.

As if sensing her wavering, Caitlin marched over to stand next to Sam. A helmet covered in patchy, thinning black velvet trailed from her fingertips. "Please. I want to stay."

Andie stared at her niece, who'd barely said two words to Andie since they met. All through breakfast and the drive to the barn, even while standing close as Andie helped brush her hair into a ponytail. Fiery wisps were escaping from the elastic band already. Andie's fingers itched to smooth Caitlin's hair, but the little girl would probably only pull away again. The way she'd done every time, in response to every question from "What were you studying in school back in New Jersey" to "Do you like pancakes better than waffles?"

Caitlin had sidestepped and refused to state a preference when asked, every single time—until now.

Forcing a smile, Andie said, "Okay. It's fine with me, for today. As long as you promise not to wander off, pay close attention to everything Mr. Brennan tells you—and Sam, you call me if anything happens. I mean anything."

Surprise registered in Sam's dark brown eyes before a warm grin crinkled their corners. "Sure thing, Sheriff. Hey, Caitlin . . ."

Cautiously eager eyes peered up into Sam's face. "Yes, Mr. Brennan?" Caitlin said primly, with a cautious sideways glance at Andie to make sure she was catching all this good behavior.

Andie bit back a real smile while Sam dug into the pocket of his worn Levi's and produced a few plastic-wrapped peppermints. Handing the hard candy over to Caitlin, Sam pointed at a stall further down the hall. "That mare down there, third stall from the tack room, is Peony—and she loves peppermints. You'll make yourself a friend for life if you step on over and feed her."

The way Caitlin's face opened up with eagerness stopped Andie from protesting about the dangers of being bitten. After Sam showed her the right way to present the candies to the horse—flat hand, thumb tucked in close so the horse didn't mistake it for another edible treat—Caitlin raced away to Peony's stall.

"She's the gentlest horse on the property," Sam told Andie, watching after Caitlin as if checking to make sure she followed his instructions. "Peony's one of my personal favorites."

"Is that why you always carry her preferred snack in your pocket?" The idea pleased Andie on some deep level, loosening the knot of instinctive wariness that clenched her guts whenever she was around Sam.

Kind to children and animals—wasn't that most people's definition of a good man?

But no pure, perfectly good man would be able to give such a sinfully tempting glance at her from beneath his lashes. Low and rough, his voice sent shivery shocks through Andie's body. "You said yes. I didn't really think you would."

Andie cleared her throat. "It was the first time Caitlin ever told me what she wanted. In all of this mess, with everything she's gone through—I can't think of anything more important I can do for her than to show her that what she wants matters to me."

Something soft and aching passed across his face, like the shadow of a cloud covering the sun for an instant. When it cleared, he said, "And then you told her to listen to everything I say. Aren't you worried I'll sow the seeds of anarchy in the kid, turn her into a rule-breaking rebel?"

Andie took a deep breath and plunged in. "I can't believe you sent her away to give us a few seconds to talk in private and you aren't using them to grill me about why I've never met my eight-year-old niece until now."

Interest sparked in Sam's eyes like a faceted piece of smoky dark topaz catching the light, but he shrugged his big shoulders as if he couldn't care less.

"If you think it's important to me being able to keep an eye on her for a few hours, go ahead. Otherwise, it's none of my business."

Andie surprised herself by wanting to open up. The feeling was so startling that it was easy to repress. "Okay, then. Well, I need to get going—I can't thank you enough for your offer, it's very sweet of you."

Sam smiled, slow like pouring molasses. "I'm a real sweet guy."

Andie's thighs tightened, a pulse of desire throbbing and expanding someplace deep inside her. "You have got to stop flirting with me."

One dark brown eyebrow lifted into a perfect arch. "Why?"

Because if you don't watch out, one of these days I'll take you up on it.

Luckily, Andie had sufficient control of her tongue to avoid blurting out the truth. "Because I don't date, so flirting is pointless."

"Flirting is never pointless, as long as everyone involved is having fun," Sam argued. "Wait, you don't date—as in, you don't date bad boys, or you don't date nice guys who babysit free of charge?"

"As in, I don't date at all. Ever."

"Some men might take that as a challenge."

Her heart jumped and started to race. "Men like that would do better to take me at my word. When I say I don't date, I mean it. End of story."

"Something tells me that's only the beginning of the story," Sam mused with a thoughtful expression that set off a thrill of nerves down Andie's spine. "But it looks like we're going to have to do story time later."

Caitlin bounded back to them just as Andie's gaze

landed on the wall clock mounted above the tack room doorway. Shoot, was it already eight o'clock?

"And then she licked my hand because some of the mint melted and it was sticky but her tongue was really big and kind of rough and I thought it would be gross but I liked it," Caitlin was telling an amused Sam.

When she paused to breathe, Andie broke in. "Hey, I'm going to run. My shift starts—well, now. I'll be back this afternoon, Caitlin. If you need me for any reason, ask Miss Jo to let you use the phone in her office."

"Okay," Caitlin said, glancing at Andie briefly before turning back to Sam to demand more peppermints.

Andie's heart sank, but the sympathy in Sam's molten chocolate gaze helped to stiffen her spine. There was no call to go losing faith just yet. It was only their first full day together.

Before she could dwell on the fact that Caitlin would be spending "their first full day together" with someone else, Andie made herself nod good-bye to the two of them. She walked out to her black SUV, and all the duties and responsibilities that waited for her at the sheriff's office, with the unfamiliar sound of her niece's laughter ringing in her ears.

Caitlin turned out to be a good little helper. She mucked stalls, using the short-handled rake to scoop up the horse manure from the empty box stalls, without complaint. She decorated the chalkboard nameplates next to each stall with colorful chalk flowers and not-half-bad drawings of horses. She swept the hall and polished the brass tags on the bridles and did basically whatever chores Sam could come up with that didn't involve letting her near the horses. Until Andie bought the kid a pair of steel-toed paddock boots, Caitlin wasn't setting herself up for a broken foot on Sam's watch.

Not that Sam had to watch her that closely. The kid followed at his heels like a duckling who'd imprinted on a mountain lion by mistake. She never gave him a moment's trouble—except when he introduced her to Taylor and Jo Ellen.

Eyes down, sullen twist to her mouth, silence instead of chatter. Jo and Taylor exchanged glances then tactfully left Sam to his babysitting duties. And boy, if he'd thought Caitlin was sticking close to his side before, it was nothing to the way she super-glued herself to him whenever Taylor or Jo were in view.

An ugly idea began to tickle at the back of Sam's mind, but for the most part, he managed to ignore anything that didn't have to do with earning Queenie's keep by taking care of Jo's barn duties for the day. If he let himself think about anything else, he might have to confront the fact that he was one single day into this adventure, and he'd already completely failed at steering clear of Sheriff Andie Shepard.

The worst part of it? He couldn't bring himself to regret it. In fact, he kept catching himself grinning in anticipation of seeing her again when she came to pick Caitlin up.

So when the low rumble of her SUV filtered through the cracks in the barn walls along with the late afternoon sunlight, Sam wasn't surprised to find a smile on his face. Shaking his head ruefully, he nudged Caitlin with his booted foot. She looked up sleepily from her spot on the tack room floor, the forgotten bridle in her lap jangling in the quiet still-ness of the barn.

"Your aunt is here," he told her.

Caitlin sighed, tightening her thin fingers on the bridle before pushing to her feet to hang it on the empty wooden peg in the row of bridles lining the wall. "I don't want to go with her. I like it here."

"Here's great," Sam agreed, breathing in the familiar comfort of stable smell as they walked out into the main barn. "But I'm sure your aunt's house is nice, too."

"Does my dad live there sometimes?"

Sam paused. "I don't know, sweetheart. Why don't you ask your aunt about it?"

"I'm not supposed to talk about my dad," she said with a matter-of-fact shrug.

He was willing to bet that wasn't a rule Andie had imposed. "You talked about him with me a little bit," he pointed out.

Caitlin gave him a withering look. "That's different. You're a boy."

Sam wasn't touching that one. "Well, I bet your Aunt Andie wouldn't mind telling you about her brother. You should give her a chance."

"A chance to do what?" Andie asked.

Sam couldn't help it. His body tightened in a rush when she strode into the barn. It was a conditioned response to her voice, at this point—just the sound of her brisk, no-nonsense tones reached deep into his chest and grabbed on tight—but knowing it didn't seem to lessen the impact. He turned to greet her, but the words stuck in his throat.

It was the first time he'd ever seen her out of uniform. And as gorgeous as that tall, athletic body was in crisp khakis and a black utility belt, Sam thought his heart might actually give out at the sight of Andie in dark wash jeans and a spaghetti-strap tank top. The shirt was a bright turquoisey blue color that made her eyes glow and her hair seem more strawberry than blonde. And those jeans . . .

They weren't skin tight, but they hugged her lithe hips and long, lean thighs in a way that made Sam swallow hard against the swell of desire.

"What were y'all talking about?" Andie glanced between her silent niece and Sam, who did his best to force his brain back online.

Caitlin said nothing, choosing instead to pick at a loose thread along the hem of her purple T-shirt. But when Sam opened his mouth to fill Andie in, the kid shot him a sideways look that dried the words up before he could spill them. Caitlin didn't want to talk about her dad with her aunt. Fine, it was none of Sam's business anyway.

"We were just discussing how I'm bound to be way better than you at this volunteering gig," Sam improvised, with a deliberate wink at Caitlin.

Andie's mouth kicked up at the corners as if she'd seen the wink, but she narrowed her eyes and did a convincing impression of a fierce competitor. "Oh yeah? Well, I'm planning to smoke you. So get ready, Mr. Horse Whisperer. You're going down."

Only Caitlin's interested gaze, bouncing between them like a tennis ball, kept Sam from stepping close enough to growl something in Andie's ear about just how much he'd love to go down, as long as she went down with him.

He didn't have a chance to come up with a G-rated response when Jo Ellen appeared in the office doorway with an amused grin on her weathered, handsome face. "Settle down. It's not a competition. In fact, the two of you are going to have to figure out how to work together, not against each other."

"I don't know," Sam said doubtfully, catching Caitlin's eye to make sure she was listening. "The sheriff and I are kind of polar opposites in most ways. And we don't know each other that well. It might be hard for me to give her a chance."

Andie stiffened, but as her gaze drifted from Sam's pointed stare to Caitlin's wide, wary eyes, a stillness came over her. With a dawning smile that looked like hope, Andie said, "You're right, we don't really know each other. Yet. But I'm willing to change that, if you are. And if you're not ready now, well . . . I can be patient. I'm not going to give up."

Once Andie caught on, she stared straight into Sam's eyes and never let her gaze waver. Even so, Sam knew who her words were truly meant for, and he could only hope Caitlin was soaking them up as thirstily as he was. Because even knowing he was only a proxy for the true point of this conversation, there was something about the sincerity and straight-forwardness of Andie's speech that hit him like a kick to the gut.

"I'd like that," Sam said gruffly. He held out his hand to seal the deal, and when Andie clasped his fingers, it was all he could do not to use the lever-age to reel her in for a kiss.

Wrong time, wrong place . . . wrong person. Sam didn't even know if it was Andie who was the wrong person, or if he was. All he knew was that this point he was trying to make to Caitlin had somehow got-ten turned around and skewered him instead. Right through the heart.

What would it be like to have someone in his life who loved him enough to never give up on him?

Sam dropped Andie's capable, interestingly callused hand with a low growl. Waste of time to even
think about it. That kind of love wasn't meant for
a man like Sam. He'd never had it and never would,
so why torture himself imagining it?

Chapter Eight

Andie wasn't sure what she'd done to put Sam in a bad mood, but whatever it was, he needed to get over it.

"Careful—Sam, wait for Andie! She's got a job to do, too, and there's no reason to rush around the ring."

Jo Ellen sat on the top rail of the indoor ring with a clipboard on her knee and a mildly exasperated look on her face. Her soon-to-be stepdaughter, Taylor, stood outside the ring with her arms crossed over the railing. Behind them, Caitlin perched on the highest step of the special mounting ramp they used to help disabled or injured riders get onto their horses.

"Just slow down," Andie hissed at Sam's tense back. The horse he was leading gave a loud, snorting sigh. "It's not a race."

From his position at the horse's head, Sam didn't even look over his shoulder at her. "It's not anything. It's pointless."

"It's practice!" Andie wanted to throw her hands

up in frustration, but she was determined to follow Jo's instructions about the duties of a side walker to the letter.

Your job is to walk beside the horse to support the rider. Keep one hand on the back of the saddle at all times. Be alert to the horse's movements and your rider's balance.

Just because there was no rider this time, that didn't mean Andie intended to shirk her duties.

"You need practice at walking?" Sam demanded. "I guess you must, since I'm going too fast for you."

Andie felt heat prickle at her cheeks and the tips of her ears. "It's more awkward than you might think, walking twisted like this to be ready to catch someone if they fall."

"There's no one to catch!"

"It's our first time! They're hardly going to trust us with a real client our first time out. But if we master this not-very-complicated routine," Andie pointed out, "there will be someone on the horse. Someone who really needs our help and will get a huge medical or emotional benefit out of a therapeutic riding session. I'd appreciate it if you'd take this seriously."

Sam stopped in his tracks, turning on her with a face set in stark, uncompromising lines. "I take this very seriously," he ground out.

Then what was the problem?

From the fence line, Jo called, "Is everything okay?"

Andie held up her hand, eyes never leaving Sam's. "Give us a minute, please, Jo Ellen."

A muscle ticked in Sam's hard jaw. His sable brows were drawn into straight lines over his dark, shuttered eyes. "I don't need a minute. I'm fine."

"Obviously," Andie said blandly. "Look, something is bothering you. Tell me what it is so we can fix it. That's part of working together, Sam."

His gaze shifted away and one of his hands sought Peony's glossy neck, as if for reassurance. "I don't really do that. Work with other people, I mean. It's better that way."

Andie cocked her head, honestly perplexed. "How can being alone be better for you?"

"I didn't say it was better for *me*."

The derisive twist of his mouth on the last word knocked something loose in Andie's chest. "You think it's better for other people if you stay apart from them."

"I'm good with animals. People? Not so much."

"But that's not true," Andie protested.

"It is, believe me." Sam finally met her stare, and the bitter chocolate depths of his eyes were hot with an emotion she couldn't name. "You don't know me, Andie."

She felt the words like a fist to the face, but she knew how to roll with a punch and come back swinging. "How can anyone know you, when you push everyone away? Everyone except my niece. You think you're not good with people? You're great with her."

"That's not . . . I mean, Caitlin is different. I get her."

"Well, she's a mystery to me. But something about you makes her feel comfortable, makes her feel safe in a way that I haven't managed to yet."

He shrugged stiffly, as if redistributing a heavy weight across his broad shoulders. "You'll get there eventually."

"I hope so. At least she knows I'm trying, thanks to your help. That's the beauty of having a partner. You have someone to watch your back, to help you when something turns out to be too much to handle alone. You're more comfortable with the horses than with the idea of the clients? That's fine, because I'm pretty good with people, and I'm the one who'll deal with them the most. Until you get the hang of it, I'll cover you. And vice versa, until I get my bearings around the horses. Right? We'll be fine. So long as we work together."

"Together," he said, low and deep as his large, square-palmed hand flexed and turned under hers until their fingers twined together. "I'll give it a try."

Heat fluttered around Andie's belly. Mouth suddenly dry, she nearly moaned when Sam's gaze dropped to follow the flicker of her tongue over her bottom lip. Her mouth felt swollen and sensitive under Sam's hungry stare. She drifted toward him, her grip on his hand tightening compulsively, the lure of his huge, hard body irresistible.

Until Jo's voice broke through the fragile web of sensual tension. From only a few feet away, Jo said drily, "I think it's time for a new approach."

Trailing uncertainly a few paces behind her was Caitlin.

Andie got under his skin like no other human being Sam had ever met. He hadn't meant to tell her any of that stuff. She had enough ammunition already without handing over new ways to strike at him. But instead of turning her newfound weapons against him, she'd somehow turned his head around so that he was agreeing to work together and coming within a hair's breadth of kissing her.

Thank God for Jo Ellen and her new idea.

"Steady now," Andie said softly from behind him. She was the one with nerves in her voice now, he noted. It was a little different having a flesh-and-blood person in the saddle, being responsible for that person's safety. Especially when that person was a niece you barely knew and desperately wanted to take care of.

Caitlin squirmed enough to make the saddle creak. Sam exchanged a look with Peony, who sighed patiently and planted her hooves in the sawdust covering the floor of the training ring. She was as steady a ride as Caitlin would ever find. Perfect for a beginner.

Especially a beginner who was eager to skip right over the lessons on walking and trotting and head straight for a four-foot jump at a breakneck gallop.

"I don't need you to walk with me. I'm not a baby," she insisted impatiently, kicking at Peony's sides a little. Her small, sneaker-clad heels didn't make much of an impression on Peony, who worked the bridle in her mouth as if she was bored.

"I know you're not, but it's not up to us. Miss Jo says this is how we do it, and it's her barn," Andie explained. There was no trace of hurt or upset in her even voice, but when Sam snuck a peek over his shoulder, her fingers were white-knuckled on the back of the saddle.

This wasn't going to get easier until they dove in and gave it a try, so Sam clucked at Peony and led her forward in a slow, stately walk.

Caitlin shrieked with glee, making Peony's ears flick back and forth.

"Don't be too loud, remember what Miss Jo Ellen said," Andie fretted. "Sam, are you sure you've got a good hold on her?"

Sam checked his grip, about eight inches down the lead rope attached to the bottom of her halter, but there was no need. "Look. Peony is as steady and even-tempered as they come, but unpredictable accidents happen, even with the gentlest horses. I'd stake my reputation as a trainer on this mare's temperament, but there are no guarantees in life."

"What if I want a guarantee?" Andie muttered.

"Get used to disappointment." Sam paced their little group around the perimeter of the ring, passing Jo and Taylor by the closed gate. Taylor gave him a grinning thumbs-up while Jo pointed to the four rails laid out parallel to one another in the center of the ring.

For the first exercise, Sam was supposed to slacken his grip on the lead rope and allow Caitlin to take more control with the reins. With Andie constantly by her side for support, Caitlin had to guide Peony to step over the rails. It all sounded pretty simple, but Sam wasn't surprised when Peony balked at the first rail.

"She won't go," Caitlin said, frustration pitching her voice higher than usual. "Why won't she go?"

This, Sam knew how to do. Without dropping the lead rope, he twisted to assess the situation. "She's confused because you're sending her mixed signals. You're squeezing with your legs and nudging with your heels like Jo told you, right?"

Caitlin nodded, her pale brows a fierce line of concentration. Her whole body was tensed, wiry muscles standing out on her thin frame.

"That's good," Sam told her. "But look at the way you're grabbing onto those reins. They're connected to the bit in Peony's mouth. You're pulling on those reins—pulling on her mouth—so hard that she actually wants to back up to relieve the pressure."

"What should I do?"

"Relax a little, kid." Sam gave Caitlin an easy smile that slid over and encompassed Andie without him intending it. "Remember this is supposed to be fun. I know how much you love horses and how much you want to learn to ride, but don't let that make you nervous. Nerves are contagious and horses are pretty sensitive. She'll pick up on your mood, so try to project confidence. Trust. Good things."

The rueful curl of Andie's lips told Sam she'd realized that this speech was meant for her, too. Her grip on the saddle loosened at the same moment Caitlin dropped her hands down to her lap, easing up on the reins. "That's good," Sam praised them both. The twin smiles he got in return were sunny enough to blind him.

"You can do this, Caitlin." Andie sounded so sure, so calm, it was like she'd never doubted it for a second.

Caitlin pressed her lips together and nodded once, short and sharp.

Keeping his breath and heart steady was a challenge, but he had lots of practice. Facing forward once more, Sam said, "Okay, let's try that again."

This time, when Caitlin urged Peony forward, she clucked softly at the horse in imitation of the way Sam did it. And it worked for her the way it always worked for him. Peony lifted her hooves and daintily picked her way over the rails as if she were born to be a high-stepping show horse.

After the fourth rail, Andie burst out, "You did it! Great job, Caitlin!"

Sam turned in time to catch Caitlin's small, tentative smile at her aunt. From the way Andie's whole face lit up, he had the feeling it might be the first smile Caitlin had given her since arriving on Sanctuary Island.

Caitlin's fingers tightened on the reins once more, but when Peony tossed her head up and down, Caitlin wrinkled her nose and relaxed. Looking down at her aunt, she asked, "Can we do it again?"

Sam felt Andie's thrill at being asked, at being part of this moment, as acutely as if she'd thrown her arms around him and squeezed the breath from his lungs. These two females were going to be the death of him.

An hour of exercises later, Caitlin was finally starting to droop a little. When she confessed that her butt and her knees hurt, Andie hustled them over to the gate where Jo was waiting for them. "Taylor went up to the barn—Sam, I think your cousin, Matt, is here. You three did a wonderful job!"

"Four," Caitlin said. She went beet red when they all looked at her in surprise, but she lifted her stubborn little chin and elaborated, "Peony did a good job, too."

Nothing could have charmed Jo Ellen more. "That's exactly right. You have the makings of a real horsewoman, Caitlin."

Caitlin ducked her head and busied herself with hauling her leg over the saddle to climb down, but Sam could tell she was pleased. Pleased enough, it turned out, to ask Jo if she could be the one to lead Peony back up to her stall. The look of pride on her face as she carefully took the rope from Sam, and the way she listened so intently as Jo explained how to walk on Peony's left and to keep the long end of the rope from trailing and tripping the mare . . . it made Sam smile.

He dropped back to walk with Andie, who had her arms wrapped around herself like she might fly apart with happiness if she didn't contain it. "That was amazing," she said, her eyes shining.

"It was, kind of." Sam rubbed a hand over his undeniable smile. "Your brother is lucky. Caitlin's a good kid."

The mention of her brother seemed to cast a shadow over Andie's face. "I wish Owen could've been here to see how well Caitlin did."

Even knowing that every question he asked made it more likely Andie would start to expect some answers from him in return, Sam couldn't stop himself from saying, "What's he off doing that's more important than this, anyway?"

Sam winced a little at the belligerent way that came out, but Andie didn't get offended. Instead, her chin lifted and her spine went straight. "He's in the army, special forces. My kid brother, Owen, is a Ranger."

Respect slowed Sam's steps for a few paces. "Rangers lead the way."

"You know the Ranger motto?"

"I even know where it comes from," Sam countered. "I may not have served, but I can read a book."

"I didn't mean it that way. It's just that the armed forces aren't for everyone."

They definitely weren't for men with felonies on their records. Pushing down the bitter surge of remembered disappointment, Sam attempted a shrug. "Probably for the best. As you know, I don't do so hot when it comes to dealing with authority figures. It's a hard thing to put your life on the line when you aren't sure you can trust the people making the decisions."

Which was true, and Sam's distrust of authority had been cemented before he hit puberty. But none of that had lessened Sam's desire to join up, to know that he was making a difference and doing his bit. To feel a part of something larger than himself.

There are plenty of ways to make this bad old world a better place, he reminded himself. The voice in his head sounded a lot like Amelia's, and Sam got a sudden flashback image of her broad, sturdy shoulders and salt-and-pepper bun at the front of the history classroom. Straight-backed, no-nonsense Ms. Amelia Endicott, who'd saved Sam's life—in more ways than one.

"I'm surprised you even made it through high school, with an attitude like that," Andie said.

The stiffness of her voice reminded him that she was one of those authority figures he usually avoided like the plague. Guilt tugged at him enough to widen a chink in his armor. "I had help. The same history teacher who taught us about Rangers and the part they played in World War II, actually."

He felt some of the tension go out of Andie on a soft breath. When the hell did he get so attuned to her every inhale and exhale?

"Is that where 'Rangers lead the way' comes from?" she asked curiously.

Relieved to be back on more neutral ground than his history with Amelia, Sam nodded. "They were an American unit modeled after the British commandos, and of the first five hundred volunteers, less than a hundred survived World War II. They were some of the first boots on the ground with some of the deepest penetration into enemy territory."

Andie blinked. "Wow. You weren't kidding when you said you've read about this. Tell me the rest. How did the Ranger motto get started?"

Sam dug his hands into the pockets of his heavy canvas jacket, his fingers automatically searching out the smooth, round circle of metal. "It was during the invasion of Normandy that Brigadier General Norman Cota looked out across Omaha Beach and stalked up to ask Major Max Schneider what outfit he was standing with. 'Fifth Rangers, sir,' Schneider replied. And Cota said, 'Well goddammit then, Rangers, lead the way!'"

"And now my brother is one of those guys leading the way." Andie sounded dazed, but proud.

"When's his hitch over?" Sam probed, wondering how long he had to get Caitlin up to speed on her riding.

Not that Sam was staying on Sanctuary Island forever, he remembered with a dull ache. Just until the heat died down and he figured out what to do with Queenie.

"I don't know." Andie flushed red, her teeth worrying at her bottom lip. "Owen and I haven't . . . my family isn't close. Let's just say it's been a while since the last reunion."

Sam peered into the dim barn where Caitlin was learning how to curry comb Peony under Jo's watchful care. "About . . . nine years or so?"

Andie huffed out a breath. "Not quite that long, actually. The reason I'd never met Caitlin until recently is that my brother didn't know about her until her mother died, leaving Caitlin on her own. He was overseas already, about to head out with his team."

"What if you hadn't been available? What would have happened to Caitlin?"

"I don't know," Andie admitted, hugging her arms around her ribcage. "They might have been able to track down my dad. Or maybe they would've dumped her in foster care until Owen comes home."

"That sucks," Sam said bluntly. Everything in him revolted at the thought of quiet, fragile Caitlin getting dumped into the same system that had chewed him up and spat him out years ago. "It's not right."

"It's not ideal, but what's the alternative?" Andie shivered, even though the waning spring sunshine had taken the chill off the lengthening shadows of the pine trees. "Owen should abandon his team, the people who count on him, and possibly derail an operation that has who-knows-what importance in the grand scheme of our national security?"

Sam clenched his jaw and lowered his head stubbornly. "Someone ought to put Caitlin first, is all I'm saying. I don't think she's had a lot of that in her life."

The sudden stillness of the woman next to him made Sam tense before risking a look at her. Andie watched him with her head tilted to one side. "What makes you say that?"

"Nothing," Sam evaded. "Call it a hunch. And look, I don't mean to imply that you're not putting Caitlin first. One phone call and you dropped everything to take her in and try to make her feel welcome. That's more than a lot of people would do."

"Thanks, although I haven't exactly dropped everything. I left her here with you all day."

"You've got a job," Sam pointed.

"I do, and it's an important one. It's a job I believe in"—Andie shot him a half-smile—"even if you don't. But I've got deputies, and I haven't taken a single day off since I was elected three and a half years ago. Maybe you're right. Maybe it's time someone put Caitlin first."

Chapter Nine

Even after a year of being friends (with, sadly, no benefits), Taylor's heart still fluttered into her throat at the sight of Matthew Little's car pulling up the gravel lane to Windy Corner. Granted, when they first met he'd been driving his mom's used hatchback and now he had a shiny, candy-apple red convertible, but that's what happened when your mom married an honest-to-Oprah billionaire.

The spring breeze ruffled Matt's dark blond hair as dust billowed behind his slow-moving wheels. He knew better than to zoom up the drive, scattering gravel and spooking the horses, and it warmed Taylor from the inside out that he remembered Jo's rules and did his best to follow them. Of course, between Taylor and Matthew, she was definitely the rule breaker. Matt was good—dutiful and helpful to his mom, hard working and attentive at school, loyal to his friends—even when they didn't deserve it.

Before Matt, Taylor would've said "good" was

synonymous with "boring." But Matthew Little was the opposite of boring.

He stopped the two-seater convertible in front of the barn doors and let it idle while he grinned up at Taylor. With his tanned left arm propped on the open window frame and the fingers of his other hand loosely circling the wheel, he looked like a shot from a music video for a song about hitting the road and being free.

"Hey, Tay. You done?"

Making an effort not to be self-conscious about the fact that she was probably red and sweaty from raking hay, Taylor wiped her hands on her jeans as casually as she could before walking over to the car. "What's it to you?"

Matt tipped his head down to peer over the tops of his aviator sunglasses, giving Taylor that weird shiver of anticipation as she wondered if he'd finally hear the flirtation in her tone for what it was. For a moment, she thought she saw an answering spark of heat kindle in his green-gold eyes, but then he laughed and shook it off. "Don't be a brat. I'm here to give you a ride if you want."

Fighting down disappointment, Taylor forced a smile. "Well, my car *is* in the shop again . . ."

"I know." Matt drummed his fingers on the car door. "That's why I'm here. That, and I . . . come on, d'you want the ride or not?"

He knew her car was in the shop. Something inside Taylor thrilled to the knowledge that Matt kept as close tabs on her as she did on him. "Sure, let me grab my stuff and tell Merry I'm leaving."

Ten minutes later, Taylor was tilting her face up to catch the feeble spring sunshine and shivering pleasantly as the wind whistled past her ears. Happiness bubbled up in her chest, so much she felt it leaking out of her, but she couldn't stop it. Didn't even want to try.

They raced down Shoreline Drive with the ocean on one side and the salt marsh on the other, taking curves just fast enough to get Taylor's blood racing. Matt was a great driver, she thought dreamily. He handled the sports car like he'd been born to it, shifting smoothly and working the clutch as if he hadn't just learned how last summer. His stepfather, Dylan, taught him as a consolation prize when Matt's mom vetoed Matt learning to ride Dylan's motorcycle. Nestled into the leather bucket seat with the winding road purring mere inches below her butt, Taylor felt like Matt actually got the sweeter deal. She glanced over at him, relaxed and handsome behind the wheel, and started when she realized they'd passed the turn-off for her house a few miles back. "Hey. Where are we going?"

"Our spot. You have time?"

Struggling not to beam with dorky delight, Taylor shrugged. "Sure. Not like I'm aching to rush back to my calculus homework."

Our spot. They had a spot. And as Matt carefully pulled off the road and onto a dirt track through the scrub grass, Taylor acknowledged that it was a pretty effing romantic spot.

Heartbreak Cove. The place where they'd first hung out on purpose—until the sheriff showed up and hauled them in for trespassing. Since then, they'd spent a bunch more time out here picking up trash and tending to the overgrown foot trails as part of their community service punishment. At this point, Sheriff Shepard was used to finding them out there, and so long as they didn't go down to the cove after dark and they didn't disturb the wild horses, she didn't mind.

"Funny how we got in trouble for hanging out at Heartbreak Cove and now we don't," Taylor observed.

"It was never really about trespassing," Matt said, parking by a big loblolly pine. "It was about being out after curfew . . . and I seem to remember someone pinching a bottle of rum from her dad's liquor cabinet. That definitely helped seal the deal."

"And thus began my criminal career." Taylor kept her voice light, even though her stomach was flipping at the fact they were talking about That Night.

They usually steered clear of reminiscing about how they met or how close they'd come to being more than friends. But every time they went to Heartbreak Cove, Taylor remembered the clear midnight sky and pinprick stars, the tingling burn of rum, and the soft brush of Matt's hand on her cheek. And every time, without fail, she wished Sheriff Shepard had been just ten minutes later on her patrol.

Maybe if she had, Taylor wouldn't still be eating her heart out over a guy who'd moved on months ago.

"Let's hope that was the end of your criminal career, too," Matt said mildly, swinging out of the car and grabbing a wadded up blanket from the trunk. Taylor followed him down to the edge of the thicket and helped him find a spot that wasn't too marshy to spread it out.

"Don't try to tame my wildness, Matthew." Taylor plopped down on her back with a sigh of pleasure. "A bad girl's gotta do what a bad girl's gotta do."

"You've been turning over a new leaf since the day I met you. How long does it take to make a fresh start?"

"Maybe it takes more than time." Taylor suppressed a shiver as Matt sat down beside her, close enough to touch and yet so, so off limits. "Maybe it takes distance, too."

"That's one thing I'm definitely looking forward to about college. A whole new crowd of people with no preconceived notions about Fatty Matty."

A hot flush of shame washed over her at the old nickname. She hadn't been one of Matt's primary tormentors—too caught up in the hellstorm of crap that became her life after her mom died—but she'd used the name casually. All the kids at Sanctuary High had.

When she got up the courage to look over at Matt again, there was something grim about his mouth, a cynicism that had only grown when the popular kids who used to make fun of him suddenly morphed into his friends at the beginning of this school year. And the in crowd hadn't glommed onto Matt just because he was rich now, related to the wealthy Harrington family whose ancestors originally owned Sanctuary Island. No, it was mostly because the summer between junior and senior year, Fatty Matty had a growth spurt.

Or, more accurately, a hotness spurt. Taylor stared at his sharp jawline and wide shoulders, his deep chest and tightly muscled forearms, and wondered how blind she'd been not to notice him before he grew six inches and shed twenty pounds of baby fat practically overnight.

"I don't think I'm going to go to college," Taylor blurted. "At least not right away."

Matt turned to her sharply, hair flying into his eyes in that way that made her want to brush it back. "What? I thought you were applying to all the same schools as me, so we could get in together."

An odd little burn of anger flamed in her belly. Taylor sat up and hooked her arms around her knees. "I know we talked about that, but I didn't promise anything."

"Taylor, come on. You have to go to college. I mean, what are you going to do instead, get a job flipping burgers?"

The anger burned a little hotter. "I may not be a billionaire's stepkid, but I have options. And besides, what's so bad about getting a job after high school? I work at the barn now. Does that make me less than you?"

Matt's shoulders slumped. "No, of course not. That's not what I meant. I just . . . whenever I picture what next year will be like, at a new school in a new city with new people, you're right there with me."

He would miss her. Taylor knew that. Didn't doubt it for a second, because Matt was a good friend. But if nothing changed in the next few months, if this summer didn't show him how wrong Dakota was for him and how the perfect girl for him was sitting right there on the blanket at his side . . . well. Taylor wasn't sure her heart could take another four years of watching from the sidelines as Matthew Little's best bud. "I'm just not sure school is for me. I mean, I already know what I want to do with my life. I want to work with horses. What do I need a college degree for?"

"Jo Ellen has one," Matt argued. "I bet it helps her all the time, with grant applications and keeping the barn's books. Stuff like that."

"Sounds enthralling." Taylor rolled her eyes. "I don't want to be stuck in an office all day, even one that's attached to a barn. I want to be in the ring, in the stalls; I want to get my hands dirty and experience the whole world. I want to travel."

She paused, peeking at Matt from the corner of her eye. "I was actually thinking of asking Sam if he needs any help at Blue Ridge Horse Rescue."

"Are you asking me to talk to him for you?" Matt gave her a narrow frown. "Because I'm still not sure this is a good idea."

Taylor knocked her shoulder against his. "Don't worry about it. I'm not exactly shy, I can figure out how to approach your cousin on my own."

"And you don't need my permission," Matt finished for her.

"Yeah, it's not like you're my boyfriend."

The "B" word dropped onto the blanket between them like a rock, something with physical weight and substance that they'd have to maneuver around.

"If I were your boyfriend," Matt said carefully, after a heavy pause, "I wouldn't try to control you or stop you from doing what you want. But I would hope you'd think about me when you made major life decisions that could affect us both. Like splitting us up for four years."

Agitated, Taylor got to her knees, then up to her feet, to pace around the blanket a little. Her legs got restless sometimes, needed to move, and she'd learned to listen to her body. "Good thing you're not my boyfriend, then, so you don't have to care what I do for the next four years. It doesn't affect you at all."

Another weighty silence as they both absorbed

the fact that there was nothing much Matt could say to that. He had a girlfriend already, and it wasn't Taylor. And while part of Taylor desperately wanted to turn and yell at him that he was an oblivious idiot if he hadn't figured out that she was in love with him, the larger part of her was putting up red flags and caution signs all over the place.

If she exposed her heart to Matt now and he turned her down, it wouldn't matter how sensitive and caring and regretful he was about it—she'd never get over the humiliation and heartache. They'd spend what was potentially their last summer together not speaking or hanging out or seeing each other at all, and then he'd go off to college and marry Dakota Coles, and Taylor would never see him again. She couldn't deal with that. All her grand plans to take a chance and make a play for Matt's heart suddenly seemed stupid. Childish.

Better to be friends who kept in touch occasionally than distant strangers.

So Taylor changed the subject. "What did you want to come out here for, anyway? It wasn't to grill me about my post–high school plans."

"Oh. Yeah."

The change in Matt's voice, from exasperated affection to careful flatness, had Taylor whirling to study him. He was splayed out on the blanket like the best dream of her life, long legs in dark jeans and ripped, lean chest stretching the thin cotton of his expensive T-shirt. But when he met her questioning gaze, nerves shone clearly in his bright hazel eyes.

"Matt? You okay?"

He shrugged one shoulder, plucking a blade of grass to thread idly through his nimble fingers. "Sure, just got a lot on my mind. With graduation coming up."

Taylor perched on the edge of the blanket, the rough wool scratchy under her knees. "It's still more than a month away."

"I know. But did you hear the announcement on Friday? They're issuing tickets soon. We're supposed to tell them how many we want."

"My dad and Jo." That much was easy, obvious. Taylor sat on her heels and thought about it. "Maybe Ella and Grady, Merry and Ben and baby Alex. Wow, when did my family get so big?"

The happy glow of that dimmed a bit when Matt split the blade of grass with his fingernail and tossed it aside with a jerky motion.

"Yeah, me too. I've got Mom and the Harringtons. Sam." Matt looked up at her, misery tugging the corners of his wide, expressive mouth down. "So why am I obsessed with calling up my dad and asking him to come?"

"Ooh, big stuff." It all made sense now. Matt's dad had been out of the picture for a while—his parents had gotten divorced before he and Penny moved to Sanctuary Island a few years ago. Matt and his dad didn't talk much, and Penny didn't make it any easier. Matt had blamed her for the divorce for a long time, and while things were better now that Dylan was in the picture, there was still a big old question mark about why Matt's mom packed their crap in the middle of the night and hauled her kid away to some hidden-away island off the coast of Virginia.

"When was the last time you talked to your dad?" Taylor asked hesitantly.

Matt gave that one-shouldered shrug again, leaning back on his hands and blinking up into the swaying evergreen overhead. "I don't know. It's been a
while, I guess."

Watching Matt closely without seeming to was
one of Taylor's areas of expertise. If it had been
offered as a class at Sanctuary High, she'd have aced
it. Hell, she could teach it. Employing her best casual side eye now, Taylor said, "So, not even on your
birthday last month?"

"You sound like my mother." Matt kicked at the
rumpled corner of the blanket where a gust of wind
had folded it over itself and looked annoyed. "No,
okay? He didn't call on my birthday. He's busy. He
has a job and a life, and we left him. It makes sense
that he's mad."

"At your mom, maybe," Taylor said skeptically.
"But not at you. You were a kid! What were you
supposed to do, run away from Sanctuary Island
and hitchhike back to the mainland?"

"There were times when I thought about it, believe me."

Taylor could relate. There were times after her
mother's death when all she could think about was
the bone-deep desire to be somewhere else. Anywhere but where she was, in the middle of all that
pain. But eventually, she'd realized that even if she
managed to get away from the big, silent house on
Shoreline Drive and the empty look in her dad's sad
eyes, she could never actually outrun her own sense
of loss. So she'd stayed put, and distracted herself
from her grief in other ways. Stupid, unhealthy ways,
she saw now when she looked back. But at the time,
underage smoking and drinking and getting into

trouble with her previous best friend, Caleb Rigby, had seemed like a great idea. Right up until Caleb's dad tossed him into military school while Taylor's dad started dating Jo Ellen Hollister.

It was Jo who changed everything for Taylor. Not by replacing her mother—no one could ever do that—but by being someone Taylor could talk to about all the stuff that made her poor dad go all red-faced and bewildered. Jo got her, right from the very beginning, and Taylor needed that desperately. Almost as desperately as Matt seemed to need some kind of reconciliation with his dad.

Maybe reconciliation was impossible. Taylor had gotten to know Penny Harrington a little bit, and she saw in Matt's mom a fiercely independent, strong, loving woman who'd fought through tough times without ever losing the ability to laugh. Taylor had an inkling that if Penny up and left Matt's dad in the middle of the night, there must have been a pretty good reason for it. But Penny never bad-mouthed the guy and was so vague about the end of her marriage that Matt had a ton of unanswered questions.

If he couldn't reconcile with his dad, Taylor thought, at least he could get some closure. "So why don't you call him up? Or just send him the invitation and see what happens."

Matt brightened, shoving his sunglasses up onto his head so he could squint at Taylor. "You think I should?"

Suppressing the satisfaction she always got when Matt demonstrated how much he valued her opinion, Taylor reached over to grab his outstretched foot and shake it encouragingly. "What's the worst that can happen?"

Ticking off his fingers, Matt said, "Dad could show up and upset my mom, get in a fistfight with Dylan, be mad at me for not trying to spend more time with him . . ."

Which was a two-way street, Taylor wanted to point out, but she didn't want to hurt Matt. Instead she said, "Or you could warn your mom ahead of time so everyone is on their best behavior, and when he arrives, maybe they'll work out some of their issues and make it easier for all of you from now on. I mean, amicable divorces happen. That's a thing, right? Blended families and all that."

"It's a nice idea," Matt said, obviously unaware of how clearly he was telegraphing his longing. "I don't know, I'll think about it."

"When you really want to make it work, almost nothing can stop a family from coming together," Taylor said with unshakeable conviction. "I should know. My dad and Jo and I have been through a metric ton of crap, including me being a total brat. If that wasn't enough to detonate my family, yours should be able to get through one little high school graduation."

Matt smiled, the slow, fond smile he seemed to reserve only for Taylor. "You're not such a brat. In fact, I'd say you're kind of amazing. And thanks for the advice. I'll add my dad to the list of ticket requests for graduation."

Beaming proudly, Taylor squirmed into a more comfortable position and relished the soft breeze and distant lapping of waves against the shore. "It's time your parents figured out how to deal with each other. They're adults! I'm sure they'll work it out."

And if Matt's dad did show up and turned out to

be as big a jerk as Taylor suspected . . . well, maybe it was time Matt realized the truth about that, so he could move on with no regrets. The way Taylor planned to do at the end of this summer.

Chapter Ten

The Firefly Café was jumping when Andie pulled into the parking lot. She cruised around slowly, looking for an empty spot and listening as Caitlin recounted—for the hundredth time—every moment she'd spent on Peony's back. Even two weeks later, it was as fresh in Caitlin's memory as if it had just happened, and the kid seemed to spend every waking moment either reliving her experience riding Peony or asking when she could do it again.

Andie grinned when Caitlin got to the part about stepping over the rails. Even though Andie had been there to personally witness the triumphant moment, she still liked to hear Caitlin's bright, happy chatter.

Of course, she'd like it even better if Caitlin would chatter that way to her, but they were working on it. And in the meantime . . .

Andie's gaze flicked up to the rearview mirror automatically to catch the gleam of Sam's mysterious eyes. He noticed her looking and his lips curled up in a grin, sensual and dark with shared secrets.

She shivered, enjoying the tingling anticipation and the jump of her nerves. They'd spent a bit of time together over the last few weeks, training as volunteers and working with their first few clients at Windy Corner, but she hadn't yet accustomed herself to the way he made her feel. Maybe she never would—maybe Sam Brennan would always be the one man who made those butterflies in her stomach start zooming around.

The thought was strangely appealing.

Tearing her attention away from the huge, muscular man in her backseat, Andie spied a car leaving one row over and hurried to slide the SUV into the vacant space.

"Tight fit," Sam commented, eyeing the tan convertible mere inches from the right passenger-side window. "Am I gonna have to climb out through the trunk?"

"Yeah!" Caitlin popped up in the front seat to peer over the headrest as if contemplating making a break for it.

Andie narrowed her eyes at Sam's reflection only to see his grin morph into a smirk. "No need. We'll fit just fine."

"You could've parked on the grass over there." The helpful tone was at odds with the teasing glint in Sam's eye.

Andie frowned repressively. "That's not a real spot."

"Who's going to ticket the sheriff's car?" Sam laid one brawny arm along the back of the bench seat, for all the world like a king surveying his domain. "It's not a crime if you don't get caught."

"Actually, that's not true." Andie threw the SUV into park and turned to make sure Caitlin was listening. "That's the exact opposite of true. Whether or not you get caught, it's important to follow the rules."

"Why?" Caitlin asked, looking skeptical.

Maybe instead of silently cursing Sam and his mocking smile for getting her into this conversation, she should be thanking him. This was a perfect opportunity to explain to Caitlin—and, incidentally, to Sam—why Andie cared so much about being sheriff.

It didn't escape her that so far she and Sam were doing quite a bit of communicating through other people. If they ever found themselves alone in a room together, they might have a hard time making conversation.

Although, Andie admitted to herself, if she had Sam Brennan alone somewhere private, polite chitchat would be the last thing on her mind.

Wrenching herself out of that tempting fantasy, she focused on Caitlin's expectant face. "We follow the rules because they help us live with other people. The rules are there to remind us that we—our own thoughts and desires and needs—are not the only thoughts and desires and needs in the whole world. Other people matter, and what we do can either hurt them or help them. Do you see what I mean?"

There was a long pause while Caitlin thought this through. She frowned like she didn't like it much, but her voice was small and serious when she said, "I don't want to hurt anyone."

A little taken aback by Caitlin's intensity, Andie exchanged a lightning-fast glance with Sam . . . who looked sad, but not shocked. Interesting. "That's good," Andie finally told her. "That's a good way to be. So then, what if I parked over there, where it's not really a spot and I'd be blocking that gray minivan from getting out easily? What would happen if the person who owned that van needed to leave the restaurant suddenly—"

"Why?" Caitlin demanded.

"Er, why what?"

"Why are they leaving the restaurant? Are they in trouble? Did they steal something?"

Andie blinked. "I was thinking more like, what if the man who owns the van found out his wife is sick and needs his help at home."

"Oh, okay." Caitlin relaxed back into her seat as if her strings had been cut. The vibrating tension of a few seconds before dissipated in the air like smoke.

"So if we blocked that spot," Andie finished lamely, wondering where this conversation took a wrong turn, "that man and his wife would be hurt by it. But if we follow the rules and do the right thing, no one gets hurt."

"Stealing is wrong," Caitlin announced, her gaze directed out the passenger window. "It gets you in trouble and people get mad."

Was this what it was always like with kids? You thought you were having one conversation, but they were on their own plane, doing their own thing. Andie decided to trust that she'd laid the groundwork for the whole right versus wrong lesson. "That's exactly right. People shouldn't take things that don't belong to them. It's wrong, and it hurts both people—the victim and the thief."

The back door of the SUV closed with a clap, and Andie glanced over the console to see Sam standing at the rear of the vehicle. His wide, muscular back was turned but it looked as though he was staring up at the sky. Probably starving and wondering how long he was going to have to wait for the fried chicken Andie had promised him weeks ago as thanks for his help with Caitlin.

Andie hurried to get Caitlin zipped into her hoodie and out of the truck. Beckoned by the warm glowing lights strung around the seaside patio, Caitlin ran down to the low fieldstone wall at the far edge to get a look at the beach. Sam and Andie followed more slowly, and he didn't seem impatient, after all. In the dusky twilight, his strong face looked thoughtful, as if he were processing what she'd said.

"Nice sermon back there, Sheriff."

The words stung all the more because Andie had hoped for a few seconds that she might have gotten through to him. "I don't mean to sermonize, but it's important to me that Caitlin understand how the world works."

He tilted his head back again, his fathomless gaze searching for answers among the stars. "And you truly believe that's how the world works."

"Absolutely."

"Even the part about how if you never break the rules, you'll never get hurt? If that's truly been your experience of the world—well, you and I must live on different planets."

The rueful twist to his handsome mouth tangled Andie's tongue. "I guess . . . no, you're right, I can't claim that my rule-following lifestyle means I've never been hurt. But the worst things that have happened to me have all been a direct result of breaking some rule or other. And I don't think it's a coincidence."

Sam's eyebrows slashed down. "I don't like the idea of bad things happening to you."

"Bad things happen to everyone," Andie said, her lungs so tight she barely gasped it out. "The trick is learning something from it and moving forward."

A darkness deeper than the gathering night pooled in his eyes, and for a moment, the light laughter and clinking silverware of the few couples at the patio tables faded away. All Andie could hear was the rhythmic wash of the surf—or maybe that was the tidal rush of her own blood in her ears. Either way, the moment narrowed in until Andie forgot they weren't alone.

"Damn it, Andie." He lowered his forehead until it brushed hers. "You deserve better."

Seduced by the intimacy and intensity of Sam's bent head, his steady gaze, his granite jaw, Andie drifted closer to the muscular heat of his big body. "Better than what?" she demanded, her fingers taking over for her brain and stretching to clasp the body-warm flannel of his shirt.

"Better than me." Sam punctuated the raw confession by seizing her mouth with his in a hungry kiss that jolted through Andie's body with pure, perfect pleasure.

She filled Sam's arms, and when she moaned, open-mouthed, into the kiss, Sam squeezed his eyes shut tightly enough to see bursts of colored light explode behind his closed lids.

Desire rode him unmercifully, galloping through his system, impossible to halt. Any thoughts about how wrong this was, how stupid and reckless and unfair it was of him to kiss Sheriff Andie Shepard— all of that was trampled beneath the rampaging lust coursing through his blood. Sam's body went heavy and tight, harder than iron and hotter than sin.

He'd never known anyone like Andie. No woman had ever impressed him so much, so fast, with her strength and purpose. There was a bright, unwavering light at Andie's core, and Sam wanted to warm himself at that fire more than he wanted his next breath.

This kiss was inevitable. Maybe it had been unavoidable since the first time he met her—but it was the way Andie was with her niece, the vulnerability she couldn't hide combined with the guts it took to keep trying, that sealed the deal. He had to have her.

Even if it meant losing her.

Because Sam knew he'd never be able to live with himself if he went down this road with Andie blind and deaf to the truth about him. His poor, overworked conscience couldn't carry another burden.

He'd have to tell Andie the truth about why he was on Sanctuary Island, and hope that she understood.

A shaft of despair slid between his ribs like the tip of a knife, piercing the heat of their embrace. Sam lifted his head, his chest clenching at the way Andie followed his lips with hers, chasing his kiss. It took everything he had to grip her shoulders and put cool night air between their overheated bodies.

"Andie," he forced out, before he could second-guess it and come to his senses. "There's something I have to tell you."

She blinked away the haze of passion. Sam saw the exact moment she realized where they were and who she'd just kissed. Awareness flushed over her cheeks, but if she felt embarrassed or regretful, she didn't let it show. Andie tilted her chin up and met his gaze without flinching. "Yes?"

The words wilted in Sam's suddenly parched

throat. He swallowed with a dry click, searching for the words to admit to an officer of the law that he was everything she stood against. But before he could come up with anything that seemed liable to keep him out of handcuffs, Caitlin's voice broke them apart.

"Are you her boyfriend?"

Sam jerked and stared down at the kid. The outraged betrayal on her pale, thin face was like a headbutt to the diaphragm. "Hey, Caitlin—look, your aunt and I . . ."

He ran out of steam but Andie saved him, with a sideways look that said she wasn't going to forget the conversation that had been interrupted. "We're friends, sweetie. Friends who are interested in finding out if they can be something more. But whatever we decide about that, it won't change anything for you."

There it was again, that weary, knowing expression that seemed way too adult for such a young girl. "That's dumb. Boyfriends change everything. They move in and . . ." Caitlin buttoned her lips tight, refusing to finish.

"Did your mom have a lot of boyfriends?" Sam asked gently.

Caitlin shrugged as Andie caught his gaze, a big question mark swimming in the blue depths of her eyes.

Sam wanted to tell her his suspicions. The way Caitlin avoided being around adult women but had trusted him immediately, the way she'd wolfed down half the granola bar he'd given her at lunch then hidden the other half in her sleeve when she thought he wasn't looking, that slip about stealing, back in the car.

But these weren't Sam's secrets to tell. He put one

hand on Caitlin's head, smoothing down her wind-tossed red hair. When she didn't shrug him off, Sam prompted her. "Caitlin? What happened when your mom would get a boyfriend?"

Caitlin shrugged again, her skinny shoulders coiled tighter than springs. "Nothing. They'd go off together and do stuff. Grown-up stuff."

And where had Caitlin been while her mom and whatever loser she shacked up with had been off doing "grown-up stuff?" Sam's heart ached for the lonely, forgotten kid he saw inside Caitlin.

He wondered if Andie saw it as clearly as he did. She might have the training to read between the lines of a confession—but maybe she didn't have a lonely, forgotten kid inside herself to be able to recognize the signs.

At least she was trying. Andie was studying Caitlin's averted face like if she stared hard enough, she'd be able to read her niece's history written on her freckled cheek. "It's okay," Andie said at last. "You don't have to talk about your mom if you don't want to. But . . . whatever happened with your mom's boyfriends, I promise you that Sam is not moving in with me anytime soon. So you don't have to worry about that."

Visibly struggling, Caitlin glared out over the reflection of the moon on the waves. "I don't care. You're not my mom. I only have to stay here until my dad comes to get me."

A muscle flexed in Andie's jaw, but her expression and voice were nothing but soft and caring. "I'm not going to lie to you. I don't know how long it will be until your dad can come home. So you and me, we're going to have to figure out a way to get along until then."

"That's easy." Caitlin sniffed dismissively. "Not like we have to see each other, even if we live in the same house."

Come on, Andie, Sam prayed silently as his heart squeezed tight. *Listen to what she's saying.*

A stillness had come over Andie, watchful and alert, but the straightforward caring in her stance and voice never changed. Sam had the fleeting thought that she'd make a good horse trainer.

"But that would make me sad," Andie told Caitlin. "You're my niece. You're family, and from the minute I found out about you, I loved you. So that means I *want* to spend time with you."

Caitlin vibrated with tension like a plucked rubber band. Sam couldn't tell if she wanted to run into Andie's arms, or run away.

"You can't," the kid countered, crossing her arms over her chest. "You have a job. That's how you make money. You can't just stay home and hang out with a dumb kid all day."

Swift and graceful, Andie crouched to put herself at Caitlin's level. "Don't ever call yourself a dumb kid," she said fiercely. "And don't act like you don't matter. You matter very much to me. In fact—I'm going to do whatever I can to spend as much time with you as possible. Even if it means I need to take some time off my job to do it."

Caitlin's eyes were wide and wary as she shrugged one more time, but when Andie reached out tentative arms to enfold the kid in a hug, Caitlin didn't squirm out of her grasp. She stood quietly and let herself be hugged. Andie didn't see the way Caitlin closed her eyes and smiled as she rested her head on Andie's shoulder for a brief moment, but Sam did.

The glow of satisfaction warmed him from the inside out. These two were going to be fine. And he couldn't help thinking that maybe, just maybe, if Andie took a break from being Sheriff Shepard, it might be easier for her to come to grips with Sam's secrets.

"Come on, ladies," he said as they broke apart and Andie got to her feet. "I was promised a fried chicken dinner."

"And fried chicken you shall have." Andie's bright, beaming smile lit up the night. "Caitlin, what are you hungry for?"

It was an odd feeling for Sam, walking up the steps to the homey little restaurant with a vulnerable child and a beautiful woman at his side. They weren't his to protect or cherish, but Sam felt those urges anyway. He wasn't sure if it was something about this woman and this kid or maybe it was this lovely island that always made Sam achingly aware of the possibility of a different kind of life.

Maybe it was the wild salt breeze and the careening constellations of stars overhead, the new moon over the water, or the boisterous noise and light spilling from the café, but Sam felt an unfamiliar optimism breaking through the hard-caked soil and taking root in his heart.

It was heady and exciting, thrumming through his blood with the same primal beat as the unsated desire that rekindled every time he look at Andie. And it lasted exactly until the moment they opened the café door and stepped inside to see a crowd of cheering folks under a white banner that read NASH TUCKER FOR SHERIFF.

Something told Sam that Andie wasn't going to

be taking any time off of work for a while. If there
was a newcomer in the sheriff race, she couldn't afford to.

She also couldn't afford to associate with the likes
of Sam Brennan . . . unless no one found out about
his past—and present—mistakes. He'd have to stay
away from her, for real this time.

Sam had told her the truth right before he kissed
her. She deserved better than the trouble he'd bring
her, and it was up to him to see that she got it. Even
if the thought of pulling away from Andie and Caitlin now felt about as painful as cutting out his own
heart.

Chapter Eleven

Shock clobbered Andie over the head, leaving her stunned for an awful moment. "Who is Nash Tucker?"

"That would be my grandson." Mr. Leeds emerged from the crowd, leaning on his cane and practically radiating smug satisfaction. "A Sanctuary Island boy, born and raised. He left for college and made a name for himself on the force in Atlanta, but now he's come home where he belongs!"

Andie felt her grip on her temper loosening. "And I don't belong, because I wasn't born here?"

She was grateful for Sam's steadying presence at her shoulder as Mr. Leeds stretched his tight, puckered mouth into a grim smile. "Now, now, Miss Shepard. I don't have to tolerate sass from an outsider."

Outsider. The word scraped Andie on the raw. "I've worked hard to make a place for myself here, among these people," she said, staring Mr. Leeds down.

"That's the difference, right there." Mr. Leeds

tapped his cane on the floor smartly. "My grandson doesn't have to work at it. He belongs here. Always has, always will."

Andie decided she'd be damned if she showed how hard those shots hit her. "If you think I'll back down and let the sheriff's badge go without a fight, you're wrong."

"Is that so?" Mr. Leeds drawled, his watery gaze slipping down to rest on Caitlin's red head. "I thought you might have discovered some new priorities."

Something about the way he said it made Andie stiffen. In the tilt of his head, she saw echoes of her father's dismissive headshake on the worst day of her life as a cop.

Women are too emotional for police work, I guess. I thought maybe you'd be different, but you're the same as all the rest, Andrea. You've embarrassed this family.

She was responding to her absent father as much as to Mr. Leeds when she shot back, "You thought wrong. I'm not giving up on being sheriff, and I can win this election without abandoning my niece."

Mr. Leeds didn't look too concerned. "I guess we'll see, won't we? Oh, look, Nash is about to take the podium."

Applause erupted from the packed booths and tables lining the walls of the small diner. Andie stared around her at the eager faces of people she'd served and protected for the past three years. Mr. Leeds gave her one last smug smile before he stumped over to the dais someone had constructed in front of the counter.

"You were counting on these people to vote for

you." The low rumble of Sam's voice held no question, but Andie nodded anyway.

"That's Cora Coles." She tilted her chin at an expensively dressed bottle blonde who'd tottered up on her stilettos to get a better view. "I gave her daughter a five-hour defensive driving tutorial instead of writing her a ticket when she backed over a fire hydrant. And over there, pulling out his camera? That's the editor of the *Sanctuary Gazette*. I mediated a dispute between the paper and the lawyer's office next door."

"Ungrateful idiots," Sam growled. "What are they so excited . . . about . . . ?"

He trailed off as a tall, golden Adonis climbed the steps to the podium, muscled arms raised and million-watt smile firmly in place. Andie's heart sank to the soles of her boots as she took in Nash Tucker's handsome, clean-cut appearance. "My competition," she said numbly.

Sam made a scoffing noise. "That guy? Captain America over there? He's no competition for you."

"Oh sure," Andie choked out as Tucker laughed and waved his hands in an unsuccessful attempt at calming the cheers and wild clapping. "What would the Sanctuary Island townspeople want with him?"

"Your track record here has to count for something," Sam argued.

Andie swallowed around a lump of emotion. "I hope so. But 'local hero returns' is a pretty compelling story. Elections have been won on much less."

Nash Tucker beamed around the crowded café and shouted over the applause, "All right, all right. It's good to see y'all too! It's been way too long."

Of course, his speaking voice was clear and deep,

confident and compelling, with just enough of a rasp
to sound appealingly masculine. Andie steeled herself for a charming speech. Not that she wanted to
stay for it, but pragmatically, she knew she ought
to hear the words he'd use to sway votes his way.
She couldn't fight back if she didn't know what she
was up against. Besides, how would it look if she
walked out now? She couldn't bear for Mr. Leeds
or anyone else to think she was intimidated.

But before Tucker could do more than thank the
crowd for welcoming him home so enthusiastically,
Andie felt a prickle at the back of her neck that lifted
all the hairs along her nape. Darting a glance down
to check on Caitlin, Andie sucked in a gasp. The girl
was gone.

Between one heartbeat and the next, everything
changed. Suddenly Andie couldn't care less what
anyone thought of her. All she cared about was finding Caitlin. She craned her neck to check the restaurant, her lungs freezing when she didn't see a trace
of her niece's flaming red hair. "Come on," she hissed
to Sam. "Caitlin's run off again, we have to find her."

Sam, hard on her heels, reached over her shoulder to shove the café door open. They spilled out
into the cool night air, Andie's heart pounding a
rough drumbeat against her ribcage at the thought
of what might happen if Caitlin wandered down to
the beach by herself and decided to wade.

"There, down by the water," Andie breathed out,
rushing around to the patio on shaky legs and scour-
ing the deserted beach for a small, fragile figure
kicking at the sand.

Sam was right by her side as she scrambled down
the scrubby hill to crunch over the broken shells of

the high-tide mark. His solid presence there gave Andie strength. When they reached Caitlin, he hung back a bit as if wanting to give them a moment alone. Without even thinking about it, Andie grabbed his hand and pulled him forward with her.

"Caitlin! You have to stop running off like this, you nearly gave me a heart attack," Andie said, dropping Sam's hand to throw her arms around the little girl's slumped, unresisting shoulders. Andie tensed inside, wondering if she'd be rebuffed, but Caitlin sniffled into her shoulder and let herself be hugged.

"I didn't think anybody'd notice," she muttered. "You have a boyfriend now, and your job is hard."

Andie's heart expanded so fast and hard, it made her ribs ache. Leaving aside the tricky question of whether or not "boyfriend" was the right way to describe Sam, Andie zeroed in on the main issue. "I'm sorry, Caitlin. I know I said I'd try to take some time off, but I guess you figured out that's probably not going to happen now. Still, I'm going to spend as much time with you as I can. I want to get to know you, and I want you to get to know me."

Caitlin pulled away to stare up at her, blinking furiously as if holding back tears. "Why? I'm not even your kid."

"No, but you're still my family." Andie heard the wobble in her own voice, but she couldn't do anything about it. "Neither one of us has so much family left that we can afford to lose each other."

Caitlin cocked her head. "What happened to your family? Are they dead like my mom?"

What a complicated question. Andie bit her lip and glanced up at Sam helplessly. She had no idea how honest she should be. How could she explain to someone so young that there were families that splintered into pieces for all kinds of reasons. And no matter how many regrets a person had, sometimes there was no way to fix it. Sam spread his hands in a sorrowful gesture that told Andie he had, if possible, even less of an idea how to deal with the sticky subject than she did.

Begin as you mean to go on, Andie thought, the words drifting through her brain in her father's brisk, no-nonsense voice. It was good advice, and Andie drew in a steadying breath before she told Caitlin the truth. "My mother is dead, like yours. My father is still alive, but he doesn't talk to me or your dad, for different reasons. And your father and I . . . well, it's been a long time since I saw him."

"I never saw him," Caitlin said, staring down at her sandy sneakers. "But I still miss him. Do you miss him?"

Tears thickened Andie's throat, making it hard to talk. "I do, sweetie. So much. The same way I'd miss you, now, if you left. So I need you to promise me you'll stop trying to run away, Caitlin. I would notice. And I would miss you like my heart was breaking—just like you miss your dad."

Maybe it wasn't fair to use Owen that way, but she and Caitlin had the exact same hole in their hearts where Owen Shepard was supposed to fit. And Andie was desperate to get through to this closed-off kid—she'd use any tool that came to hand.

It paid off when Caitlin's blue eyes filled with tears and her face crumpled like tissue paper. With a soft wail, Caitlin pushed into Andie's arms and buried her face in Andie's chest, right over her pounding heart. When Andie held her niece close and let Caitlin sob, she felt that heart crack right down the middle.

They were going to be okay. They'd muddle through until Owen came home—and then they'd decide where to go from there. Tears tracked cool and wet down Andie's cheeks, but she smiled as she glanced up to share the moment with Sam . . . only to find that she and Caitlin were alone on the empty beach.

The buzz of the cell phone in his hip pocket jolted Sam out of his hypnotic brushing of Queenie's black coat. Running his fingers over her glossy flank, Sam ruefully acknowledged he'd probably been brushing the mare more to calm his own stormy mood than in an attempt to clean an already-clean horse. Usually nothing chilled Sam out like spending time in the barn, connecting with his horses. But ever since the night he'd kissed Andie and then walked out on her, no amount of curry combing or hoof picking seemed to settle the raging torrent of emotion in Sam's chest. Even now, ten days later, whenever Sam closed his eyes he felt the phantom brush of Andie's lush, sweet mouth against his.

He was surprised and a little dismayed to find that he missed his miniature barn shadow, too. But Caitlin had started at Sanctuary Elementary this week, and at least he got to see her after school when Taylor picked her up and brought her to the barn for her riding lessons.

Maybe it was stupid to continue with those lessons, considering he was determined to ignore his heart and get back on track with what he should have done all along—avoid Sheriff Andie Shepard.

It sucked, worse than he could have imagined. But he had to face reality—this was the only way he could protect her from his past. Especially now that she was in a serious race for the job of sheriff of Sanctuary Island, she really couldn't afford to hook up with a guy like Sam.

Still, whatever mistakes the adults in Caitlin's life made, that kid didn't deserve to have yet another promise broken. So Sam carefully arranged his schedule so that he gave her lessons on the weekdays when Andie had an afternoon work shift and couldn't come to watch, and he made himself scarce when it was time for her to pick Caitlin up. It was harder than it should have been.

He sighed. Slapping a hand against Queenie's gleaming flank, Sam palmed his phone out of his pocket and grimaced at the text from his business partner back home. Although, as Lucas Ricker himself would say, calling their horse rescue operation a "business" was a big enough stretch to pull a muscle. The text read:

> *Gimme a call when you get a chance. Had an offer on the old trailer.*

Sam stiffened, his eyes automatically scanning the message again. Yep, that was the code they'd agreed on. If their phone records were subpoenaed later, Sam wanted no trace of a chance that anyone could go down for this except him. If Sam got arrested, at least Lucas would still be there for the horses.

Ducking out of the stall with an absent-minded pat on Queenie's rump, Sam thumbed in Lucas's number and listened to the ring. He took a quick glance around the quiet barn—it was Saturday, so Taylor was probably fooling around in the ring with her favorite gelding, Jeb. Jo Ellen was out to lunch

with her fiancé while her daughter, Merry, was in
the office across the hall typing away. Pretty private,
but maybe not private enough for Lucas's news. Just
as Lucas answered with a terse "This is Ricker,"
Sam's gaze turned to the ladder leading up to the
hayloft.

"Hold on a sec," he told Lucas, tucking the phone
into his pocket and setting his boots to the ladder
rungs. The air was still and close up in the loft, and
dust motes danced in the shaft of light from the high,
square window. He breathed in the warm, yeasty
smell of fresh-cut hay and let it brace him for the
call ahead.

"Okay, I'm here," Sam said, kicking a rectangu-
lar bale into place so he could sit on it and lean
his back against the stack behind it. "What's going
on?"

"Cops came by yesterday, asking questions."
Lucas never wasted time on chitchat and how-are-
you's. He got right to the point, and Sam appreci-
ated it.

"What did you tell them?"

"Exactly what we decided—you're consulting at
the Windy Corner Therapeutic Riding Center, and
you traveled there with a horse that needs rehab. I
showed 'em Queenie's documentation."

Sam's left knee jittered and he blew out a breath.
"Then what?"

"Then nothing," Lucas grunted. "They left. You
sure those papers will hold up?"

There was no way to be sure, but it wasn't like
Sam had any other options. "So long as they don't
dig too deep, I should be okay. I've got a history of
coming out to Sanctuary Island with problem horses,

and if they call the therapy riding center, Jo Ellen will tell them the truth—which confirms what they've already heard."

"I don't like it."

The roar of a pick-up truck's engine in the background gave Sam a picture of his partner. Lucas was out on the road where he liked to be, running down rumors and investigating complaints about mistreatment and neglect of horses. Folks called in or left anonymous tips on the Blue Ridge Horse Rescue website, and Lucas crisscrossed the state to check them out. Weeks could go by without the two men laying eyes on each other, but that suited them both just fine. They weren't friends—they were more like cell mates. Two loners thrown together by the choices they'd made, who shared a common goal. Only in their case, the shared purpose wasn't to survive prison and get out, it was a burning hatred of people who abused the animals under their care.

"Sorry you had to deal with the cops," Sam said, scrubbing a hand down his face. "I hope they don't hassle you again."

"Not that," Lucas growled, the grinding of his teeth audible over the line. "I don't like that you're the one taking all the risks. I'm as guilty as you are."

Sam grinned a little, more touched than he'd like to let on. Maybe they were friends, after all. "Give it a rest, Ricker. We agreed it's better this way."

"You agreed. I still think I've got a better reason for being out traveling around with a broke-down horse."

"But you've never been to Sanctuary Island," Sam pointed out patiently. "And this is the perfect place for Queenie to hide out. Who'd ever think to look for a stolen racehorse in a therapeutic riding stable?

She'll be safe here, if I can just get her to the point where she can work with kids. And we can't leave now, anyway, because it would be dangerous to her health to make her travel again. It's done. So shut up with your second-guessing and tell me what's going on at the farm. How's Galahad progressing?"

As Lucas grudgingly shifted gears into updates about their latest rescue, Sam forced himself to follow along and pay attention. It should've been easy—that was his real life, the work he'd dedicated himself to and the calling he believed in. Rescuing abused animals was Sam's redemption. If he didn't have that, what was he? Just another drifter, ghosting through life without leaving a mark on the world to say he'd been there. He'd made a difference. He wasn't worthless, the way his old man always said.

Sam wished to God that felt like enough anymore, because it had to be enough. There was nothing else for him. He wasn't cut out for love and family, or even friendship. He was better off alone.

And, Lord knew, Andie and Caitlin were better off without him.

Taylor froze with one hand on the loft ladder. She made a frantic shushing gesture with her other hand as her mind dipped and swirled with new information. Little Caitlin's baby blues went wide and worried, but she mimed zipping her lips and throwing away the key as if she'd seen that a lot in her young life.

On her way to find Sam and ask if he had time for a quick riding lesson, since Andie'd had to work a double, Taylor had heard his deep voice coming from up in the loft. She'd been about to climb the ladder and poke her head up to let Sam know she wanted to talk to him when the content of his conversation had filtered through. Taylor couldn't believe her ears.

Still in shock, Taylor stared down at Caitlin and whispered, "Did he just say 'a stolen racehorse'?"

Chapter Twelve

"Ivy, I'm calling it for the day. Got to go pick up my niece from the barn." Andie strode into her office just long enough to grab her jacket from the back of her desk chair, then pivoted and walked out again. She stopped by the dispatcher's desk to appraise her friend and coworker's red cheeks and furious eyes.

"You do that, Sheriff. I'll stay here and hold down the fort until Deputy Fred manages to haul his sorry butt in to work." Ivy rummaged under her desk and came up with a handheld compact mirror. The face she made when she flipped it open to check her makeup told Andie her dispatcher was more than a little off her game.

"Go easy on Fred," Andie begged. "I can't handle him quitting again this week."

Fred Stanz was older than dirt. He'd been a deputy for the last five sheriffs, and he was known for having so little ambition to be promoted to the office of sheriff himself that he periodically quit, just to keep people's expectations low. He'd quit on Andie four times before she hired Ivy Dawson to run the office and handle the phones. Now Deputy Fred, as everyone called him, was known for two things: total lack of ambition and total obsession with the pretty new dispatcher who dressed like a fifties pin-up girl and had a smile for everyone—usually.

"He better just stay out of my way," Ivy grumbled.

Andie frowned. "You're usually so sweet and patient with him. If his flirting is starting to get to you, I'll put a stop to it."

Sighing, Ivy gave up on dabbing at her smudged black winged eyeliner and snapped the compact closed. "No, he's fine. Fred's harmless and I usually don't mind a bit of target practice myself, but I'm not looking for another useless man to hit on me today. I filled my quota when I picked up lunch from the Firefly."

"I've never heard you talk like this." Amusement tickled at Andie's mouth but she held back a smile. "Has Sanctuary Island's biggest flirt finally met her match?"

Ivy sat bolt upright in her chair, green eyes flashing. "If Nash Tucker is my match, I'll flush all my Chanel lipsticks down the toilet, stop showering, and start wearing a bonnet."

"Nash Tucker?" Andie froze, the name running through her like a sword. "Dabney Leeds's grandson."

"And the new horse in the sheriff race." Ivy twisted her mouth guiltily. "Okay, I know technically he's your nemesis, not mine, but please—can't I have this one? I promise I'll hate him forever and completely! No one could be a better mortal enemy for Nash Tucker than I will be."

Andie blinked, a little dazed by all the dramatics.

"Hold up. Let's be clear. Did he threaten you in some way? Make you feel unsafe?"

Ivy tucked her tongue in her cheek. "If I say yes, will you throw him in the pokey?"

"If it's true," Andie emphasized, staring her flighty friend down. "Then there's nowhere he can hide that I won't hunt him down and make him pay for scaring you."

The rhythmic click of Ivy's long, scarlet-varnished fingernails drumming against her desk punctuated the way her gaze shifted around. Bless her, Andie thought fondly, but Ivy was not a good liar.

"What if I told you he's a jackass?" Ivy said, wheedling. "Like, a big one. . . . Pokey time?"

"Sadly, being a jackass is not on the books as being against the law in Sanctuary," Andie told her, finally breaking a grin at her friend's outraged growl. "Hey, if you don't like it, take it up with the town council. Or run for mayor and change the laws yourself. I don't make the rules, I just enforce them."

"Well, there ought to be a rule against waltzing into the town you swore you'd never go back to looking all gorgeous and handsome and charismatic and charming, and talking to your ex-girlfriend in a diner. I mean, anyone would agree that's beyond the pale. Right?"

"Nash Tucker should be tarred and feathered," Andie agreed, filing all this interesting info away for later thought. "If it were up to me, he'd be run out of town on a rail, along with his self-serving, money-flaunting grandfather. But it's up to the people of Sanctuary Island to choose who they want as their sheriff. So we'll see what they say come election time. I'm willing to abide by the people's decision."

Easy to say, Andie reflected as she made the now-familiar drive across the island to Windy Corner. *Harder to live up to.*

If she lost this job, what would she have? Nothing but the bitter knowledge that a whole town full of people agreed with her father that she wasn't a good cop.

The only positive thing about her worries over her job was that they took her mind off her worries about her personal life. She hadn't heard from Owen since that one, too-short phone call, but Caitlin was actually settling in okay. They were learning to rub along smoothly, the two of them, and Andie counted it a big step forward that her niece no longer looked ready to bolt at the first sign of affection. They'd graduated to an actual kiss good night, on the forehead or cheek. Caitlin still didn't exactly come flying into her arms when Andie showed up at the barn to take her home after her riding lessons, but that was mostly because Caitlin would happily bed down in the sawdust outside Queenie's stall and live there full time if Andie would allow it. So all of that was going well.

As long as Andie didn't allow herself to think about Sam Brennan, or the fact that after one scorching hot kiss, he'd basically disappeared off the face of the earth.

Oh, he was still around. She heard stories and tales about his ease with the horses, his amazing ability to get them to do whatever he wanted without even touching them, his comments to Caitlin as she mastered the basics of horseback riding. But though Caitlin saw him almost every day, it had been more than a week since Andie had caught even a fleeting glimpse of Sam. For such a big, heavily muscled man, he sure could slip into the shadows when he wanted to.

At first, Andie hadn't understood. She'd thought maybe Sam was giving Caitlin and Andie time alone together, to get used to each other without him around as a distraction. And then she'd started to wonder if he regretted that kiss . . . and once she considered the humiliation of that, she supposed she ought to be grateful that Sam was so obviously staying out of her way.

Maybe he meant to spare her the embarrassment of throwing herself at him again. Maybe that was the gentlemanly thing to do—maybe that was how it usually worked on the dating scene. Andie wouldn't really know, considering that her one foray into adult relationships had ended with her quitting the Louisville police force, breaking ties with her father, and running away to Sanctuary Island.

Clearly, Andie was no expert when it came to relationships. But she still wished Sam had the balls to talk to her, face-to-face, and tell her straight out that he wasn't interested. And if she ever managed to run into him again, she was going to have to seriously work to keep herself from confronting him about it.

I thought we had the start of something good, she imagined saying as she pulled up to the barn and climbed out of her SUV. *Maybe we don't know each other all that well, but I wanted to know more. And I thought you did too. What changed?*

She was so intent on silently rehearsing a conversation she was, realistically, never going to have, that she almost tripped over Caitlin. Curled around her own skinned knees, bony arms clutching tight, Caitlin was waiting just inside the barn doors. Alarm pushed every other thought out of Andie's head. She crouched down to run a quick, assessing hand over the girl's shoulders and head. "Hey there! Are you okay?"

"I'm ready to go," Caitlin told her, pushing to her feet and flipping her pink backpack onto one shoulder.

Andie let her hand drop. "Sure. But I usually have to drag you away from Queenie kicking and screaming, or bribe you with promises of mac and cheese. Did something happen during your riding lesson?"

"Didn't have one. Sam was . . . busy."

The brief hesitation sent up a signal flare, but all Andie said was, "Is Taylor around? I should pay her for babysitting."

"I'm not a baby," Caitlin snapped. "I don't need a babysitter."

Brows climbing, Andie opened the car door and stood back rather than helping Caitlin get in and situated. Something was going on here, and Andie was going to find out what. "Hang out for a sec, I'll find Taylor and then we can go home."

But once she marched into the dim, cool interior of the barn, it wasn't hard to figure out where Taylor was. A murmur of voices from the office drew Andie in. She raised her hand to knock on the cracked-open door just as she heard Jo Ellen Hollister say, "How could he not tell us? Does he think we wouldn't understand?"

Sam. They were talking about Sam.

Andie breathed in, a slow, silent breath and shifted her weight closer to the opening . . . and a board creaked under her foot. She winced, and there was a beat of silence from inside the office before the door swung open and Taylor peered out at her.

"There you are," Andie said, pasting on a nonchalant smile. "I was looking for you."

"Why?" Taylor glanced over her shoulder hastily, nervous fingers tucking her tousled blonde hair behind her ears. "I mean, here I am. What's up?"

"What's up with you?" Andie countered, still smiling.

Taylor smiled back, a little too bright. It reminded Andie of the expression the teenager wore that night she busted Taylor and Matt Little for underage drinking. "Nothing's up! Just a regular old boring day here at Windy Corner."

Andie looked past Taylor to make eye contact with Jo Ellen, who looked calm, if a little tense. Jo nodded briskly. "Sheriff."

They'd closed ranks, Andie understood. Whatever was happening with Sam, they weren't going to tell Andie—the Sheriff—about it. Doesn't matter, she decided, returning Jo's nod and reaching for her wallet to fork over Taylor's babysitting pay. Andie would find out on her own.

From the moment she met Sam, she'd sensed he was dangerous. She should have listened to her gut. It was time to do her job and investigate what he was hiding. Even if it meant finding out that she'd been taken in, yet again, by a handsome face and a sizzling attraction.

The next day, when Sam's borrowed truck backed out of the Harrington House driveway onto Island Road, Andie was ready for him. From her position across the town square, in an unmarked sedan, behind sunglasses and a baseball cap, she carefully tailed Sam all the way down Main Street and out of downtown. They were heading in the direction of Windy Corner, and she fully expected him to drive there. Her plan was to park off the road nearby and surreptitiously stake out the barn to see if she saw anything unusual or illegal taking place.

She planned, also, to stubbornly ignore how much she hoped she saw nothing out of the ordinary. This was her job, like it or not, and if it gave her a little bit of vertigo to blur the lines between her personal and professional lives, so be it.

But Sam didn't take the turn for the barn. Instead, he maintained his course along the coast road, taking them deeper and deeper into the island. As other vehicles thinned out around them and the road narrowed to a single lane, Andie pulled back to keep plenty of distance between her sedan and Sam's truck. She lost sight of him for moments at a time as they wound around curves and up and down hills through the thick maritime forest. She had to trust that when he finally made a turn off, she wouldn't miss it completely.

She came close to missing it when it happened at last, but as she rolled quietly past the barely-there dirt track that led out to Heartbreak Cove, something made her pause. Cutting the engine, she rolled down her window and listened to the sound of a truck engine grumbling off to the left.

What in the world was Sam Brennan doing out here? Her gut clenched. There was no reason she could think of. No business he could have, on his own or for the barn or for his family. It was a tiny, out of the way pocket of nature nestled in the heart of Sanctuary Island. The way the island curved created a small inlet and cove, complete with gritty pebbled beach and calm, lapping waves cut off from the wind that crashed towering surf against the rocks on the eastern shore. No one came to Heartbreak Cove except the wild horses.

Well, the horses and a couple of teenagers, looking for privacy. But what did Sam need privacy for, all by himself like this? Something was definitely weird. Maybe not illegal weird, but off enough to get her heart hammering and adrenaline pumping.

Andie wheeled the car into a U-turn and parked it a couple hundred feet up the road, off to the side and sheltered under a big wax myrtle. Then she doubled back and took the path to the cove on foot.

With every step, she wondered if she was being paranoid. Maybe Sam just wanted to see the wild horses! Was she was so busy berating herself for trusting the wrong guy—as if she'd learned nothing from the worst event of her entire life—that she was inventing reasons to be suspicious?

Her brain was buzzing back and forth so rapidly by the time she caught up to Sam, it took her the space of a few quiet breaths to understand what she was seeing.

From where she'd crouched in the underbrush, her boots sunk in marshy wet ground and nothing but the waving willows to shield her if Sam turned around, Andie watched him stride purposefully down to the edge of the marsh and out onto the glittering sand. Broken shells crunched under his boots as his steps slowed, his gait going liquid and graceful in a way that tightened Andie's body and made her breath come shaky.

No man that big should move like that, like a dancer or a warrior, light on the balls of his feet and every muscle loose and ready. She blinked, registering the change in Sam's posture—it was the way he looked when he went into the ring with Queenie. It was the way he moved when he wanted to be ready for whatever came his way.

Standing up a little taller, Andie did her best to melt into the sparse coverage of the swaying willow branches. She needed a better view, but there was a dip in the land that hid Sam from her. What was he doing?

Probably nothing illegal, she admitted to herself. Yet somehow, she couldn't look away.

Andie set her foot on the lowest branch and tested her weight against it. Seemed sturdy. Swallowing hard, she stepped up onto the branch and clung to the smooth bark of the trunk, praying for enough breeze to part the trailing willow branches and let her see what Sam was up to. As if on cue, a salt-scented wind rolled in from the water, smoothing the cordgrass in billowing waves and making the weeping willow dance. Through the shower of pink blossoms, Andie caught a glimpse of Sam, and he wasn't alone.

There was a wild horse inches away from him. And not the "wild" horse he'd brought with him to train—no, this was one of Sanctuary Island's free-roaming stallions, rangy and built to endure exposure to the harshest storms and coldest winters. The entire island was dedicated to protecting these animals, but that didn't mean they were pets. On the contrary, it was against the law to feed them or interfere with them because their survival hinged on being free to form their own bands and make their own way.

Each wild horse band consisted of one stallion to every five or six mares. The stallion would lead and protect his brood from predators, he'd find food and shelter when the weather turned bad, and he'd keep them safe and together. Horses were herd animals—you never saw one of the Sanctuary Island wild horses on its own. They ran together, relied on each other, as social as any human. More so, in fact, because humans could survive living alone.

Horses couldn't. If a horse lost his place in his band and was left alone, he'd find his way to this secluded spot on the island's coast, lie down, and die of loneliness.

That's why it was called Heartbreak Cove. And that's what Sam was doing here, Andie understood in a flash as she realized what was bugging her about the scene unfolding on the beach below.

The horse was alone. He'd lost his band and come here to die.

Sam wasn't doing anything wrong. He was saving this stallion from dying of a broken heart. Joy bloomed up from her chest and into her throat, making her want to laugh or sing or shout Sam's name. But she wouldn't do anything to jeopardize the delicate dance of trust between man and beast.

She hadn't caught Sam doing something wrong. She was going to get to help him do something right. And when the horse was safe and cared for, Andie and Sam were going to talk. She'd misjudged and misunderstood Sam Brennan for the last time.

Chapter Thirteen

Sam breathed out a steady stream of nonsense noise and soothing sounds, his eyes tracking every flex of muscle and flicker of tension under the colt's shaggy, dappled coat.

When the call came in that morning, he'd been expecting to hear the update from Dr. Ben Fairfax's latest vet check on Queenie. He hadn't expected to hear how Ben's friend, Grady, who apparently functioned as some sort of unofficial Guardian of the Wild Horses or something, had witnessed a fight for dominance between a grizzled old chestnut stallion and a young Appaloosa colt. And when Sam heard what that meant for the colt . . . before he knew it, he was heading out to Heartbreak Cove.

And there was the wild colt, shivering and limping, with the marks of battle standing out bloody against his dappled gray flanks. Sam knew how long it usually took to get a wild animal to trust him—days, weeks, even months of slow, gradual progress. Of leaving out treats and standing in the horse's sight line, moving incrementally closer every day until finally the horse stood still and let him close enough to touch.

They didn't have months. This colt was injured, but worse than that, he'd given up. Every line of his body showed defeat; despair dimmed his sunken brown eyes. So Sam took his shot. He approached from the side, walking slow and gradual with his eyes down. No eye contact—he wasn't pushing for dominance here, but trust.

The colt shuddered and took a single, faltering step but when his injured right foreleg nearly collapsed under his weight, he stilled. Head down, ears back, the colt waited as Sam reached out a careful hand, fingers curled under, and brushed the backs of his knuckles against the colt's withers.

His gray flanks trembled as if the colt were shaking off a fly, but Sam kept the pressure of his hand light and steady as he began to smooth carefully over the horse's back and sides. He took his time, and when he finally made it to the colt's head and face, Sam was ninety percent sure he wasn't about to get bitten. He was less sure how the colt would react to the halter in his other hand, but it wasn't until the thing was on and buckled that the colt really reacted.

Jerking his head up and away from Sam's hands, the colt backed up a few nervous paces, breathing hard through his nose at what had to be terrible pain in his buckling foreleg. Sam let the halter go, let the lead rope trail on the ground, and focused on calming the colt . . . until the sound of footsteps registered in Sam's consciousness.

He glared over his shoulder, about to issue a firm command to back off, no matter who it was. But the sight of Andie smiling at him, with Dr. Fairfax and his mobile medical kit right behind her, stopped the words in Sam's chest.

"What are you doing here?" Sam asked hoarsely.

Andie tilted her chin at the veterinarian. "Bringing help. You don't have to do this all on your own, you know."

As Ben shouldered past them and started his examination, aided by a little sedative, Sam stared at Andie. Her red-gold curls tossed in the wind, blowing tendrils into a face flushed with an emotion Sam could hardly stand to read. In well-worn jeans and a heather gray T-shirt, Andie Shepard was the most beautiful thing he'd ever seen. Wait.

Sam frowned. "Aren't you on duty today? Where's your uniform?"

A dark flush washed across her cheeks, but Andie didn't drop her straightforward gaze. "I wore plain clothes and drove an unmarked car to follow you. I wanted to find out what you were up to."

Heart-stopping panic seized Sam's chest, but Andie only smiled ruefully and dipped her chin. "Now I know," she said softly. "You were helping an injured colt who lost his band."

Sam forced air into his lungs. "I want to take him back to Windy Corner once the doc is finished with him," he said thickly, doing his damnedest to keep the conversation focused on the business at hand—and not on how badly he wanted to close the distance between them and pull Andie down onto the sand for the kiss of her life.

"We have regulations about interfering with the wild horses," she said, but when he looked at her sharply, she held up her hands in surrender. "But in the case of injury, it's different. We can't help every wounded wild horse, but when we get the chance, we have to take it. These horses are part of our island—it's our responsibility and our privilege to protect them."

The passion firing her voice and brightening her eyes reached into Sam and wrung him out. He managed a faint smile. "You sound like me, when I talk about the horse rescue operation."

"I liked seeing you in your element," Andie confessed softly. "Actually rescuing this horse. I could tell you know what you're doing. I mean, I've seen you at the barn. You're amazing with all the horses. But this, getting him to trust you when he's never had any human contact in his entire life . . ."

Sam shrugged even though he wanted to pull his shoulders straight with pride. "Thanks," he said, training his eyes on the veterinarian's competent hands checking out the colt's injuries. "That means . . . a lot, coming from someone I respect. And thanks for bringing Dr. Ben here. I was going to call him on my cell when I got the colt ready to move, but this is better."

Andie came close enough to lay a hand on Sam's arm, and he felt the contact all the way to the marrow of his bones. "Like I said, you're not alone in this. There are people who want to help the colt, and help you. I'm glad I got the opportunity to prove it."

He flexed his forearm, mesmerized by the sight and feel of her pale, slender fingers against his sturdy, work-roughened tan. "It's your job to take care of the island and all the creatures on it. You're damn good at what you do."

"For as long as it lasts." The wry twist to her smile slid between Sam's ribs like a knife. "Come November, I guess we'll see if the residents of Sanctuary agree with you or not."

"They'd be fools to let you go."

It wasn't until he saw the slight widening of her ocean blue eyes that he realized what he'd actually revealed.

"Sadly, there are plenty of fools in the world," Andie said lightly, but her gaze was thoughtful.

"Come on," Ben broke in before Sam could figure out how big a fool he was about to be. "This guy needs a warm barn and a more substantial leg brace than I've got with me. Let's get him back to Windy Corner."

Sam knew he should be grateful for the interruption, for the chance to pull back and think through what it meant that Andie's suspicions had been raised to the point of tailing him—and how completely he'd allayed those suspicions, apparently, without even meaning to.

But as the three of them worked together to help the stumbling, lightly drugged colt up the hill and into Ben's horse trailer, all Sam could think about was the admiration and respect on Andie's lovely, strong face, and the way it made him feel.

Andie made him achingly aware of life's possibilities. She made him want more than he'd allowed himself to have in years. She made him forget that he wasn't the man she thought he was.

More than anything, she made him want to be the man who could deserve her.

Queenie had graduated to one of the more permanent stalls a week ago, leaving the integration pen in the middle of the barn free. It was the perfect place for the injured colt. There was a little more room to move around while he got used to four walls and a roof, and close proximity to the other horses in

the barn so he could grow accustomed to them—
and vice versa—before they were all turned out into
the pasture together.

Andie grinned at the curious way Queenie eyed
her new neighbor. The mare hung her head over the
top of the stall door, craning her long, black neck
to get a look at the barn's latest addition.

"I think she wants to be friends," Andie said as
Sam ducked out of the pen and left Dr. Fairfax to
his work. "Do horses make friends?"

"Sure." Sam crossed the central hall and bent to
turn on the hose attached to the wall between a set
of crossties. "Horses are very social. They can form
intense, lasting bonds with other horses . . . and with
other things."

"What do you mean?" Andie asked, mildly
amazed that she was able to form a complete sentence, considering how every scrap of her consciousness was suddenly focused on the riveting sight of
Sam Brennan lifting the hose and gulping down
some water before directing the stream over his head
and face.

Rivulets trickled down his temples and soaked his
T-shirt, molding it to the chiseled definition of his
pecs and abs. Sam shook his head, spraying drop-
lets everywhere, but some still clung to the dripping
ends of his dark brown hair.

All that water, and Andie's mouth had never been
so dry. She swallowed hard, an inferno of desire raging to life in her core, a fire so intense it would take
more than a splash of water from that hose to cool
her off.

"Horses are funny," Sam said, apparently oblivious to the fact that he was providing Andie with
a show that was going to make multiple return

appearances in her midnight fantasies from now on. He blinked water out of his eyes and smoothed a hand over his close-cropped beard. "They'll buddy up to cats, dogs, goats—there are racehorses who have to travel everywhere with their goat best friend because if their owners leave that goat behind, the horse won't run."

"That's very . . . interesting," Andie said, her gaze tracking the progress of a particular water droplet as it ran down Sam's throat and disappeared where the stretched-out neck of his T-shirt gave a glimpse of the strong, sturdy wings of his collarbones.

Sam paused in the act of tugging his shirt hem up to wipe at his damp face. Andie wanted to drag her eyes away from the taut sliver of hard-muscled belly he'd exposed, but she honestly couldn't. The most she could manage was not to lick her lips like a hungry cat staring down a bowl of cream.

The noise Sam made in the back of his chest rumbled through Andie like thunder, charging the atmosphere between them with the sizzling ozone of a lightning strike. He took a step toward her as if she'd dragged him close, and Andie lost her mind.

Grabbing his hand, she hauled Sam out of the hallway and away from the colt. She didn't even know where they were going, just that she had to get him somewhere dark, somewhere private, somewhere she could look at him and feel safe, even knowing that everything she felt and everything she wanted was naked on her face.

"Here," Sam urged, tugging her over to the ladder that led up into the hayloft, and Andie didn't even think about it. She climbed, with Sam following close behind. The knowledge that if he looked up, he'd get an incredibly intimate view of her back-side made Andie glad she'd worn these jeans.

Six inches from the top of the ladder, her foot slipped off the rung, and Sam's broad-palmed hand was instantly there, cupping her rear end and boost-ing her gently into the loft. Breathless, head spin-ning, Andie turned back to the ladder in time to see Sam vault over the loft threshold and stalk forward like a hunting panther. He was gorgeously, over-whelmingly masculine. The powerful lines of his big body advancing on hers made Andie want to swoon back, to lean against the hay bales and let him rav-ish her. But she was too impatient for that.

Meeting Sam in the middle of the loft, Andie speared her hands into his wet, curling hair and dragged his head down for a kiss. The searing heat of his mouth contrasted with the cool of his damp skin, making Andie shudder with the need to feel more of him.

"You make me crazy," she admitted, husking the words against his open lips before licking into his mouth for another greedy kiss.

His only reply was to bend her back over his strong arm so he could plunder deeper. Andie felt herself go pliant and soft, every part of her trusting Sam to hold her up, to not let her fall.

She trusted him.

The realization blinded her, caught at her breath—or maybe that was the hunger for Sam clawing at her insides and urging her to take hold of this man and never let him go. Andie bit at his jaw, delight-ing in the rough bristles of his beard abrading her tender lips, and when she sucked a soft love mark into the hollow of his throat, Sam made that noise again. The same noise that lit Andie's fuse and set her off like an explosion—a deep, grating growl of pure need.

Grinning with triumph, Andie pulled back far enough to gasp, "We could have been doing this every day for a week, if you hadn't decided to avoid me."

Sam stiffened in her arms, but she wasn't having it. Hooking a foot behind his knee, Andie tumbled them to the floor of the loft, trusting the thick carpet of hay to soften their fall. But at the last second, Sam twisted to get his body under hers so she landed with a pleased "oof" on his wide, heaving chest.

"I wasn't avoiding you," Sam denied, wetting his kiss-swollen bottom lip with the tip of his tongue.

Andie shivered and let her legs slide open so that she straddled his lean hips. "You were. But that's okay, I forgive you since it was obviously not about you never wanting to kiss me again."

He surged up and caught her mouth with his, the motion sending shocks of pleasure through her molten liquid core as she squirmed against the denim-covered bulge between his massive thighs. "No," he rasped. "It was never about me not wanting you."

Rational thoughts swirled through Andie's sensation-soaked brain like dandelion fluff scattering on a breeze. "What was it about, then?" She managed to ask. "Why have you been hiding from me?"

Sam sat up in a swift, fluid move that made Andie tremble at the hard crunch of abdominal muscle she could feel working against her own belly. She was still splayed around him, clinging to his broad shoulders and crossing her ankles behind his back. They were pressed so close together, Andie had to focus on one of Sam's bittersweet chocolate eyes at a time or risk going cross-eyed. Part of her knew that a little bit of distance would improve her view and help her read what was really going on, but she didn't want to let go. She was sick of letting go of Sam.

"I wasn't hiding from you," Sam grated out. "I was hiding from myself. I've been on my own for a long time—my whole life, basically. I wasn't ready to admit I might want more. Or that I might be able to have it."

"You can have more," Andie told him, heart pounding. "If you want it. If you're willing to take a chance."

"I'm pretty good at risk-taking." Sam nuzzled the words into the crook of her shoulder as if he couldn't bear not to be kissing her. "In the past, I've risked my livelihood, my freedom, even my life. But nothing and no one has ever gotten me this close to risking my heart."

The litany of Sam's past risks echoed through Andie's head, even as her heart leapt uncontrollably to meet his declaration with the passionate press of her mouth on his. When she could think again, much less breathe, Andie rested her forehead on Sam's and cradled his rugged jaw in her hands.

"There's a lot we don't know about each other," she said softly. "There are things I should tell you, so you'll understand why this is such a big deal for me. And I don't know how long you're planning to stick around—or how much longer I'll be here on Sanctuary Island, for that matter, if I lose my job. I know there are obstacles and difficulties—there are probably a million reasons why it's a terrible idea to get involved in a romantic relationship right now."

Sam drew back, his brows knitting and a sort of grim agreement shadowing his eyes.

"But I don't care about any of that," Andie said urgently. "I just want to get to know you better, and see where this thing between us goes. I want to go on a regular date, just the two of us, and I want to go on a picnic with you and Caitlin, and I want to kiss you. Every day."

The clouds behind his eyes didn't exactly scatter—there was a lingering darkness Andie didn't understand. But the crinkle at the corners of his eyes and the wicked curve of his smile, the sweep of his huge, hot hands down her spine . . . those things, Andie understood.

"Daily kissing," he purred, low and sexy. "I can live with that."

Andie's breath quickened. "You know, it's been a week since the first time we kissed."

With a subsonic groan, Sam tucked her against him and rolled them both back down onto the hay-strewn floor. This time he put Andie on her back and loomed over her, blocking out her view of everything that wasn't him. She arched helplessly against him, breathless with desire as Sam lowered his head to whisper in her ear, "Hmm. Seems we've got a few days to catch up on, now don't we?"

Chapter Fourteen

"Why did I agree to this?" Sam wondered aloud as a bead of sweat trickled a ticklish path between his shoulder blades. "Kissing every day, sure. A picnic with the kid, fine. Even a date. I can do that. But whatever happened to dinner and a movie?"

"There's no movie theater on Sanctuary Island," Andie pointed out languidly from the prow of the rowboat. "And I told you I'd take a turn at the oars when you got tired."

Sam lifted the oars from the water and let them cross over his lap so he could rest his elbows on them. "Yeah," he said, eyeing her long, athletic form reclined against the cushions with an appreciative eye. "You look like you're ready to jump up from there and start rowing."

Guilt stirred across Andie's beautiful face. "I'm sorry. I thought this would be fun, but if you want to head back to shore we could just go to the Firefly and have lunch."

It was the damnedest thing, but Sam would do anything to take that look off Andie's face. "Nah, that's all right," he said, dipping the oars in and pushing the rowboat forward across Lantern Lake's placid surface. "It's just hot out here, and I'm in a mood. Ignore me."

It was hot, the warmest day they'd seen all spring, but it wasn't the cheerful sunshine beating down on Sam's head and illuminating every pale freckle on Andie's creamy skin that had him in this ugly mood. No, that was all thanks to another cryptic text from Lucas, back home. The cops had been by again, looking for Sam.

It was an unpleasant reminder that no matter how perfect the last few days had been, no matter how much he wanted to change his life—he was still caught in the tangled web of his past choices. And if he wasn't careful, those choices would chase him all the way to Sanctuary Island.

For the thousandth time, he told himself he should quit while he was ahead, before any of the crap in his life touched Andie or Caitlin. It would be the right thing to do, and he knew it. But as he studied the concerned look on Andie's beautiful face, Sam despaired. He couldn't pull away from her now. He couldn't bear to hurt her like that. Even the fact that he'd let his dark mood affect this date with Andie made Sam hate himself.

"I don't want to ignore you," Andie protested, sitting up and gripping the sides of the boat as it rocked. "I want to know what's going on with you."

"I'm just worried about Queenie," he settled on, grimacing at his own cowardice. "She's not progressing as well as I'd hoped."

"I thought things were getting better, now that she and Lucky are joined at the hip."

"Lucky" was what they'd all started calling the

rescued colt once it became clear that his injuries would have been life threatening if Sam hadn't found him in time and delivered him into Dr. Fairfax's very capable hands. To Sam's surprise, the wary, untamed horse had immediately taken to following Queenie around—so much so that he'd started to worry Queenie was going into heat.

She hadn't yet, but he was keeping a careful eye on the situation. Barely more than a filly, she and the colt were a funny matched pair. They both tended to shy away from human touch; they both had the instincts of prey animals surrounded by predators. But they trusted each other. In the week since they'd brought Lucky into the stable, they'd become inseparable.

"Their connection is healthy and good for them," Sam agreed, "but it's not doing much to make Queenie safer around people."

Andie frowned and trailed a hand over the side of the boat, her fingertips dancing across the water. "Caitlin won't be happy about that. She loves that horse."

"It's inevitable at her age," Sam said, pulling more easily on the oars as his shoulder muscles warmed and loosened. "She's horse crazy in general, but lots of horse-crazy kids tend to focus on one specific animal more than any other. It's like falling in love—irrational and insane, maybe, but when you're in the midst of it, nothing feels better or more vital."

Andie shot him a half smile that made his blood tingle. "Insane, huh? I take that to mean you've been in love before."

Laughing, Sam shook his head. "No, actually. I'm not speaking from experience, just from a lot of observation. You?"

The smile dropped off Andie's face. "Me what?"

Sam noted the stiffness of the words, the slamming down of a barrier behind Andie's clear blue eyes, but he didn't back off. "Have you ever been in love?" he asked deliberately.

"That's complicated." Andie looked away as if the tree-lined shore was suddenly extremely fascinating.

Sam wasn't sure why he was edging closer and closer to the warning signs Andie was giving off, but he couldn't seem to stop himself. "I don't know. It kind of sounds like a yes or no question to me."

"Spoken like a man who's never been in love." The bitter twist to her mouth couldn't be called a smile. "It's complicated because it turned out badly. Part of me knows it wasn't love, but if I'm honest, what I regret the most is that I blew my whole life apart for something that wasn't even real."

The rowboat skimmed the surface of the lake. With one last strong push, Sam lifted the oars again and let the boat drift so he could focus on Andie. "What happened?"

She waved a hand as if it were unimportant. "Boring, predictable story. I fell for the wrong guy—he was handsome and charming and exciting, but he also turned out to be a liar and a crook. Which was a big problem, since I was with the Louisville police department."

It was worse than Sam had guessed. Her past was repeating itself like a scratched record. Fate couldn't have sent a worse man than Sam to Andie Shepard. "Is that why you left Kentucky?"

"I left because I found out my fiancé wasn't an insurance adjuster—he was a highly placed member of the Dixie Mafia who'd been ordered to get close to me to exploit my position in the department."

The words were flowing fast and furious now, a waterfall Andie couldn't stop, and Sam wondered if this was the first time she'd told the whole story to anyone.

"I'm sorry," Sam said, painfully aware that there were no words he could say to close the raw wound in Andie's heart. Even worse, by his very existence in her life, he was doing more to hurt than to heal her. Guilt scraped at his insides. "Please tell me you busted your ex and he's serving time right now."

"That's the worst part. I never caught on. My dad was the one who figured it out—he was head of the department, and it turned out he was really the one my ex wanted to get close to. I was just his way in. It was never about me, but all I could see was what Damien wanted me to see. And when the dust finally settled, I'd lost more than a fiancé and a future I'd dreamed about and planned for—I'd lost the respect of every person I worked with. Especially my father."

Clenching his fists around the oar handles was the only way Sam could keep from launching himself across the seat to grab Andie in a hug that would capsize the boat. "I'm no expert on how good parents are supposed to act, but it seems to me that your dad should've been on your side, backing you up through the worst that life had ever thrown at you."

Andie's eyes went bleaker than a winter sea. "You've obviously never met my father. Owen and I were both disappointments to him even before I nearly married a felon. After? Well, let's just say our relationship has improved since we stopped speaking."

Casting around for some way to meet Andie's incredible openness and honesty, Sam took a deep breath and deliberately cracked himself open. "I guess that's one good thing about having no parents—no parental expectations to live up to."

Andie sat up straight. "Sam." Her voice was soft and yielding, something Sam could fall into if he let himself. "I didn't know—I'm sorry."

"Hey, everyone's got it bad, somehow, some way." He squinted at a rough spot on the starboard oar, worrying a splinter up with his thumb. "The way I grew up . . . it wasn't so bad. Taught me independence, self-reliance."

"It taught you that you were completely alone in the world," Andie realized. "That no one's there for you. But someone should have been. How old were you when . . ."

"When the state finally figured out the bruises and welts all over me weren't from a normal boy's rambunctiousness? About thirteen." Sam shrugged. "I hardly remember my parents—my memory of my dad is like something out of a nightmare, huge and hulking, unpredictable and angry. Always angry. I don't know what happens in a life to make a man angry like that, all the time, but I know I was lucky to get away from him when I did. If my ninth-grade teacher hadn't red-flagged me, I'd probably be dead now."

Andie sucked in air, distress lining her beautiful face. "Sam, my God. What happened to you?"

"What happens to any kid who's too old to be adopted by a couple looking for a cute baby?" Sam shrugged, feeling the pull of sore muscles along his shoulders. He made a conscious effort to not tense up. "I went into the system. Even though there actually was a couple that wanted to take me."

Her eyes widened. "What? Who?"

This was the only bright spot in his sob story, and

even this was bittersweet at best. Still, Sam smiled thinking of Ms. Endicott with her no-nonsense bun and kind eyes. "My teacher. The one who made the call to child protective services. Amelia Endicott. She and her partner fostered me for six months while they built a case to take away my parents' custody permanently."

"Her partner?"

"Sherry Rayborn, a gym teacher at the high school," Sam said, his vision suddenly filled with Sherry's big, booming laugh and short, cropped black hair.

"A lesbian couple," Andie said softly. "They were the ones who wanted to adopt you?"

"The only ones," Sam agreed, forcing his mouth into an ironic smile. "But it was a small town, twenty years ago. The authorities, in all their wisdom, decided I'd be better off shuffling from house to house with foster families who took in eight, nine kids at a time for the money they brought in, instead of living in a stable home with two women who actually gave a damn about me."

Andie's eyes slid shut as his harsh words resonated between them. "No wonder you don't seem to have much faith in laws or rules. The authorities that should have protected you failed you when you needed them most."

Sam gripped the oars until the rough wood bit into his palms. "I don't have faith in the system because the system is broken. It takes care of the rich while ignoring the people who most need help, and it rejects anyone who doesn't fit the mold of the so-called normal. And yeah, the system screwed me over in a bad way when I was a kid, but that's not the only reason I have to hate it."

"I get that," Andie assured him, and Sam had to glance away from the earnestness in her eyes. "But don't you see that all of us, you, me, Caitlin, everyone—we're the sum of our experiences. The things we believe, the choices we make, they come from somewhere. I'm honest enough to admit I chose my path, devoting myself to serving and protecting in law enforcement, because it was what my father expected. But I grew to love it for its own sake, because I see over and over the difference I can make in the lives of the people who elected me."

"It must be nice to have that faith."

"But you have it too!" The boat rocked heavily as Andie knelt up in the bow, gripping the sides. "I mean, your whole life is about making a difference and protecting those who can't protect themselves. We're more alike than you want to admit."

"I'm no hero," Sam grated out, every part of him straining forward as if he could shove the words into Andie's head and make her believe. "Remember that. You think we've got something in common, but I'm nothing like you."

Heedless of the way the small rowboat swayed and threatened to tip them into the lake, Andie crawled over the forward bench seat to get her hands onto Sam's granite-tense shoulders.

"I don't believe that," she said fiercely. "I may not know everything about you, Sam, but I know the core of you. Actions speak louder than words, and the things I've seen you do, the way you are with Caitlin and the horses—I know what kind of man you are."

The words hammered at Sam's guilty heart, cracking it right down the middle. "You don't, Andie."

"Yes, I do," she hummed, ghosting kisses across

his cheekbones and down the slope of his nose. She held him so lightly, the caress of her fingers like the flutter of a butterfly wing, but Sam couldn't move a muscle to save his life.

Andie drew back to stare tenderly into his eyes, letting him see far down into the depths of her beautifully honest, transparent soul. "The kind of man you are, Sam Brennan, is the kind of man I could fall in love with."

And instead of doing the right thing, pulling away and telling Andie exactly why she was wrong, Sam proved her wrong. He kissed her.

Chapter Fifteen

"Somebody had a good day off," Ivy commented archly, flipping her coal-black Bettie Page waves off her shoulders with a petulant pout. "Good, that makes one of us."

Andie wanted to ask how Ivy could tell, but she was a little afraid of the answer. Realizing she'd lifted a self-conscious hand to her tidy French braid, Andie dropped it and cleared her throat. "Yes, well. The weather is warming up, it was nice to spend some time outside."

"Oooh, Sheriff!" Mischief flashed behind the black-framed cat-eye glasses Ivy wore some days, purely for fashion purposes. "Isn't there a law against public indecency?"

Frowning repressively, Andie changed the subject. "Any calls for me?"

"Wyatt Hawkins, from the *Gazette*. He's got some questions."

Apprehension prickled a cool chill over Andie's scalp. "I'll call him from my office. Anything else?"

Ivy tilted her chin down to stare meaningfully

over the tops of her glasses. "Not unless you're willing to let me live vicariously with some down and dirty details about your date with Sam Brennan."

All it took was one mention of Sam to restore Andie's good mood. That afternoon on the lake had changed everything between them. Sam had let her see beneath his gruff, tough-guy shell to the bruised heart and lonely solitude at the core of him—and she'd told him her worst secret, but he hadn't looked at her like she was an idiot or should have known better. He'd been angry at her father for not supporting her.

Sam's anger on her behalf was like being taken by shoulders and shaken awake. Andie could look back at that time in her life now and see that while she'd certainly made mistakes and trusted where she shouldn't—her crimes hadn't been so terrible that she deserved to lose everything. She hadn't deserved being abandoned by her father.

On the other hand, Andie couldn't regret the way things had played out. If her father were a different man, if he'd been more understanding and loving, Andie would never have picked up and moved to Sanctuary Island.

She'd never have met Sam. At the moment, that seemed like a worse fate.

"Oh fine," Ivy grumped. "If you're not dishing the dirt, you might as well head out to the Firefly. Wyatt said he'd meet you there."

"Perfect! I'm supposed to have lunch with Sam," Andie said without thinking.

Ivy brightened instantly. "Oooh, a nooner! That's promising."

"If by 'nooner,' you mean splitting my usual order of cheese fries with another human being so I don't start the afternoon shift feeling like a blimp, then yes." Amused despite herself, Andie flicked her fingers good-bye at Ivy's stuck-out tongue, and headed out.

At this hour, before the lunch rush, the Firefly Café was almost empty. Other than Lonz, the owner and head chef, and an older waitress Andie didn't recognize, the only person Andie saw when she stepped into the restaurant was slouched into the back corner booth, nursing a cup of coffee and scowling at the waitress's attempts to get him to order anything else.

"I'm here for a meeting," Wyatt groused, shoving ink-stained fingers through his disheveled brown hair. "Not to clog my arteries with animal byproducts and spike my blood sugar with high fructose corn syrup."

"I see," the waitress retorted, propping one hand on her hip above the flare of her sea-foam green uniform skirt. "So I'll just keep the free coffee refills coming, and you can fill your veins with caffeine—which is so all natural and healthy, it's basically medicinal. Is that right?"

Andie felt her eyebrows shoot up as she checked the woman's nametag. Florene. Andie thought Florene might last—after the previous waitress left to get married, the Firefly had become a revolving door of women looking for work but unable to deal with the idiosyncratic demands of Sanctuary Island's quirkier residents and Alonzo's tendency to conduct every conversation at top volume. Florene was older than most of Lonz's applicants—in fact, as Andie studied the woman, she had to revise her original estimate of middle-age up by a decade or two.

"That *is* right," Wyatt insisted, sitting up straight

and emphatically holding out his mug. "Coffee is the nectar of the gods, and besides that, studies show—"

The waitress cut him off by rolling her eyes and filling his mug to the brim from the pot she carried. "Next you'll be telling me people aren't designed to eat meat or gluten or what have you."

"As a matter of fact," Wyatt began, but Florene only rolled her eyes again.

"I don't know how you got muscles like that, eating no meat."

"Whey protein shakes," Wyatt shot back.

"That's revolting," she said in a bored tone. "You're cute. But I'm seventy-three and I've eaten steak and fried chicken and biscuits my entire life. Still here, still kicking."

"I bet you'd be kicking higher if you lived healthier," Wyatt retorted.

"Boy, you don't want to see me kick. I'm liable to aim it at your backside."

"Lonz!" Wyatt yelled. "Your new waitress is threatening me."

"Aw, write an exposé about it then," Alonzo shouted from the depths of the kitchen.

"Maybe I will," Wyatt grumbled as Florene carried her empty coffee pot back to the pass in triumph. "I'm sure the residents of Sanctuary Island would like to know the poison this place regularly serves."

"I like her," Andie commented as she slid into the booth across from the newspaperman.

"Hi, Sheriff." Wyatt gulped at his coffee, dark eyes studying her over the rim of his mug. Wyatt Hawkins might be a vegetarian health nut, but he backed up his nutritional choices with a sharp mind and a body honed at the gym. As Ivy liked to say, Wyatt treated his body like a temple . . . and she was ready for worship.

Andie could see how Wyatt's lean musculature and stern, serious eyes would appeal to some women. Her tastes ran more to slow, gentle smiles and big shoulders broad enough to carry the weight of the world.

"Mr. Hawkins," Andie said, making an effort to rein in her focus. "How's the newspaper business? I hope you're still managing to get along with Barry Fillmore."

"He's still a whiny jerkwad, if that's what you mean."

"It wasn't, but I can read between the lines. As long as nothing major has changed, I'll leave you two to enjoy your feud. Let me know if you need another mediation, and I'll bring my riot gear and handcuffs."

Wyatt's mouth quirked like he wanted to smile, but instead he put his Serious Reporter face on. "Will do, Sheriff. Of course, that's assuming you remain sheriff after the upcoming election."

Suppressing a sigh, Andie sat up straight. "I can't say I'm looking forward to this interview, but I've been expecting it."

Interest sharpened Wyatt's gaze. "Have you?"

"Sure." Andie shrugged. "It's the first sheriff election with two real-live candidates this town has seen in more than a decade. It stands to reason the *Gazette* would run a story. And I'd certainly be curious to read any interview you run with my opponent."

"Don't worry, I'll be talking to Nash, too," Wyatt assured her, "but this piece isn't just about the election. It's more about . . . you."

Andie blinked and took a too-hot sip of coffee to hide her surprise. "Me. What, like an interview? I've been sheriff for three years, the people of Sanctuary Island already know what I stand for and how dedicated I am. They know me."

"I think there's more to know." Wyatt clicked the end of his pen a few times, studying her. "For instance, no one seems to know much about your personal life."

Her personal life. As in Caitlin, and the circumstances of her birth, and how Owen hadn't even known about her for the first ten years of her life? No. "My personal life is off limits," Andie said sharply.

Wyatt's gaze bored into her face as if he were trying to drill a hole through her forehead to get a peek at her secrets. "The people deserve to know."

"The people deserve a competent, intelligent, experienced sheriff who takes the safety of this island seriously," Andie snapped. "That's it in a nutshell."

"Okay, but they've got a choice in the matter this time. Don't you want to give them a chance to make an informed decision on election day?"

"I've more than proven myself over the last three years of my term in the sheriff's office. What happens when I'm off duty is my own affair."

"Affair. Interesting word choice." Wyatt scribbled something down as Andie absorbed that comment. She frowned. Wait. Was this about Sam?

"I don't have anything more to say here."

But before she could rise from the cracked vinyl seat, Wyatt pinned her in place with a calculating stare. "I'm going to print this afternoon with an article about you, Sheriff Shepard. I'd like to be able to quote you and let you tell your side of the story, but if you walk out of this interview, I'm comfortable running with what I have. I've corroborated my information with multiple sources."

Andie froze, already picturing a storm of gossip about to slam into her niece. Caitlin was only just settling in, still fragile, and she certainly didn't need to deal with rumors and ugliness about things she couldn't help. "What information?"

Clipping the words briskly, Wyatt said, "Are you involved with a man named Sam Brennan?"

So it wasn't about Caitlin. Relief that her niece was probably safe made Andie lightheaded for a minute, but deep inside her chest something heavy coiled and waited. Sam. What about Sam?

Wyatt clicked the pen again. "Should I just mark your response down as 'No comment'"?

"It's complicated," Andie retorted. "I guess you could say we're involved. It's a fairly recent development. What about it?"

"So you don't know Mr. Brennan very well?"

"If this turns out to be some morality thing about how it's indecent that I'm not married, I'm going to cancel my subscription to the *Gazette*."

"Please." Wyatt sat back in the booth, outrage deepening his voice. "I'm hardly going to haul my paper back into the dark ages by running some ridiculous opinion piece about how unmarried ladies ought to stay home. But as a public figure, you come in for more scrutiny than the average person. Your choices affect the rest of us. Which means that even if I happen to like you personally and think you're a better candidate for sheriff—the truth has to come out."

"What truth? What's this all about, Wyatt?"

For the first time, a fleeting emotion softened the hard angles of Wyatt's face. Regret.

"You really don't know, do you? I'm sorry, Sheriff. I really am, but . . . better you find out from me than when you pick up the paper tomorrow morning."

Something about Sam—Sam and all his secrets. There was more to him than met the eye, depths she hadn't begun to plumb, but what could be bad enough to make Wyatt Hawkins look at her like that? Half of her wanted to shake the truth out of him immediately, while the other half wanted to bolt out of the booth and flee the café so she never had to hear it.

Andie clenched her fingers around the coffee mug until a chip in the ceramic dug into the side of hand hard enough to break the skin. "Tell me."

Pity gentled Wyatt's voice. "Sam Brennan served four years in the California penitentiary system for animal cruelty. Sheriff, you're dating an ex-con."

Taylor was going on day seven of keeping a secret from Matt, and she was about to lose it.

What was that all about, anyway? Used to be, Taylor McNamara was the town champion at hiding things and putting on a who-gives-a-crap face, but with Matt . . . she'd never been able to pull it off. He'd seen through her right from the beginning, even before she'd noticed him or spoken to him.

Matthew Little had watched her spin out of control, talk back to teachers, skip class, get suspended for vandalism of both the regular and cyber varieties . . . and he'd seen someone he wanted to be friends with.

Taylor shook her head in despair. How was she supposed to combat that?

With days of ducking his calls and sending only terse, monosyllabic texts back and forth, that's how.

She just didn't want to go to Matt with half the story. When she'd told Jo Ellen what she and Caitlin had overheard from Sam's phone call in the loft, Jo had advised patience. With that distant look that came over her sometimes when she thought about her struggles with alcoholism and her stint in rehab, Jo had said, "Let's give Sam a chance to come clean. Lord knows, I owe him that. I owe him my life—because I'd never have the life I lead now if he hadn't helped me."

And okay, that was convincing. Taylor was grateful to Sam too. She even liked the guy, for the gruff, affectionate way he treated Matt and for his gentle care with the horses.

But that didn't mean Taylor was willing to let things lie.

So when Matt called her for the third time since school got out, Taylor bit her lip, let it ring through to voicemail, and turned back to her laptop . . . the secret one she'd built herself, so her dad couldn't take it away when he grounded her.

Yeah, okay. She was kind of a closet nerd. She'd learned to deal with it . . . mostly by literally sitting in her closet on top of a pile of shoes while she gleefully hacked her way around the world.

Not that this is cyber terrorism or anything, she comforted her writhing conscience. *This won't even involve hacking . . . probably. Just research. I'm like a private investigator digging for facts!*

That felt better, she decided, attacking Sam's online records with renewed vigor. She wasn't even sure what she was looking for—some clue to the stolen horse's rightful owner, maybe, or how much he was worth. But just as she linked into a news article that looked promising, her phone buzzed with a text from Matt.

[Where r u? Pick up ur phone! Big news—D coming to grad]

"D" . . . for Dad. Matt's dad, who he hadn't seen in literally years, was coming to graduation. This was officially too big for texting.

Matt answered on the first ring. "Finally! Where have you been? I never even saw you at school today!"

"I've been around," Taylor said vaguely. "Matt! Come on, tell me more about your dad. Did you talk to him? How did he sound?"

"We didn't talk, but he PMed me on Facebook. I don't know why we never chatted that way before, it was great! He said he's definitely coming for graduation and he can't wait to see me. I told him all about school and Dakota and you . . . it was awesome."

Dakota first, of course, Taylor thought with a trace of bitterness. She shoved it down to find a delicate way to ask, "And . . . what did you tell him about your mom?"

There was an awkward pause on the line and Taylor could just picture Matt's lanky form squirming slightly. "He asked about her, but . . . it was too weird to tell him about her marrying Dylan. I don't know, I kind of gave him the impression we were still living in Harrington House as the caretakers, not like it's our, you know, actual home."

Something pinged at Taylor nerves. She frowned. "So he knows where you live now?"

"Well, yeah." Matt sounded confused. "I mean, the invitation says graduation from Sanctuary Island High—pretty sure there's only one of those."

"And only one Harrington House on the island," Taylor finished, her fingers moving swiftly over the keyboard almost on autopilot.

She listened with half an ear as Matt went through the conversation beat by beat, peppered with his worries about what his mom would think. Although he seemed less concerned about that than maybe he should be, Taylor considered as she quickly hacked into Trent Little's records.

Matt's dad was . . . not a nice guy, if his rap sheet was anything to go by. Bile surged into the back of Taylor's throat, sour and shocking, as she read the list of charges that ranged from public drunkenness to assault to . . . and there it was: domestic disturbance. The others were more recent, but the date on the domestic was years back. Taylor swallowed. It was around the time Matt and Penny Little first showed up on Sanctuary Island.

That's what Penny had been running from when she packed up her son and left her life for the uncertainties and hard work of a new future in a new place. Something happened in that house to make her run, and it was bad. Sickened, Taylor covered her trembling lips with the fingers of one hand and gripped her phone with the other.

What now?

What was she supposed to do with this information? And seriously, what the hell was up with every man in Matt's life turning out to be a criminal!

"And that was it," Matt finished. "He said he'd

be there. And I know it's a month away still, and man, I wish it was tomorrow. But it's good, I guess. Maybe those weeks will give me a chance to figure out how to tell my mom he's coming."

"You have to tell her," Taylor agreed, maybe more vehemently than she'd meant to. "Like now, Matt. Seriously, your mom deserves to know that you contacted your dad, that you invited him here . . ."

That you told him where she lives now and implied that she's alone and defenseless. Oh, man.

"I know." Matt's frustration echoed down the line. "I know it's kind of crappy and I don't want to upset my mom—but don't I deserve something here, too? I think I deserve to know my own father, and I thought you agreed with me."

Even if he's a wife-beating scumbag? Why, oh why did I tell Matt to go for it and call his dad? We should have left it alone. What if he comes here and hurts someone? It'll be all my fault!

Taylor had no idea what to do next. She clutched her head, too full of secrets and nerves and fears to think straight. She had to tell Matt *something* or she was going to explode.

"Sam's a horse thief," she blurted out, then immediately winced. Smooth, McNamara, very smooth.

"Wha—what? Are you crazy, Sam is not a thief."

"Not according to him."

"What do you mean?" Matt tried to laugh it off, but it sounded tense. "Sam came to you and told you he's a horse thief? Come on."

"Of course not. I overheard him talking to his partner back at the horse rescue place. At least, I think that's who it must have been. Jo says—"

"You told Jo about this?! I can't believe you, Taylor!"

"Jo's like a mom to me," she defended herself, trying not to get upset.

"I know, but even if it's true, I'd hate to see Sam get in trouble. Whatever he's done, I'm sure he had a good reason for it. He's a good guy."

"I like him, too," Taylor said, something inside tearing like tissue paper at the knowledge that Sam Brennan might be a good guy who'd done something wrong for all the best reasons, but Trent Little was not. "And for what it's worth, Jo agrees with you. She thinks he'll come clean when he can, and until then, she wants to wait and give him space. So I haven't told anyone else. I almost didn't even tell you."

The way Matt sighed gave Taylor a mental image of the jittery way he ran both hands through his messy hair when he was upset. "Is it lame to say I kind of wish you hadn't? With everything else that's going on—it feels like too much, you know?"

"Yeah. Sorry. I just didn't want to keep this major thing from you. It felt wrong." Taylor's stomach lurched. She was keeping way worse stuff than this to herself, but maybe that's what was best for Matt. Maybe it would be selfish to unload the truth on him . . . as long as she could figure out another way to avert disaster.

"Yeah. About that." The long, sheepish pause made Taylor sit up straight in her chair. Matt cleared his throat. "I got a letter from Stanford today. I got in."

Taylor's heart clenched but the grin that spread over her face was real, too. "I can't believe you're only telling me this now! That's amazing, I'm so happy for you. And for Stanford, too—if you pick them, they're the luckiest college on earth."

"I don't know," Matt said slowly, as if the words

were reluctant to leave his mouth. "Stanford was my number-one choice, even after I got into UVA. But Dakota wants me to seriously consider UVA because, you know, she's going to Sweet Briar. So we'd only be an hour apart."

Taylor's smile stiffened until it felt like a mask. "Well. Isn't that just a little slice of heaven, right there?"

"Don't be like that," Matt sighed. "I haven't decided anything. I'm still weighing my options."

"What options?" Taylor demanded. "Stanford wins, hands down. You've wanted to go there since you were a kid! It's one of the top-ranked schools in the country!"

"UVA is pretty highly ranked, too. And a way better deal, financially, since we're in state."

Taylor threw up her hands, so agitated that she nearly pitched her cell phone across the room. "Dude. Matthew. Your stepfather is a freaking billionaire. I think he can swing footing the bill for Stanford. And UVA's undergrad isn't nearly as big a deal as their grad schools, so don't even."

With a weird, unreadable note in his voice, Matt asked, "Since when do you care about college rankings?"

Since you started applying, Taylor thought, but didn't say. Instead, she sniffed disdainfully. "Please. You think I haven't gotten the talk from Jo Ellen and Dad? They'd be thrilled if I applied to UVA, believe me."

"Why don't you?" Matt asked excitedly. "If you got in, and Dakota would be down the road . . . it would be awesome! Nothing would change."

That's exactly why I can't, Taylor thought with a pang. But even more importantly, "Matt. Listen to yourself. You can't choose a college based on sticking close to your high school friends, or even your girlfriend. This is the first big step into the rest of your life, and I know you're weighing your options, but I think you should go ahead and tip considerations about me *and* about Dakota right off the scale."

And if Dakota's not telling you the exact same thing, she's a selfish idiot who doesn't deserve you, Taylor finished silently.

"Easier said than done," Matt grumbled. "I know I said I was looking forward to meeting new people in college, and I am, but the truth is, I don't make friends that easily. And the ones I have now . . . I could never replace you. I wouldn't even want to try."

The seriousness of his voice made Taylor clutch at the phone and dig deep for lightness. "Obviously you can never replace me. I'm irreplaceable. And no matter what college you pick—you won't have to replace me, because you're not going to lose me."

"Promise not to disappear on me, even if I'm three thousand miles away?"

"I promise."

Even if it would be better, safer, and healthier for me to use that distance to try to dig myself out of the pit of Unrequited Love Despair.

Taylor had never excelled at making the smart, healthy choice.

Chapter Sixteen

Sam blinked awake with the smell of hay and horses in his nose. When he went to roll over, he had to stick out a booted foot to stop himself from tumbling off the pile of straw he'd been propped against.

What the hell am I doing sleeping at the barn?

A plaintive whinny from the stall behind him dispersed the mental cobwebs. Right, Queenie's bellyache. When he'd let her out into the outdoor pen yesterday afternoon so he could muck out her stall, he'd noticed a distinct lack of anything to muck out. That was the first warning sign, followed quickly by the way Queenie kept lying down, rolling on her back and getting up—only to repeat the process over and over.

Sam knew what that meant: bellyache. He could only pray that with a little TLC, he could keep it from turning into the kind of colic that required emergency surgery. He'd run out to the pen to stop her from rolling anymore and possibly tangling her poor insides up any further. Then he settled in for a long night of dosing the groaning filly with

Banamine and hand-walking her up and down to distract her from the pain and to encourage her pipes to start working again.

Around four in the morning, when he knew she was out of danger, Sam had contemplated heading home to Harrington House. But after sixteen straight hours on his feet, it was all he could do to slump down with his back to Queenie's stall and pass out right there on the stable floor.

A fact which his back and neck were not so happy about this morning. Tilting his chin sharply enough to crack the tension in his spine, Sam grunted at the eye-watering pain in his shoulders. He heaved himself to his feet just as Jo Ellen Hollister rolled back the barn's double doors and strode in, with a take-out cup of coffee in one hand and a folded newspaper in the other.

She stopped dead in her tracks when she saw him, and Sam palmed the back of his neck. He must look like a homeless bum off the street. "Colic," he said, gesturing at Queenie's stall.

And, of course, that was all he had to say to get a nod of understanding from Jo. Any horsewoman as accomplished as Jo knew the score. A horse's digestive tract was a more delicate machine than the most temperamental European racecar, and any little problem in that area could explode into something life-threatening with no warning.

Jo headed for her office, tucking the newspaper under her arm, but she hesitated at the threshold. She glanced over her shoulder at Sam, worry and concern and something more deepening the shadows around her eyes.

"Your mare. She okay now?" Jo asked.

"Started acting interested in hay and her water bucket again around three thirty," Sam reported. "And then she gave me the ultimate proof a half hour later. I swear, I've never been so glad to shovel up a big pile of horse sh—"

"Sam," Jo broke in, turning to face him and holding out her newspaper. "I'm sorry. There's a story in here I think you ought to see. But first, can I ask—when was the last time you talked to Sheriff Shepard?"

With a start, Sam pulled his cell phone from his jeans pocket only to find the screen blank and unresponsive. "It's dead. Mind if I use the charger in your office to plug in?"

"Of course, but Sam." Jo followed him into the office like a terrier nipping his heels, but Sam was intent on getting his phone turned on so he could check for messages from Andie.

"I should have checked in last night," Sam explained, fumbling the cord for the charger with sleep-clumsy fingers. "I usually at least call to say good night to Caitlin. I bet they're wondering what happened to me."

Before Jo could reply, Sam's phone came to life with a buzz. It latched onto the Windy Corner Wi-Fi and instantly downloaded—holy geez. Sam stared down at the screen, then up at Jo's tight-pressed lips.

"I've got a dozen texts from Andie and just as many voicemails," Sam said tensely, crushing the phone in a grip so hard, he heard the casing groan. Forcing himself to ease up, he met Jo's worried gaze and grated out, "You asked about Andie before. What do you know? Is she okay?"

Jo's eyes widened and she rushed to reassure him.

"Yes! Andie's fine and so is Caitlin, as far as I know. But Sam, I really think you ought to read her texts, or at least the newspaper article, before you call her."

Sam had forgotten the newspaper completely. This time, when Jo Ellen held it out, he took it and scanned for a headline that made sense. It didn't take a lot of scanning.

Blaring from the front page was two-inch-high boldface type screaming

"SHERIFF IN BED WITH A VIOLENT CRIMINAL ELEMENT?"

Sam's blood congealed into ice slush. Violent criminal element. That meant him. That meant they knew, the whole town knew . . . Andie knew. Black and white type blurred to gray in front of his eyes, but it took him a long, sluggish heartbeat to realize that it was because the paper was crumpled in his tight, straining fist.

"How many people have seen this?" he asked, the words tearing their way out of his throat like shards of glass.

"Everyone in town. He sent out a special bulletin, so even the people who don't take a print subscription got an email with that article."

Sam closed his eyes as his world came crashing down.

"It's about your past," Jo said quickly. Her voice sounded like it came from a distance, and Sam squinted over at her with an effort. She put an urgent hand on his elbow. "Did you hear me? The reporter, he found out about your record, the arrest and the jail time from years back. That's all."

The words echoed through the empty wasteland of Sam's head where they struck like ringing a bell. "That's all."

Jo was watching him steadily, the calm strength of her presence enough to ground Sam in the moment and jumpstart his brain back into gear. She dipped her chin in a nod, raising her eyebrows significantly. "Yes, that's all. As in, the newspaper reported on matters of public record from your distant past. No one in town, including Andie, knows anything more than that."

Something in the way she was studying him finally sunk in. He straightened his shoulders and squared his jaw. Jo had always turned a blind eye before, and that was as far as he cared to involve her. "There's nothing more to know. And how do you know Andie's seen the article already?"

Jo didn't roll her eyes, but it looked like she wanted to. "Believe me, everyone looks at special bulletins, when Wyatt sends them. But beside that, Andie's quoted in the article. And fine. We'll play it your way. I just didn't want you going off half cocked, hearing some of your secrets spilled and spilling the rest yourself without thinking."

"I appreciate that," Sam said carefully as the last bit of hope he'd had to somehow mitigate the damage of this before Andie found out some other way died a swift death. He thumbed through her texts with a sinking heart.

[I need to talk to you. Call me. Please call or text me as soon as you get this.]

They were all variations on a theme, no indication of her mood other than a rising sense of urgency as the timestamp got closer and closer to dawn and the daily delivery of the *Sanctuary Gazette*.

Maybe she'd wanted to give him a heads up, which was more than he had a right to expect. Or maybe she'd wanted to yell at him in person before he had a chance to read her angry reaction to the news of his past in print. If so, he owed her at least that much.

Steeling himself to make the call that would no doubt end any chance of a relationship with Andie, Sam gave Jo Ellen a rueful glance. "Give it to me straight. How bad is it?"

Jo's brow furrowed. "What do you mean?"

"Andie's reaction." Sam shook the paper. "Does she promise to head the pitchfork posse and light the torches herself? Or does she just deny that we were ever together?"

Instead of the pity he dreaded, Jo's eyes tightened with righteous fury, the kind a woman feels on another wronged woman's behalf.

"If that's what you think, you don't know her at all," Jo said calmly, aiming each word with precision. "She didn't deny you or condemn you. She defended you."

Andie dropped a subdued Caitlin off at Sanctuary Elementary and waved at the traffic monitor with exactly the same level of cheer she used every single morning. King Sanderson, the self-proclaimed monarch of the island, wore a battered brass crown over his neon-green crossing guard vest and usually smiled back with the unfettered joy of a man who didn't have a firm grasp on reality—and who therefore tended to love any and everyone he came into contact with.

Except, apparently, Andie. Today, instead of a wave, she got a wide-eyed look of alarm and a quick hop backwards out of the crosswalk and onto the curb. As if she might be tempted to run him down if he didn't get out of her way.

A stone dropped to the bottom of Andie's belly, but she held her head high and drove slowly past King and a gaggle of gaping moms still waiting in the drop-off line. Andie wouldn't give any of them the satisfaction of showing that she hated being the subject of gossip, but inside she was squirming. She felt the eyes on her, the judgment and curiosity and disappointment. For a brief, dizzying moment, Andie's mind tossed her back to the last time she'd been the scandal of her department.

Both times, over a man. Andie met her own wry gaze in the rearview mirror. On the surface, the situations were awfully similar—the differences were all deeper down. The difference was that this time she was sure Sam Brennan deserved her trust and support. This time there was no doubt in her heart.

That reminder enabled Andie to calmly, carefully navigate her way to her office. Climbing out of her SUV and adjusting the fit of her crisply pressed uniform shirt, Andie braced herself for her deputies' reaction. And Ivy, what would Ivy have to say?

Actually, Andie thought she might enjoy that. She had a feeling Ivy would be on her side, no matter what. And no one put things in perspective quite like Ivy Dawson. Andie quickened her pace until she was moving briskly, brushing through the front door and nodding briefly to Deputy Fred, who stared but managed to tip his coffee in a casual salute.

Bolstered, Andie headed for her office since Ivy wasn't at her desk. But just as she put her hand on the doorknob, it twisted and Ivy slid out, cheeks mottled pink and eyes glittered with anger. Andie felt herself waver, wondering if she could truly count on her friends the way she'd hoped, but she didn't have time to freak herself out about it.

Ivy grabbed her by the elbow and seethed, "He just walked right in! No appointment, wouldn't wait out here, and what could I do? He's got a cane! I can't smack a man with a cane. If he falls, his six-hundred-year-old bones will crumble like a mummy's and he'll sue me for everything I'm worth! Which, granted, isn't that much. So maybe the joke's on him."

A considering look narrowed her eyes, but Andie stopped her before she could rush back inside and assault whoever it was. "Ivy! Get a grip, and please don't smack anyone. Any concerned citizen who saw that article this morning has the right to come in here and make a complaint. I'd prefer them to wait in the bullpen, but . . ."

"Oh, this isn't just any old—and I do mean *old*—concerned citizen," Ivy groused, crossing her arms over her lemon-yellow sweater set. Tiny red cherries were embroidered along the collar, matching the enameled cherry barrettes pinning up the sides of her black hair and the red gloss on her snarling mouth. Today, Ivy looked like the pretty teacher in a fifties rerun sitcom, except for the snap of fire in her expression.

Fire that wasn't aimed at Andie, who breathed a tiny sigh of relief and gratitude. "Listen, whoever it is, I'll go talk to him and we'll clear everything up. It's going to be a rocky couple of days, I'm sure, but this will all blow over."

"You think so." Ivy arched a skeptical, perfectly

plucked brow. "Well, I'm behind you either way. Whatever happens, I believe in you. We'll face it together. I'll even come in there with you, like backup!"

"I don't need anyone to watch my back," Andie said gently, touched to the bottom of her heart. "But I appreciate the sentiment. You're a good friend, Ivy."

"Hmph." Ivy retreated to her desk and perched on her chair like a sentinel on guard. "It doesn't take a good friend to see what's going on here. Small towns—everyone knows your business and has an opinion about it."

"I have faith in the people of Sanctuary Island," Andie said, to remind herself as much as to calm Ivy down. "They have a right to their opinions. And come election day, they'll make the choice that's right for them. Until then, I'm going to hold my head up and do my job. That's all that matters."

Ivy grinned, sudden and sly. "Sure, that's all that matters. That, and spending time with your hot, hot honey. I swear, for a man that choice? I think I could overlook an arrest record or two myself."

That brought a heated flush to Andie's cheeks, but it also lifted her mood. So when she shook her head and pushed open the door of her office to confront whatever elderly citizen wanted to make his displeasure known, she was smiling.

"Good day, Miss Shepard," Dabney Leeds said from the chair behind Andie's desk. That was her chair he was sitting in, as smug and self-satisfied as an emperor looking down on a supplicating peasant. "I'm so pleased to see you looking well and happy this fine morning."

Andie kept the smile in place through sheer force of will. "It's Sheriff Shepard," she replied, proud of the steadiness of her voice. She shrugged out of her jacket and hung it on the hat stand in the corner. "What brings you to my office, Mr. Leeds?"

"It's Councilman Leeds," he countered, his faded blue eyes avid on her face, searching for signs of weakness. "For the purposes of this meeting, anyway. Have a seat, please."

Gritting her teeth against the gall of being offered a chair in her own office, Andie took the one closer to the door. She gave Leeds a cool stare that masked her inner chaos of confusion and caution. Unwilling to let him set the entire tone of the meeting, Andie took charge. "Did you really make your driver carry you all the way over here just to gloat over my embarrassment? Go right ahead if it makes you happy, but keep it as brief as you can. I have real work to do today."

His pinched lips tightened briefly. "How admirable and hard working of you. Shall I call Wyatt Hawkins and see if he wants to run a story about how dedicated you are?"

Andie let her spine touch the back of the chair. "Don't bother. The truth is rarely as exciting as a sensationalistic piece of . . . journalism."

"Ah, but what Wyatt published was the truth as well. Or are you disputing the facts?"

She snorted. "I'm not saying Sam was never arrested or in prison—as I said to Wyatt and as he quoted me word for word, I don't believe for a second that Sam Brennan has ever in his life been guilty of cruelty to an animal."

"But he was convicted of that charge," Leeds trumpeted, eyes gleaming. "Among others."

Andie cocked her head. "I realize you've never worked in law enforcement yourself, Councilman Leeds, but I would think even you would be aware that occasionally a man is wrongfully imprisoned. I believe in the law with all my heart—but that doesn't mean I'm blind to its faults. The worst of which is the fact that the law can be twisted and manipulated by those with power, causing innocent people to suffer."

A vision of Sam's handsome face, dark with the pain and secrets of his past, swam in front of her mind's eye. Sam, with his passion for protecting the weak and making his own rules . . . She wondered if he realized how much he'd changed her?

The banked coals of anger in Leeds' gaze flared a little hotter. "I don't know what you're implying—"

"I'm not implying anything." Andie leaned forward with her hands on her knees. "I'm coming right out and asking. Did you dig up that story about Sam and feed it to Wyatt Hawkins? Did you drag a good man's name through the mud merely to score a political point?"

The way Leeds sniffed and glanced away for an instant told Andie her instincts were dead on. "Whatever I've done, it was in service of giving the people of Sanctuary Island all the pertinent information to choose the best possible person as their next sheriff."

"And you believe that if I care about a man who once had trouble with the law, that makes me a liability to the sheriff's department in some way. Or at least, you're hoping the voters will think that." Andie leveled him an unimpressed glare. "We'll see, I suppose. Personally, I think that even if people want to believe the worst of Sam, they should also keep in mind that he served his time and paid his debt to society. Which means he deserves a second chance, like everyone does."

"A second chance to do what?" Leeds scoffed. "To con his way into the bed of one of our town's top elected officials so he can get away with whatever crimes he's planning? You may be a naive little girl, led by her emotions, but I'm confident the voters won't be thinking with their hormones."

That dart hit home, right in the part of her heart still bruised by her father's contempt. Struggling to stay seated, Andie gripped the arms of her chair. "If that's all you've got, I think it's time for you to leave. The paperwork is piling up even as we sit here."

The slow smile that stretched over the old man's face was so triumphant, it made Andie's flesh prickle with warning. "Oh, that's not all I've got. I'm here to relieve you of all that dull paperwork—and every other responsibility of the position of sheriff, as well."

Andie's body turned to stone, a monument to shock and disbelief. "You can't force me to resign."

"I don't have to." Leeds creaked to his feet with the help of his cane and one gnarled hand on the edge of her desk. Leaning over it, he said, "You're not being forced out of office . . . yet. No, you're being put on administrative leave, effective immediately, while the Town Council investigates the situation. Once the furor dies down, and depending on how you comport yourself while on leave, you'll be eligible for reinstatement."

Her throat was so dry, she couldn't swallow. "How long—"

"That depends on you, doesn't it?" Leeds inspected the brass bulldog-shaped head of his cane with an air of satisfaction. "If nothing else comes to light that might give the council cause to doubt your suitability for the sheriff's office, we could be talking four weeks. Maybe more, if the investigation drags on for any reason."

And with Dabney Leeds heading the council, Andie realized with a sickening roll of her stomach, there was no way any investigation would be swift, efficient, or fair. "And the entire council voted on this?" she clarified, desperately wishing she didn't already know the answer.

"Of course," Leeds said, righteous as a saint at prayer. "I am merely their representative in this meeting."

"Which I'm sure you were happy to volunteer for," Andie snapped, surging to her feet. "Fine, I'll go. But I want to officially state, for the record, that this is a travesty and I plan to appeal the council's decision and be reinstated as soon as possible."

"Noted. In the meantime, Deputy Stanz has been appointed to take charge in your absence. I assume he's up to date on all your current, pending, and ongoing investigations?"

Andie held in a hysterical laugh. Deputy Fred was up to date on today's special flavor of pie at the Firefly Café. That was about it. "Probably not, but Ivy Dawson, my dispatcher, can help get him up to speed."

Through the closed door came a muffled squawk of outrage. "She will do no such thing!"

Andie ripped open the door, and Ivy all but fell into the office. She tottered a little on her red-patent stilettos but caught her balance with the grace of a woman who wore four-inch heels to the post office and grocery store. "If you think I'm sticking around and working here without you," Ivy said defiantly, her eyes bright with unshed tears of anger, "you're crazier than that old goat."

"I never! If this is the way you run your department," Leeds started, hobbling around the desk furiously.

"It's not my department for the next few weeks," Andie said, feeling the crevasse open up in her heart as she said the words aloud for the first time. Putting her hands on Ivy's shoulders, Andie looked at her gravely. "I can't make you do anything, and I don't want you to act against your conscience—but in all honesty, I'd appreciate it if you held down the fort here while I'm gone. You're already the one in the office that everyone goes to for gossip and updates. Really, no one will even notice I'm gone, probably, but if you stop showing up at the dispatcher desk . . . chaos!"

Ivy sniffed, the corners of her red lips turned down. "That's true. And lord knows that idiot, Deputy Fred, will need my help. I guess I'll stay."

"I'm sure we're all very relieved," Leeds snapped. "Now if you'll come along with me, Miss Shepard, I'm to escort you out."

Under her hands, Ivy stiffened all over again at the implication that Andie needed to be watched and prevented from absconding with office supplies or something. Andie felt the grate of humiliation across her raw nerves, but she mustered up a smile for Ivy. "Thanks for staying. Call me anytime, for any reason. Even if it's just to have lunch at the Firefly."

Ivy nodded, squaring her shoulders, and stepped back through the door to let Leeds and Andie by. "I'll make sure the office is still here waiting for you when this stupid leave of absence is over," she promised.

Andie held onto that vow as she walked down the corridor of desks toward the door. Most of her deputies and the admin assistants found busy work to look at, papers to shuffle—Roberta Andrews hastily picked up her silent, unringing desk phone as Andie passed by and said "Sheriff's Department" into the receiver. But Deputy Fred met her eyes squarely and stood up from his chair. With military precision, he brought his hand to his forehead and saluted Andie. She was the one who had to break eye contact or risk breaking down in tears in the middle of the office. She paused by his desk long enough to unhook the five-pointed star from her belt. The badge was cool and heavy in her palm, weighted with the responsibilities and cares of the office, and when Andie placed it gently on Fred's desk and walked away, she felt a hundred pounds lighter. As light and insubstantial as the apple blossoms showering from the trees lining Main Street, as if a gust of wind could sweep her up and swirl her away at any moment.

For a woman who defined her life and her self by her dedication to duty, it wasn't a pleasant feeling.

Chapter Seventeen

By the time Sam pounded on Andie's front door, he was cursing himself for not just driving straight to the sheriff's department. That's where she was likely to be by now, but he couldn't help hoping she had the afternoon shift today so they could have privacy for what he needed to say.

Not that he knew what he was going to say. Not that it mattered, since her SUV wasn't parked in the driveway, so she wasn't here anyway.

Sam clenched his fists in his pockets. He didn't want to do this over the phone. He needed to see Andie's face, to be there with her to read her emotions and reactions. He was so engrossed in imagining how it might go down that he didn't hear the engine behind him, at first. The slam of a car door made him turn around, and there she was.

Andie. The woman who'd defended him.

She looked as exhausted as he'd felt waking up on the barn floor, but the sight of her gave Sam a second wind. She stopped in her tracks, blinking as if she didn't believe her eyes.

"You're here," she said, taking a step toward him. Sam's throat closed. "If you want me to leave—"

"No." Andie shook her head and trudged up the steps past her tiny side yard garden until she stood directly in front of him. "I definitely don't want you to leave."

She was only inches away, but it might as well have been miles. Sam curled and straightened his fingers restlessly, aching to touch her, to hold her, but until he knew where her head was at . . . "I'll stay as long as you want," he told her, and even he didn't know what he meant by that. He'd stay today? Or forever?

When Andie shut her eyes and tears leaked from the corners to track down her smiling cheeks, forever didn't seem like such a crazy idea. She blinked her eyes open and said, "Come inside, Sam."

What could he do but follow her? And when the door shut behind them and the close, intimate silence of the house echoed in their ears and Andie whirled to press herself full length against Sam, what could he do but gather her in close and open her lips with a deep, searching kiss?

His hands closed on her hips, dragging her into his body as his back slammed against the door. Andie's fingers were in his hair, clutching hard enough to pull, hard enough to sting, hard enough to make Sam gasp with the sharp pleasure of it.

"I know we need to talk," Andie panted in between tiny, biting nips at his jaw and throat. "But right now, all I want is this. All I want is you, right here, with me."

Whatever was between them—Sam's past and his secrets and Andie's decision to stick up for him—everything faded out of existence except for the solid, undeniable reality of Andie's warm skin beneath his fingertips. The slim, lithe clasp of her thighs around his hips when he lifted her into his arms and turned so that she was the one with her back to the wall.

It wasn't how he'd pictured their first time together—and yeah, Sam had absolutely pictured it. In detail. But as eager fingers shoved clothes aside, delving for skin and sending shocks of pleasure zinging back and forth between them like heat lightning, Sam had no regrets.

Pinned to the wall, yielding to Sam's thrusts and welcoming him in, Andie had never seemed stronger or more sure of what she wanted. Sam couldn't stop kissing her, hips rocking and arms holding tight, until she cried out. Only when she convulsed around him did Sam allow himself to follow her into mindless pleasure.

When the strongest climax of his life finally let him go, Sam gasped back to consciousness with Andie's head on his shoulder and his muscles locked where he'd lifted her against the door.

That couldn't be comfortable, he thought muzzily, straining his sore shoulders to lift her higher against his chest. She laughed into his neck when he nearly slipped on the condom wrapper, then murmured something as he carried her to the bedroom, soft words he couldn't make out through the haze of afterglow.

Maybe words were irrelevant in that moment. Sam certainly couldn't think of any that were worth breaking the warm, connected silence they settled into as he undressed her, then himself, and slid into the rumpled bed beside her.

When he opened his eyes again, the shadows on

the wall had moved. The light streaming over the bed from the window was buttery and soft, afternoon sunshine that picked out strands of platinum and copper in Andie's red-gold hair. He blinked again, and so did she, long eyelashes fluttering over her ocean-wave eyes. She was awake.

"Hi there," Andie whispered, tucking both hands under her pillow and staring at him.

"You're so beautiful, it's like looking into the sun," Sam said, squeezing his eyes closed again and opening them to the dazzle of Andie's languid smile.

"Is that why you had your eyes closed for the last four hours?" she teased.

Sam winced. "That long, huh? Sorry I passed out. I was awake all night with Queenie, walking her through a stomach upset."

Andie went up on one elbow. "Is she okay?"

Sam nodded, struck momentarily speechless by the way the sheet had slipped down to expose the taut, round curves of her breasts. He couldn't believe they'd had sex standing up, clothes askew, without him ever catching a glimpse of this creamy flesh, without touching the tightly furled buds of her little pink . . . wait. Snapping his gaze back up to her face, he said, "Are you okay? We went at it pretty rough back there."

"I'm fine," Andie said, lying back down. One side of mouth kicked up. "Or couldn't you tell?"

But Sam was lost in a memory of how hard he'd pushed her against that door, the rough, unyielding wood against her soft, soft skin. With a jerk, he pulled the sheets down and clenched his jaw at the finger-shaped bruises on her pale hips. He was an animal. What had he been thinking, treating her that way?

"I lost control," he rasped, his throat raw and tight. Sam traced one blooming finger mark with his thumb, covering the rest with his palm, but nothing could hide his shame. "I'm sorry."

Andie stretched lazily, almost purring. "You should be. That was just the worst. I can't remember the last time something so awful happened to me. I'd arrest you, but I'm going to want you to return to the scene of the crime later tonight."

Relief and something dangerously close to happiness swelled in Sam's chest. "Sweetheart, I'm not going to need that long to recover."

"Mmm. Me neither. But check the time."

Time. It was daytime. Sam sat bolt upright and grabbed for his phone in the pile of clothes beside the bed. "It's two o'clock!"

"Yes. I need to leave to pick Caitlin up from school in a bit."

"How can you be here in the middle of the day? Don't you have a shift?"

"Oh yeah," Andie said, rolling onto her back to stare up at the ceiling. "*That's* the last time something awful happened—I got suspended this morning."

Sam went still. "Because of me."

"No, because of Dabney Leeds and his willingness to do whatever it takes to get me thrown out of office and to have his grandson installed in my place."

Rage tightened Sam's hands into fists. Another rich man, using his money and power and influence to get what he wanted, and damn everyone else. Sam clenched his jaw. "But if I hadn't been here to give him the perfect ammunition against you—"

"He would've dug up something else," Andie finished firmly. "I have zero doubts about that. Trust me, Sam, this is not your fault. This is about me, and the choices I made."

The back of Sam's throat felt raw and tight. "The newspaper article."

There it was, suddenly, like a third person in the bed with them. The bulk of Sam's past mistakes and his current secrets was enough to push him off the mattress. Tugging on his jeans, Sam started to pace.

Andie sat up and rested her crossed arms on her sheet-covered knees, her russet hair cascading over one bare, freckled shoulder. "I could have chosen to protect myself by telling them we weren't together, that you were nothing but a casual acquaintance, someone I barely knew."

"That's exactly what you should have done." The words tore from Sam's chest, taking bits of himself along with them.

"It would have been a lie."

When he paused in his restless pacing to stare at her, Andie was calm, her beautiful face a picture of serene acceptance. He shook his head in disbelief. "Are you that much of a girl scout? So what if it's a lie, it would have protected you."

Never mind that the best protection for Andie would have been if Sam stayed far the hell away from her. He hated himself, in that moment, as he'd never hated anyone or anything.

"I made my choice," she told him gently. "Instead of protection—safety—I chose you."

Gutted, Sam laced his fingers behind his neck and squeezed his eyes shut, straining against the impossibilities. It was the worst choice Andie could have made. It was a choice she'd made with incomplete information, a choice she'd never make if she knew the full extent of Sam's crimes.

This choice would probably ruin her life, which was already starting to unravel. But Sam was weak. He wanted this to be real so badly, he couldn't force himself to say the words that would convince Andie to reconsider. Because if Andie meant what she said, even after finding out about his past . . . maybe Sam had a chance at a future with her.

Spearing her with a look, he grated out the question that burned in his chest. "Why?"

Incredibly, even after all they'd shared, Andie blushed. The pretty pink flush spread over her cheeks and, for the first time, Sam knew that it went all the way down her chest too. "Not everything in life is a choice," she answered slowly, hesitant for the first time since Sam woke up in her arms. "For instance . . ."

His heart kicked in his chest like a fractious colt. "Yeah?"

Andie met the challenge in Sam's voice by raising her stormy ocean eyes to his. "For instance, I didn't choose to fall in love with you. But I did, and there's nothing anyone can do or say to change that now."

Andie held her breath. Across the bedroom, it looked as if Sam might be doing the same. He didn't move, but a hundred emotions seemed to flash through his eyes so fast, Andie couldn't get a read on which emotion might be in the lead.

I'm on your side, she pleaded silently. *You're not alone anymore.*

"How can you say that?" His voice was a ragged, broken thing with edges sharp enough to cut her if she wasn't careful. "When you know what I did, where I've been . . ."

Andie tightened her arms around her upraised knees and kept herself on the bed by force of will. "I know why you might think I'd look down on you for having been in prison. I'm sorry it happened, sorry you went through it, but Sam, it doesn't make me feel any differently about you."

He shook his head again and turned away, as if he couldn't bear to believe her. Struggling for a way to make him understand, Andie said, "The law is black and white—that's what makes it comforting. But I know that people who commit crimes are *people*. And there's a reason we stopped making people wear the mark of their crimes for the rest of their lives. Whatever happened back then, it's over now, and you have moved on with your life in such an amazing way. If anything, I admire you more, knowing what you've overcome."

"If you knew the whole story," Sam rasped, the indentation of his spine ramrod straight between the hard, tensed muscles of his shoulders and back.

"It wouldn't change anything." Andie believed that with her whole heart, but she knew Sam didn't. He couldn't. Frustration welled up, tightening her fingers where she'd tangled them in the sheets. "Fine. So tell me the whole story, then, and I'll prove it to you."

Silence filled the room, squeezing the oxygen out and making it hard for Andie to breathe. Maybe she'd pushed too hard and Sam would just walk out of her life, away from Sanctuary Island.

"I was nineteen when it happened," Sam said abruptly without turning to face her. "I'd been on my own, out of the foster system for a couple of years, and I thought I was tough. Thought I knew how the world worked. But I had no idea."

Nineteen, Andie thought, gut clenching. *Old enough to be tried as an adult instead of a minor, but still so terribly, vulnerably young.*

Bitterness roughened his voice as he began to pace again. "I'd gone out to California to look for work, got hired on as a groom by a guy who ran a boarding and training barn. People would send these crazy expensive show horses and racehorses to my boss—Arabians, Tennessee Walkers, Thoroughbreds, Friesians. Beautiful horses, and it was my job to take care of them when they weren't out on the circuit. Some of these horses were big-time winners, insured for more money than the whole barn made in a year. I bet I know what you're thinking."

"I bet you don't."

Sam finally turned his head, just far enough to shoot her a hard stare over his shoulder. "You're thinking I got greedy, stole a big purse-winner and tried to ransom him back to his owner."

That would fit with the charges Wyatt had read her . . . but it didn't fit with what she knew of Sam Brennan.

Andie tilted her head as her brain leaped from clue to clue, making connections and spinning theories. "What I'm thinking is . . . I wonder which of those horses was being mistreated by its owner."

Sam reacted as though she'd zapped him with her Taser. Reeling around, he stared at her with his hard jaw clenched and his eyes blazing with some emotion she couldn't name. "How did you—?"

"It wasn't that big a leap." Andie smoothed the edge of the sheet, satisfaction pouring through her belly like warm honey. "I told you, Sam. I know you."

"It was one of the Arabians," Sam said, eyes riveted on her face. "Sultan's Dream, handsomest chestnut stallion you ever saw. Light step, gorgeous head . . . and heart. He'd run himself to death if you asked him, pour every ounce of himself out onto the track and leave it all behind."

"You loved him," Andie said without thinking, and wished she could take it back when Sam's face immediately shuttered.

"When Sultan first came to us, he was . . . look, Arabians have a well deserved rep for nerviness. They're often high strung, and Sultan definitely fit that mold. But the difference I saw when he came home after his first race with his new owner was a huge red flag. Sultan went from being this sweet-tempered, intense guy who'd eat sugar lumps out of my hand to jumping at his own shadow, kicking out in his stall, and running from me when I'd come to catch him in the turn-out pasture. Something was wrong, and I knew who to blame."

"The new owner," Andie guessed.

Sam nodded, his bittersweet chocolate eyes opaque. "Richard Mountbatten."

"Mountbatten." Andie frowned at the uncommon name. "Like the cruise line?"

"His family owns it. Ricky had a window seat at the company headquarters, but he spent most of his time and his inherited millions at the racetrack. When I went to my boss with my suspicions, he told me to keep my mouth shut. The barn couldn't afford to lose Rick Mountbatten and his cronies. So I went to the authorities on my own."

"The police?" Andie clarified.

Sam's mouth flattened into a grim line. "Turned out the local police chief was in Ricky's pocket. They tipped him off about me and he staged a botched kidnapping to explain the injuries I'd found on Sultan."

"And framed you for it." Andie's stomach heaved but she bit back bile and forced herself to hear Sam out. She had to know it all, or they were never going to get past this.

"It was easy." Sam shrugged, but the motion was so jerky it looked as if it physically hurt. "The Mountbattens are seriously connected in California. The tourist dollars their cruise line brings in, the years they've spent making backdoor deals and slicking the palms of all the right people . . . there was no way a Mountbatten was going down for animal cruelty based on the say so of a no-name kid with no money and no education. They sent in a swarm of flesh-eating lawyers who chewed up my public defendant and spit her out again, and before I knew it, I was doing hard time."

"Four years." The number was burned onto Andie's brain the way the injustice of Sam's story was burning through her heart and her stomach lining.

"I was lucky," Sam said grimly, as if in answer to the questions Andie couldn't bring herself to ask. "I've always been big for my age. Not a lot of guys want to mess with someone as big as me. I got a job in the library, kept my head down, did my time, and got out on my twenty-third birthday."

"And instead of letting what happened drag you down into a spiral of crime and punishment," Andie finished, sliding off the mattress and dragging the sheet with her like a toga, "you went out and started a horse rescue organization."

"The next time I found a horse like Sultan's Dream, I wanted to be able to actually save him." The muscle below his ear ticked as he ground his teeth on the memory of helplessness. "He died while I was inside. Sultan. It was ruled natural causes, but I know Mountbatten was dosing him with something to numb pain and make him race even with injuries. It happens all the time in racing."

Andie's mind seethed with all this new information as puzzle pieces slotted into place. Sam had learned, early and well, that the law would not protect him. He'd been on the other side of the power struggle between justice and corruption—it made perfect sense that he would trust no one but himself. "So many of our conversations, starting with that very first night when I busted your cousin, Matt, and Taylor McNamara for underage drinking, make sense now."

She approached Sam from the side, the way she'd seen him do with the young wild stallion. "The only thing that doesn't make sense is how you ever got far enough past all that to give me the time of day."

Sam's mouth twisted, but he raised his arm and made space for her to nestle against him. She tucked her head on his shoulder and slotted her fingers along the grooves of his ribcage, taking comfort in the solid thud of his heart. "I never saw a lot of evidence, before, that you law enforcement types were interested in actually helping people. Until I met you."

"Not just people," Andie felt compelled to point out. "If anyone on Sanctuary Island ever did a thing to hurt the wild horses, I'd come down on them like the hammer of the gods. I promise you that."

He squeezed her tighter and pressed a kiss to the crown of her head. "I believe it. You're good at your job. This island needs you."

A chill of dread rushed down Andie's spine. She lifted her head to fix him with a stare. "Maybe so. But that doesn't mean you should get any crazy ideas about skipping town. The voters can deal with the fact that I'm dating an ex-con, or not. It's up to them."

"I've never told my side of the story," Sam said reluctantly. "Didn't get the chance in court, and afterward, well, I never saw the point. But if it would help, I could contact that newspaper guy and offer him an interview."

Gratitude and affection swelled up from Andie's chest so fast she almost choked on it. "I love that you'd do that for me," she said softly. "But I'm not going to ask you to give up your privacy. It's no one's business what I do when I'm off the clock. I knew you were innocent of those charges. I knew the minute Wyatt read them to me."

"How did you know? It's not like it's impossible I would've done what they said and taken that horse."

"But it was impossible that you would've harmed him."

That got her a kiss on the lips, warm and soft, almost shy. "You're amazing," Sam told her.

"I am," Andie agreed, smiling up at his handsome, troubled face and wishing she could erase the worry from his eyes. "And have some faith in the Sanctuary Island voters that they know it, too! The election will work itself out and I'll be fine either way . . .

as long as you don't leave town in some attempt to reverse the damage."

"Don't worry, I'll stick around." Sam smiled, but it didn't reach his dark eyes. "I've never been a hero. Why start now?"

Chapter Eighteen

Sam wasn't used to thinking of himself as a coward. He couldn't say he was enjoying the experience.

That day in Andie's house, in her bedroom, he simply hadn't been able to make himself confess the whole truth. Because while he hadn't been guilty of stealing Sultan, he was absolutely guilty of stealing Queenie. And as much as he despised what he was doing to Andie, Sam was stuck. He couldn't take the chance that Andie's faith in the legal system would force her to send Queenie back to the owner who'd nearly killed her.

Sam was responsible for Queenie's life, her health. She had no voice, no rights, no way to protect herself. All she had was Sam. Which meant that Sam had to put Queenie first, before himself . . . even before Andie. No matter how much he hated it.

All of that was bad enough. But there was also the fact that Andie had told him she'd fallen for him . . . and he hadn't said it back. Every day since then as they spent more and more time together volunteering at the therapeutic riding center, making dinner for Caitlin, stealing moments of hushed, intense passion in each other's arms . . . he still hadn't told her the whole truth.

He hadn't told her that he loved her, too. More than he'd ever thought he could love another human being.

To be fair, she hadn't said it again either. Not that he was hoping to hear it at least one more time before this all inevitably fell apart, or anything.

Because despite what he'd told her that day, Sam knew he should still be thinking about moving on. He wasn't sure where else he could take Queenie and hope to help the mare and keep her safe, but this fantasy he was living out with Andie had to stop. If he was any kind of a man, he'd already be gone.

The trouble was, every time he made up his mind to pack Queenie's things and bundle them both onto the next ferry off the island, something stopped him. For one thing, Queenie and the wild colt, Lucky, had basically turned into a matched set. Where one went, the other followed instantly. Any separation, even the bare minimum of time it took to restrain them in crossties to be hosed down after a long day of romping in the muddy fields, led to loud, frantic whinnying and straining toward one another. Sam was genuinely concerned that if he took Queenie away from Lucky, both horses would pine to death.

He knew the feeling.

There was also the matter of Queenie's health to consider. She didn't do well with travel, couldn't be sedated, and he'd just gotten her back up to speed after her dangerous brush with colic. When Dr. Ben examined her afterward, he'd warned Sam about the dangers of even the smallest change in Queenie's routine—different food, different bedding, stress—like the stress of leaving her best friend—could set off another attack. Sam could only imagine how the veterinarian would react if Sam tried to load Queenie onto the ferry and whisk her away from the place where she'd grown comfortable.

And then there was Matt's high school graduation coming up in a couple of weeks. Sam knew the kid wanted him to be there. He'd mentioned it more than once, always with this air of agitation and nerves that was pretty unusual for such a solid, down-to-earth boy.

Sam found out why when his cousin Penny took him aside and asked if he could get Andie's help in filing a restraining order against her ex-husband. Apparently Taylor had let Penny know about Matt's communications with the guy, and the two women were determined to keep Trent Little's violent tendencies away from Matt.

In fact, they didn't even want Matt to know his dad had ever hit his mom—apparently, they'd decided it would be better if Trent simply failed to show up for graduation, thereby breaking his promise and hopefully making Matt think twice about contacting him again.

In Sam's view, they were likely only going to be delaying the inevitable, but when he'd argued that point with Penny, her sweet round face had suddenly gone all stubborn angles. Jaw jutting and eyes narrowed, she'd poked her finger into Sam's chest and glared up at him as if he didn't tower over her by more than a foot.

"Have you been talking to Dylan?" she'd demanded.

Sam held up his hands in self defense, and also to remind her he wasn't armed. "Slow your roll, cuz,

I don't talk to your hubby about much beyond how the Nats are doing."

Sam was pretty sure he and the former Bad Boy Billionaire didn't have a lot common. Except, apparently, the crazy notion that Matt was almost a grown man and could handle hearing the truth about dear old dad.

"Maybe it's a mistake," Penny allowed, standing down slightly. "But it's my mistake to make, and Matt is my kid. So I'll thank you to stay out of it."

"Penny, come on. Don't cry. That's not fighting fair."

"I don't want to fight with you at all," she said thickly, swiping at her eyes with an impatient slice of her hand.

"I know," Sam soothed, wrapping his favorite cousin up in a bear hug. "You just want me to fall in line and do exactly as you say."

"Is that so much to ask?" Penny sniffled and pulled far enough back to see Sam's reluctant smile. She made a face at herself. "Sorry, I hate blubbing. It's just, so much is going on, with one baby about to leave home . . ."

Almost unconsciously, one of her hands fluttered up to rest on the gentle curve of her belly, and Sam's heart jumped into his throat. "And another baby on the way?" he guessed hoarsely.

Penny's gaze flew to his. "Don't say anything," she pleaded. "Especially not to Matt. It's too soon to tell people, and at my age—well, at any age—anything can happen in the first trimester."

"At your age," Sam scoffed, bending down to give her another, softer hug. "What are you, thirty-five?"

"If you can't remember, I'm certainly not going to tell you. And for your information, when the mother is thirty-five or older, the doctors start using the charming phrase 'geriatric pregnancy.' Which is not designed to make you feel like a spring chicken."

"Congrats anyway, old-timer," Sam said, ducking a half-hearted swat. "Seriously, I'm happy for you and Dylan. And you know Matt will be happy too, right?"

"You really think so?" Horrifyingly, Penny's eyes filled with tears again. She scrubbed at her face and grimaced. "Ugh. These hormone surges are driving me bananas. I don't remember having them with Matty."

"But then," Sam pointed out, "that was eighteen years ago. Your memory probably isn't what it used to be."

To his everlasting relief, Penny laughed. "Oh Sam. I love having you here. Say you'll at least stay through graduation. Please?"

So that was that. He'd promised Penny, and then he'd promised Matt, who was about to get stood up by his father. To Sam, that was as good as a blood oath. He settled in for another couple of weeks, determined to use the time to get Queenie as healthy as she could be, in case they needed to leave town in a hurry to save Andie's career.

Those two weeks passed in a haze of loving, laughing, teaching Caitlin to ride, and enjoying watching her come out of her shell and latch onto Andie. Sam cherished every huge grin and relieved sigh Andie gave. He stored up every brush of her fingers and casual kiss good-bye in his memory, alongside the unforgettable moments of entwined limbs and breathless desire. Sam stockpiled sidelong glances and the downward sweep of Andie's lashes like they were all he'd have to live on—and one day, they might be.

He told himself that he could afford the time, that he could give those days to Andie and Caitlin—and himself—without risking more hurt. He couldn't leave the island until Queenie was more stable, and he'd worked out a way to bring Lucky with them. Maybe it would have been kinder in the long run to distance himself from Andie, but she'd opened up to him, more than to anyone in her life, Sam knew, and he couldn't run out on her after that.

Maybe it made him a bastard, but he couldn't let Andie believe her love meant nothing to him. And in a deep, secret part of his heart, Sam had hope that he still might be able to figure out a way through this mess. A way to keep Andie safe, and Queenie too. A way to have the kind of life he'd never even dared to dream of before.

It was possible. The same laws that gave horses no more status than livestock also tended to keep law enforcement from expending precious resources on an extended hunt for the stolen property. He had to assume the only reason the cops had been so persistent on this case was the high-profile "victim."

If Queenie had been stolen from a regular family by some criminal bent on selling her for profit, the cops wouldn't have done much more than file a report.

So if Sam and Queenie could stay hidden away on Sanctuary Island until the search was called off and the cops quit hassling Luke, there was a good chance he could actually get away with this. They just needed to hold out a little longer.

But then, the night before Matt's pre-graduation party, Andie got a call that changed everything.

Andie tucked Caitlin into bed, with the good-night kiss they were both coming to count on, as well as their traditional exchange: "When is my dad coming home?" Caitlin would ask sleepily. "Tomorrow?"

"Maybe," Andie told her, as she did every night. "Go to sleep and when you wake up, we'll find out."

She closed Caitlin's door softly behind her and padded barefoot down the hallway to the living room, where Sam was watching a baseball game with the volume turned low. Andie slid onto the couch next to him like a key into a lock, with Sam instantly making room for her and welcoming her body close to his.

"Who's winning?" she asked sleepily, her head falling heavy onto the back sofa cushion.

"The Nationals, in red."

"They're the good guys, right?" Andie smiled at the rumble of near-silent laughter she felt vibrating through the ridged muscles of Sam's abdomen.

"Yep. The Nats are the good guys. I love that you know that."

"Hey, I know how it goes." Andie's eyes drifted shut. "Love me, love my team."

Sam went so quiet next to her, it startled her awake. Replaying her last sentence in her head, Andie flinched. "I mean, when you date a guy . . ."

"I know what you meant." His voice was low, strained. Andie forced her muscles to stay lax and pliant against Sam's side.

The loud *b-r-r-ring* of the phone mounted on the kitchen wall split the silence and launched Andie into motion. She jumped off the couch wondering who would be calling on her almost unused land-line and prayed she could get to it before it woke Caitlin up.

Grabbing the receiver, Andie sent Sam a small, apologetic smile. "Hello?"

There was a pause on the other end. Then, "Andrea Shepard?"

It was a woman's voice, vaguely familiar, but Andie couldn't place it right away. "Yes, speaking. May I ask who's calling?"

"This is Loretta Phelps, Army chaplain at Fort Benning."

The woman who used her own meager time off to transport Caitlin over to Sanctuary Island. "Of course," Andie said warmly. "Lieutenant Phelps! It's so nice of you to call and check in. Caitlin is doing well, I've got her enrolled in school, although the year's almost over, of course."

"I'm very glad to hear it," Lt. Phelps replied. Something in her slow, careful voice made the smile drop off Andie's face.

Gripping the phone more tightly, Andie said, "I'm pretty sure I gave you my cell number in case you needed to contact me."

The dread coiling in her guts rolled over when Lt. Phelps hesitated. "Yes. You did. Well, for this kind of call I'm afraid the army requires that we use a landline. I have an important message to deliver from the Secretary of the Army."

White noise buzzed in Andie's ears. She didn't know what kind of sound she made, but it must have been bad because Sam was instantly at her side. His strong, sturdy presence gave Andie the courage to stand up straight and say, "All right. I'm ready, Lieutenant."

The chaplain took a deep audible breath. "Andrea Shepard, the secretary has asked me to express his deep regret that on the sixteenth of May, your brother, Sergeant First Class Owen Shepard, went missing in action."

There was more, but Andie heard it all distorted, broken by the static of the Army chaplain's sympathy and the shocked grief beating at her own heart. Wounded, presumed dead, body not recovered, so sorry . . .

"Wait," Andie rasped, breaking into Lt. Phelps' halting condolences. "Presumed dead. So you don't know for sure."

"That's correct. But I wouldn't want to give you false hope, Andie."

"Owen is strong," Andie insisted, reminding herself as much as arguing with the chaplain. "He's smart and fast—if he's still alive . . ."

"That's a big if," Lt. Phelps said softly. "His team was ambushed. There were a lot of casualties."

Andie wanted to press the point, to shout down the line and make Lt. Phelps agree with her, but she heard the subtle catch in the other woman's breath. Like a suppressed sob. And she knew Lt. Phelps wanted to believe it, too, as much as Andie did—but she couldn't say it aloud.

Rather than torture them both, Andie took a shuddering breath and said, "Thank you for calling, Lieutenant Phelps. You volunteered to notify us, didn't you?"

"Owen's C.O. is still OCONUS, that is, outside the continental U.S., but he authorized me to go ahead with the notification. Up until today, they were still working to discover Owen's whereabouts but . . ."

"The search has been called off," Andie finished, her lungs squeezing down until her voice was a faint thread. "Okay."

"I'm very sorry for your loss." The lieutenant had steadied herself and was back on script, but Andie could hear the genuine regret and sorrow throbbing through Loretta's voice.

"I'm sorry for your loss, too," Andie told her. "I know you were friends."

Maybe more than friends, judging by the fragile silence on the other end of the line. Or maybe Loretta had simply loved Owen like a sister—that was enough cause for pain, as Andie knew all too well.

They said their good-byes and after extracting a promise that she'd be notified if there was any new information, Andie hung up. Her feet felt leaden, too heavy to lift, but she was afraid if she didn't walk over to the couch and sit down, she'd collapse in a heap on the kitchen floor. She couldn't collapse. She had to hold it together.

A large, warm hand smoothed down her arm to circle her wrist, solid and comforting. Andie blinked up at the man beside her, his dark, watchful eyes and the concerned tilt of his brows, and she let herself fall into him.

She trusted that Sam would catch her, and he did. With an incoherent hum of low, soothing words, Sam scooped her up against his chest and carried her to the sofa. He lay down full length and pulled Andie over him like a shaking, gasping blanket and there, cradled against the strength of Sam's body, she allowed the first tear to fall.

Sam held Andie in his arms and felt his heart crack with every tear she cried, and he knew all those things that had stopped him from leaving town were nothing but flimsy excuses compared to this—the reality of this woman and the way he'd somehow become so connected to her that he felt her grief as his own.

He couldn't even think of leaving her now. Not when she needed him so badly . . . and not when he'd finally realized that he'd be leaving his entire heart behind with her.

Chapter Nineteen

"You don't have to come with me tonight, if you're not up to it," Sam said from the bedroom doorway.

Andie responded by turning her back and gesturing at her dress's stubborn zipper. She was determined not to sit around feeling sad. Brooding wouldn't help Owen, and it certainly wouldn't help Caitlin—who had to be her first priority now.

"Your cousin's graduation party is a good distraction," Andie said, giving him her best attempt at a smile. "Besides, I feel invested in Matt. It's always nice to see a kid you've arrested turn his life around."

The zipper hitched, then slid upwards. Sam's fingers followed it, smoothing the soft cotton of the dress and sending a clenching shiver through the center of Andie's body.

"If that's what you want to do, sweetheart. But if it's going to be too much for you, I can explain to Penny about what's going on, and no one will blame you for ditching the party."

"No!" The vehemence in Andie's voice surprised them both. Sam's hands stilled. She met his stare in the mirror and swallowed hard. "I mean, please don't talk to anyone about Owen. Not yet."

"Andie. These people here are your friends. They'd want to know what's going on so they can help you, support you. Isn't that what friends are for? That's the whole point of belonging to a community like this one, or so a certain someone keeps telling me."

Considering that she was about to get booted out of this particular community—or at least, booted out of the sheriff's office—she wasn't so sure. Andie bent down to search the closet floor for her one pair of dressy sandals. "It's not that. I'm just not ready to give up on Owen yet."

"And that's why you're still not telling Caitlin either."

"I don't want her to worry until we know more about what happened," Andie said, trying to sound confident and upbeat. "It wouldn't help anything, and might derail her when she's finally settling in here. Sometimes we have to keep things from people for their own good."

And saying it out loud to Owen's daughter might make his disappearance more real.

Andie checked, but Sam didn't seem to be listening for the unspoken true reason for her keeping this from Caitlin. Instead, his dark gaze had turned inward.

"Sam?"

He startled. "Yeah, no. I hear you. I won't say anything to Caitlin. But what about your father?"

She stiffened, crouched on the floor of her closet as if she'd heard an air raid siren. "What about him?"

"I'm not saying you ought to call him up," Sam said. "At all. As far as I'm concerned, he waived all right to hear from you when he threw you to the wolves back in Louisville. I guess I just thought, maybe he's learned something from losing both of his kids, in different ways. He must know by now, about Owen, right?"

Words jammed into Andie's tight throat. She jerked her shoulders up and down. "I doubt it. I haven't told him, and when Owen left home, he swore he'd never speak to him again. He even went so far as to put me down as his next of kin on his army intake forms. The army wouldn't even know to call Dad, or how to reach him."

Andie knew, despite not having spoken to the man in years. Her father was still in the same little row-house where her mother had dropped dead in the kitchen, an aneurysm in her brain going off like a bomb that destroyed the entire family.

The brush of Sam's body as he sat down beside her drew Andie from her memories. He put a hand on her arm, gentle and undemanding, telling her without words that he was there if she wanted to say more. She sent him a half smile that turned to a grimace as she let herself slide down to sit against the closet doorjamb.

"All the men in my family are cops. Going back— gosh, I don't even know how many generations," Andie explained wearily. "From the time we were little, Dad was always after Owen, telling him how it would be when he got to the academy, out on the beat, how if he applied himself, he could make detective. It was all he seemed to care about, once Mom was gone. Or maybe it was just the only future he could envision anymore. I don't know. But Owen was always more interested in causing trouble than keeping the peace."

Extending his mile-long legs on either side of her, Sam tugged until her curled-up body unraveled against him. Andie wasn't a small woman—she'd never pictured herself as the kind of petite, kittenish girl who sat in a man's lap—but Sam was huge, solid, and reassuring. A wall strong enough to hold her up when she needed it.

He nuzzled a kiss into her hair, making her relax deeper in his embrace. "Your dad must have been proud that you followed in his footsteps."

"You'd think so, wouldn't you?" Remembered hurt surged up, the feeling of being invisible, irrelevant, a footnote. "He sent Owen to military school to try and straighten him out before he could get accepted to the police academy, and I guess it worked a little too well. Owen quit getting into trouble—but he didn't come home and follow my father's script. Instead, as soon as he turned eighteen, he joined up. I was so proud of him . . ."

Her voice broke, all her fears for her brother pouring over her once more, but the steady circle of Sam's arms around her shoulders helped keep her head above water.

"But your dad was angry," Sam guessed, although the grim tone of his voice said it wasn't a shot in the dark.

"He didn't see that Owen was still protecting and serving, just in a different way. All he cared about was that Owen had defied him. And when I graduated from college and started the recruitment process with the Louisville Metro Police Department . . . I thought it would make things better. That Dad would get off Owen's back because he'd see that the Shepard legacy of law enforcement would live on. But Dad didn't care. I wasn't a boy, wasn't a Shepard son, so I was never good enough. Even when I beat every other candidate, including the men, at the physical ability test. It didn't matter."

Sam's fingers flexed, as if he were fantasizing about wringing her father's neck. "Andie, I'm sorry. He should've cared—you're amazing. Any police department would be lucky to have you."

"That wasn't even the worst part." Forcing herself to sit up, Andie wiped a finger under her eyes and hoped she hadn't wrecked her eyeliner. Hard enough getting it on straight the first time. "I thought joining the LMPD would put my family back together, but instead it tore Owen and me apart." Guilt and pain wrapped around her heart like climbing vines studded with thorns. Andie forced herself to continue.

"He was furious about it, like I'd personally betrayed him. He accused me of trying to replace him, to push him out of the family—and I lost it, I yelled that he'd ditched us a long time ago and maybe he should stay gone. It was awful. We were young and stupid; we both said things we didn't mean. I finally calmed down enough to apologize and convince him that I actually wanted to be a cop. We patched things up on the surface, but underneath, it was never the same."

A sob choked out of her, chest heaving, and Andie covered her streaming eyes. "And now I might never get the chance to make things right, to let Owen know once and for all that I never wanted him out of the family."

Sam leaned in, framing her face with his big hands and rubbing tears away with sweeps of his thumbs across her cheekbones. "Ah, sweetheart. He knows. Wherever he is, Owen knows you're his family. When he was in trouble, when he needed a place for Caitlin to stay, he trusted her to you. That tells me Owen Shepard is a man who knows who his family is."

The words broke through Andie's misery of regret, fear, and grief. *Owen knows, Sam said. Knows. Not knew—not past tense.* She blinked until her blurred vision cleared and all she could see was Sam Brennan's serious mouth and deep brown eyes.

"I love you," she whispered thickly.

Sam's eyes warmed, a smile touching the corners of his lips, and Andie's poor, battered heart throbbed. But before Sam could reply, Caitlin's clear voice piped in from the hallway.

"What are y'all doing on the floor?"

"Looking for my shoes," Andie called, snagging a pair of flat, gold-toned sandals and raising up on her knees to peer over the bed at Caitlin's curious face. "Found them. Are you ready to go?"

"I've been ready for days," Caitlin told her, vibrating impatiently.

"Days! Gracious. I guess I'd better hurry and catch up then." Andie climbed to her feet and held out a hand to help Sam up. "Goodness only knows what my face looks like. Stupid makeup."

Stupid hysterical crying fit. Although Andie had to admit, she felt lighter for having shared that burden with Sam.

Slipping her feet into the sandals, Andie rubbed at her cheeks and prayed she didn't have raccoon eyes. "How do I look?"

"Too gorgeous for company," Sam growled, desire heating up the tender glint in his eyes until Andie had to kiss him, nipping at his bottom lip and tasting the desire on his tongue.

"Gross," Caitlin pronounced. "Stop that. Come on, I want to go see Taylor."

"We're coming, we're coming," Andie laughed, feeling better than she had all day.

Harrington House was ablaze with lights when they pulled up. Caitlin was out of the SUV and scrambling up the porch steps to look for Taylor almost before Andie had it in park.

Sam and Andie followed at a more sedate pace so that Andie had time to admire the Victorian gingerbread trim and the stately, welcoming feel of the place. Through the sparkling golden windows she glimpsed guests talking and smiling, raising their glasses in a toast. A cheer and a wave of laughter rolled out the door when they opened it, a wall of sound that made Andie flinch.

Maybe Sam had been right. Maybe it was a mistake for her to come here tonight.

As if sensing Andie's second thoughts, Sam quietly closed the front door in front of them. He curved his arm around her shoulders and steered her around the side of the wraparound porch to the cool darkness at the back of the house.

"I'm fine," Andie tried to protest, but her feet followed where Sam led without hesitation.

"Of course you are," Sam said matter-of-factly. "You're just going to take a minute out here to gather yourself while I go in and wrangle Caitlin. We'll come find you in a few."

Filled with gratitude, Andie nodded mutely and Sam turned to leave. She kept hold of his hand though, and reeled him back in for a soft, thankful kiss.

"Enjoy the roses," Sam whispered against her parted lips. "Be back in two shakes."

This time, Andie let him go. *How did I get so lucky?* she mused, leaning both hands on the porch railing and breathing in the moonlit garden. The scent of newly budded roses wafted lightly through the cool night air, fresher and greener than the way they smelled in full bloom on a hot summer day.

Andie counted her heartbeats and breathed in and out, hoping some of the night garden's serenity would rub off on her, but she couldn't stop noticing things. The deep, black shadows at the back of the garden by the summer cottage where Sam was staying; the breeze rustling through the dogwoods and the sound their thin, spindly branches made; the crunch of a booted foot on the graveled garden path . . .

Adrenaline shot into her bloodstream, sharpening her vision and prickling at her skin. Andie peered into the darkness, every sense alert and seeking.

Someone was out there.

Andie cataloged what she had with her. She'd turned in her gun along with her badge back at the sheriff's office, but she still carried pepper spray in her purse. And the purse itself, small but heavy with her car keys and wallet, could be used as a weapon. Slipping the shoulder strap off, she casually swung the purse from her right hand and retrieved the pepper spray with her left.

Keeping the canister down by her thigh, Andie called out, "Who's there?"

No answer.

"I'm Sheriff Andie Shepard," she tried again, shamelessly using the title to hopefully intimidate whoever it was into breaking cover. "Come out and state your reason for being here."

But no one came out. Nothing moved in the

garden other than the gentle sway of the rosebushes in the lightly scented breeze, and Andie began to doubt her instincts.

There was probably no one there, she told herself as she walked down the back porch steps and out into the garden, pausing to listen. But there was nothing to hear. This was nerves and paranoia brought on by a sleepless night of worrying and praying for her brother's safety, and the emotional exhaustion of sharing her family's history with Sam. She was being ridiculous, literally jumping at shadows, because once again her emotions were clouding her judgment.

Sighing, Andie turned to go back up to the house, determined to get through this party with a good-natured smile—when a hand shot out of the darkness and hauled her roughly back against a masculine chest.

"Sheriff Shepard," the man hissed, his foul breath hot and moist against her ear. "You're the bitch that's trying to keep me away from my wife and son."

Andie regretted wearing flat-heeled sandals when she stomped as hard she could on the man's booted foot and he barely winced. He did spit out a curse and tighten his arm across her throat, trying to drag her away from the house toward the shadows behind the summer cottage. Andie knew she couldn't let that happen. As stars began to sparkle at the edges of her vision, she bent her right arm and elbowed him in the gut.

He wheezed and cursed again, his grip loosening enough that Andie could drag his forearm down and slam her head back. She felt the crunch of cartilage in his nose before he dropped his arms to bend over with both hands to his bleeding face.

Andie didn't hesitate. She followed up with a shot of pepper spray straight to his eyes, which was enough to have him on the ground and howling. Flipping him over, Andie got her knee into the small of his back and scrabbled for her purse. She unhooked the shoulder strap and used it to secure her attacker's hands just as Sam roared her name from the porch.

Once her prisoner was subdued, Andie risked a glance over her shoulder to see a crowd gathering on the porch and Sam barreling down the garden path like a berserker, the light of battle making his face fiercer than she'd ever seen it.

"I'm fine," she called, grimacing at the hoarseness of her voice. She coughed a bit and held up a hand to stop Sam from pounding the man under her knee into some kind of pulp. "Seriously, Sam, cool it. He's down. I need you to call the sheriff's office, have Deputy Fred—I mean, Acting Sheriff Stanz, send someone over to pick this guy up."

"Are you sure you're not hurt?" Sam growled, looming enough to block out the moonlight.

Andie squinted at him and called up a smile. "Just another day on the job. Well, the job I used to have."

"Who is he?" Sam demanded when the man beneath her spat a weak stream of blood and wriggled like a caught fish.

"I didn't get a chance to check his ID," Andie said, riding out her prisoner's struggles. "But I'm pretty sure it's Trent Little."

The man—Trent—groaned and tried to throw her off. "I need a doctor!" he yelled. "This bitch attacked me."

Between one breath and the next, Andie had been hauled off Trent's resisting body and set carefully aside so that Sam could slam the suddenly—and rightly—terrified man up against the summer cottage wall. "If you ever use that word to refer to any woman again, I swear to almighty God that I will hunt you down like the rabid dog that you are, and put you out of everyone's misery."

"Sam. I know you want to hit him, but you can't. Please, love." Andie put a restraining hand on Sam's back, feeling the electric tension of his muscles quivering as he fought for mastery over himself.

Finally, the tension went out of his shoulders, and Andie let herself relax too. "Someone call the Sheriff's Department," Sam called to the crowd of onlookers clogging the porch.

"What's going on?" A young man's voice carried over the sudden hush of the crowd. "Who's that? Oh my God. Dad?"

"Matty, no," Penny cried. "Don't go down there!"

Andie met Sam's anguished sideways glance. *So much for keeping Matt blissfully ignorant of just what kind of man his father is.*

Standing in Matt's house, watching Dakota Coles swan around clinging to his arm like he was an extra-large accessory she'd picked out to match her baby-pink silk dress was not Taylor's idea of a fun night. So she'd spent most of it in the kitchen, helping Matt's mom.

And she wasn't hiding out, no matter what Penny said.

Happy graduation to me, she thought as she plunged a dirty wine glass into the soapy water filling the sink.

"I hope you're enjoying that." Matt's voice behind her made Taylor lose her grip on the slippery wine glass. She caught it before it floated to the bottom of the sink.

"I love washing crystal," she deadpanned, shooting him a snooty look to cover how happy she was that he'd sought her out. "It's my favorite thing."

"Good." Matt sauntered into the room with his hands tucked into the pockets of his pressed khakis. "Because if you stick to this whole no-college plan, at least you'll have a back-up career in the food service industry."

Taylor flicked soapsuds in his direction and he laughed and danced backwards, one hand shielding his navy blue bow tie. When he dropped his hand, she saw that his tie was printed all over with little pink whales the same color as Dakota's dress.

She turned back to the sink, all her pleasure in the moment popping like a soap bubble. "You should get back to your party. I'm sure your friends are looking for you."

"Why don't you come with me? Then all my friends will be in the same place."

Yeah, because I'm just dying to hang out with your stuck-up, popular crowd who only started paying attention to you once you got hot and rich. "I'll be right there. I promised your mom I'd finish up this round of dirties, but after that I'm all yours."

I'm always all yours.

"I'm holding you to that," Matt said sternly, pointing ridiculously dorky finger guns at her. Taylor tried not to find it endearing.

She also tried not to be depressed that when she didn't leave the kitchen for the next hour, Matt didn't come looking for her again. The only person who came to find her was Caitlin.

"Taylor! Hi! See what Aunt Andie got me?"

Taylor grinned down at the plastic horse, a small chestnut mare who bore an uncanny resemblance to the barn's designated beginner pony, Peony. Andie was still on her campaign to make her niece throw over Queenie for Peony, then. Taylor dutifully admired the toy horse before asking, "Where's your aunt now? Did you run off again?"

Caitlin wrinkled her nose. "Maybe, but I didn't mean to. They were so slow! And gross."

Ah. Sam and Andie had arrived together, of course. And maybe they'd stopped to steal a kiss along the way. "I remember when my dad first started dating Jo Ellen, he was worried I'd be upset when they kissed. But you know what?"

Caitlin gave her a skeptical look, like she knew she was being taught a lesson, but she played along. "What?"

"It's actually really nice to know that they found each other. Because I love my dad, and I'm happy that he's happy, that he's not alone, and that he found someone besides me who sees how cool he is. And it helped that I loved Jo, too."

"I guess." Caitlin didn't appear completely convinced, but she obviously wasn't too concerned about it because in the next breath she was off again, telling a long, rambling story about what happened during her last riding lesson with Sam. Taylor listened enough to be able to make the right noises at the right times, but most of her attention was caught by noticing that the hallway and living room had gone eerily quiet.

Is the party over?

Grabbing Caitlin's hand, Taylor stuck her head

out into the empty hallway. A thump from the back porch had her head swinging that way. "Come on," she told Caitlin. "Let's go see where everyone is."

They followed the sounds of commotion down the hall to find what seemed like every single party guest clustered against the railings of the wraparound porch. Slipping around to the outskirts of the crowd while keeping a firm grip on Caitlin's squirming fingers, Taylor craned her neck to figure out what was going on.

Sam Brennan had some guy up against the wall of the cottage, looking rough and tough and like he'd be happy to beat the everliving snot out of the stranger. Andie was down there too, looking disheveled but basically okay. And who was the guy? Taylor strained to make out his face just as she heard Matt's voice crack as he cried out, "Dad?"

Taylor's heart dropped into her stomach with a sickening lurch. The worst had happened. Trent Little had come to Sanctuary Island, and Matt was about to find out the truth.

Not just that his father was an abusive jerk, but that his best friend, who encouraged him to get in touch with the man, had known all about it and hadn't told him.

Chapter Twenty

Taylor felt Caitlin's small body press close against her side. The kid couldn't possibly see what was going on through the thicket of adult legs and torsos cramming the porch, but she could obviously tell it was something bad.

"Matty, no. Don't go down there!" Penny's anguished cry rang over the whole porch.

Taylor had zero hope that Matt would listen to his mother. Everything in her wanted to get down there and do something, anything, to help Matt, but she had Caitlin . . .

Except, she didn't. Between one heartbeat and the next, Caitlin had dropped Taylor's hand and eeled her way through the crowd to peer through the slats of the porch railing. "Andie!" she cried, and somehow slipped under the railing to make a run for her aunt.

Crap. Taylor started after her, vaulting the porch railing. Good thing she wasn't wearing a tight skirt like Dakota's. Or heels. She ran through the rosebushes to intercept the kid, the soles of her ballet flats slipping on the gravel path and her heart pumping frantically.

Halfway there, Taylor collided with Matt, who grabbed at her arms to stop her from falling. Over his shoulder, Taylor saw Caitlin barrel straight into Andie, who dropped her phone in the middle of calling in—yikes, an attempted assault *on herself*—to swing her niece up into her arms. Andie carried Caitlin around to the front of the cottage, talking to her quietly, and Taylor relaxed a fraction.

Until she realized that Matt had pushed past her, his wide-eyed gaze trained on his father. In a voice that shook, he demanded, "What's going on here? Let go of my dad, Sam."

"Not gonna happen," Sam rumbled, never taking his attention off Trent Little for an instant.

"Matt, don't," Taylor pleaded, but he shook off her tentative touch as if he hadn't even felt it.

"Someone tell me what the hell is going on. Right now!" Matt demanded.

"What's going on is that bi—ow!" Trent broke off when Sam surged closer to him, mashing his face into the wall hard enough to shut him up. But Matt was the one who made a sound like he was in pain.

Panic shot through Taylor at the imminent freakout she sensed in Matt. He needed answers. Taylor looked around. Sam was too busy watchdogging Trent, Andie was on the phone with the dispatcher and had Caitlin in her arms, and Penny was struggling to make her way through the crowd of gawking guests.

"Your dad isn't supposed to be here," Taylor blurted.

Matt looked down at her, seeming to focus on her

face for the first time. "Tay. What do you mean? I invited him. He said he'd come."

The bewilderment in Matt's green-gold eyes slashed at Taylor's heart. "I know."

"This is all a big misunderstanding," Matt said, begging Sam to understand. "I wanted him here. I asked him to come to graduation."

"He tried to hurt Andie." Sam's voice seemed to have permanently dipped into that riled-up bear growl.

"That . . . doesn't make any sense." Matt wrapped his arms around his torso as if he were cold, even in the balmy early summer evening. "No. He was . . . Dad, were you nervous? Maybe waiting out back until the party thinned out so you could come in and say hello in private? And Andie, I don't know, thought he was a burglar and clobbered him."

But Andie was still several feet away, all her attention focused on comforting Caitlin. Taylor swallowed hard. "Andie knew who he was, Matt."

"How is that possible? He's never been to Sanctuary Island before!"

Taylor bit her lip and squeezed her eyes shut against the oncoming storm. "Because Andie helped your mom get a restraining order after I told her you'd invited Trent down here."

"You what?" Furious betrayal darkened Matt's eyes.

"I had to," Taylor cried. "You weren't going to tell her, and she had a right to know. To protect herself, and you."

"I don't need to be protected from my own father!" Matt yelled.

"Matthew." Penny's sharp tone was enough to

stop Matt short, but it took a look at her pale, set face to make him really back down. "Don't be angry with Taylor. If you have to be angry with someone, you can be mad at me."

Matt glanced back and forth between them. "I still don't understand what's happening," he said, more quietly now.

"I know, honey." Penny glanced over her shoulder to where her husband, Dylan, was attempting to herd the crowd of party guests back into the house while keeping an eagle eye on the action in the garden. "But can we please discuss it a little later?"

"When?" Matt demanded. "After the sheriff hauls Dad down to the station in cuffs?"

Penny didn't flinch. "Yes."

"Then . . ."—Matt appeared at a loss, as if he hadn't expected his mother to agree—"I'm going with him."

Oooh, bad idea. Alarmed, Taylor shot Penny a glance, but Matt's mother had her stoic face on. "There are some things you need to know first, Matty. Things I probably should have told you a long time ago. And if you still want to visit your father in jail, I won't stop you."

Matt vibrated with tension, torn between getting answers and taking care of his father. He didn't have long to be conflicted, though, because what seemed like the entire Sheriff's Department showed up right about then, descending on the summer cottage like a swarm of khaki-clad bees.

Taylor let herself be pushed to the fringes of the commotion. She was pretty sure her presence was no longer needed here—she hadn't witnessed anything, and whatever Penny had to say to Matt was a private family matter. Even if Taylor's cyber snooping had given her a decent idea of what it might be.

The only reason she'd stick around at this point would be as Matt's moral support, but since he hadn't looked at her once since he shouted at her, she was probably off duty there, too.

She told herself she didn't care, that Matt was under a lot of stress and they'd work it out when things calmed down, but the way her heart leapt with relief when he appeared in front of her told another story.

Over his shoulder, she could see the deputies leading Trent Little away, Sam and Andie following behind, probably to give their statements. Caitlin had been transferred to Sam's arms by now, and the same man who'd mercilessly restrained Trent Little held the eight-year-old girl as if she were made of spun sugar.

"I want the truth, Taylor." Matt's voice was harder than she'd ever heard it. "How long have you known about whatever is going on between my parents?"

Penny paused on her way up the back-porch steps to join her husband in shoving their guests out the door, and sent Taylor a concerned look. Neither of them was on Matt's list of favorite people right about now, Taylor thought wearily. "A few weeks."

She could actually hear his molars grinding. "You should have told me."

A tiny spark of anger sizzled to life in Taylor's belly. "Why? When I told you about Sam, you said you wished you didn't know. Make up your mind, Matt."

"That was different," he said loudly, raking both hands through his short, tawny hair. "I said that about Sam because—"

"Because you love sending me mixed signals," Taylor concluded, with a bitterness that went deeper than she even she had known.

Matt rocked back on his heels, scowling. "I don't do that. Mixed signals. What are you even talking about?"

The peal of semi-hysterical laughter caught Taylor by surprise. "Are you punking me? Is this being filmed? Where's the camera, in the rosebushes?"

"Stop making jokes," Matt yelled. "I'm serious about this! You're my best friend. I tell you everything, Taylor. I can't believe you would keep something like this from me. It's *about* me!"

"Oh, come on, Matt." Fed up, Taylor started searching her pockets for her car keys. She needed to get out of there before she said something she couldn't take back. "You don't want me to tell you everything. Trust me."

"Wait, there's more? What else are you not telling me?" Matt grabbed her wrist when she turned to escape, tugging her off balance so that she stumbled against his chest.

Overcome with his nearness, her senses filled with the heat of Matt's lean, strong body and the fresh scent of his expensive cologne, Taylor lost her head. She gazed up into Matt's beautiful, intense hazel eyes and blurted out, "I'm in love with you, you idiot."

Those hazel eyes widened in shock as he stepped back, putting space between them. Everywhere they'd touched felt instantly cold and empty. Matt opened his mouth but nothing came out, and with a small, hurt sound, Taylor turned and ran for her car.

So much for leaving before she said something she couldn't take back. Thank God graduation was tomorrow, and after that—she'd probably never see Matthew Little again.

Taylor told herself she was glad as she started her car and peeled away from Harrington House, that it was good to finally get everything out in the open and to stop pretending she was okay with being Matt's best buddy. That was a slow, torturous death of daily heartache. This way, she could make a clean break.

But as the tears started to fall, she knew she'd give anything to go back for her daily serving of heartache if it meant seeing Matt smile at her again.

Andie's official statement was a clear-cut case of self-defense. Sam's was more problematic. Trent Little had complicated it by swearing it was Sam who'd broken his nose—probably because he was embarrassed to have anyone know that a woman had taken him down—and it took time to straighten out everyone's stories and get to the truth.

By the time Acting Sheriff Stanz let them go, it was well after midnight. When Andie walked out of her old office, still smarting a bit from the awkward interview with her former deputy seated behind her old desk, she found Sam sitting behind Ivy's vacant desk with his long legs stretched out in front of him. Caitlin was curled on his chest, and they were both fast asleep.

My little family. The thought came to her out of the blue, and she tried to dismiss it immediately. It was way too soon for that kind of thing with Sam—and Caitlin. Andie's heart just about broke remembering that she might very well be that little girl's only surviving family.

Refusing to give into the rising tide of emotion,

Andie rallied the troops and got them up and into the SUV. While she settled Caitlin into the backseat and searched for the seatbelt, the girl roused enough to say, "I'm glad Sam is coming home with us. He's not like other boyfriends. He doesn't make you forget about me."

The backs of Andie's eyes burned with unshed tears. "Nothing could make me forget about you," she said, the words as fierce as her hand smoothing back Caitlin's messy red hair was gentle. "Nothing could make me stop loving you."

Caitlin blinked up her. "Not even if you found out I did something really bad?"

"Not even that," Andie promised her, sliding the belt buckle home and tightening it securely. "You're my girl. I love you."

"I'm your girl," Caitlin repeated solemnly, like a vow, and Andie heard the unspoken "I love you, too."

Pressing a tremulous kiss to Caitlin's smooth forehead, Andie breathed through the moment and wondered if she was going to be able to get it together enough to drive them safely home.

But when she finally managed to straighten up and close the back passenger door, Sam was already in the driver's seat. Good, he'd had a nap at the station. He could drop them off before heading back to Harrington House like he did every night.

Except, Andie decided as she slid into the front seat and fumbled with her seatbelt, she didn't want Sam to drop them off and leave. Peering at him across the electronic lights of the dash, she decided to test the waters.

"I don't want you to go back to your cousin's place tonight," she said. "I want you to stay with us."

Andie blinked. That was blunt. Apparently her filters were down. But it was okay, because Sam gave her a look from under his lowered brows and said, "If you think I'm letting you out of my sight for the next twenty-four hours . . . hell, for the next year, you're losing your fine little mind."

"Does that mean you're planning to stay on Sanctuary Island for a while?" Wow, she really needed to stop talking for a bit.

But Sam wasn't looking for the ejector button or trying to bail out of the car. Instead, he took the turn toward her house and said, "Yeah. I think I am."

Chapter Twenty-One

Sam had faced down plenty of bad in his life. His childhood was no picnic, before and after Child Protective Services removed him from his parents' house. In prison, he'd been one of the youngest guys on his cellblock, and even foster care hadn't prepared him for the things he saw inside. After he got out and dedicated his life to saving abused horses, he'd witnessed the worst of humanity's selfishness, neglect, and easy cruelty.

But nothing in his life had filled him with fury and terror like seeing Andie fend off a man who outweighed her by at least fifty pounds. The fact that she'd wiped the floor with Trent Little did help. Still, Sam wasn't sure how long it would take to erase the horrible image of that beefy arm around Andie's throat as the guy tried to drag her off into the darkness. Sam hadn't seen it in real life, but now he envisioned it every time he closed his eyes.

The only remedy was to keep his eyes open and to fill them with Andie, safe and sound and close enough to touch.

"That's wonderful!" Elation brightened her smile until she was luminous enough to light the inside of the SUV. "But . . . I hope you're not staying because you think I need protecting."

Sam huffed out a laugh at the thought. "Not likely. I've literally been a witness to how well you defend yourself. And can I say, I have never found you sexier than when you beat that guy down?"

He didn't need to look away from the road to know she was blushing. "Stop it. And . . . thank you, I guess. Some men I've known have been thrown off by the fact that I'm not your average damsel in distress."

"Like the worthless sack of crap who turned out to be a mob guy," Sam supplied. "Well, lucky for you, I'm not him. I look at you and I see a strong, resourceful woman who's smart as hell and not looking to be rescued by anyone."

"That's right." She nodded firmly, but when Sam glanced over, her mouth had taken on an unhappy curve.

"But that doesn't mean you don't want someone to stand by you," Sam said, locking his hands around the wheel and concentrating on his driving rather than on how saying this felt like stepping off the roof of a ten-story building. "Someone who has your back and respects how capable you are—while giving you someplace to go where you don't have to be strong every minute."

In the moment of silence that followed, he could hear Andie swallow over the sound of the tires on the road. "Are you offering to be that place for me? Don't say it unless you mean it. Because let me tell you right now—if you promised me that and then took it away, I'm not sure I could forgive you."

That was his Andie, never backing down and taking no crap from anyone. Sam felt like he'd swallowed the sun, everything inside him going supernova in an instant of blinding recognition and affection and need. "I mean it," he said gruffly, pulling into her driveway and cutting the engine. "I love you, Andie Shepard. And I'm not leaving Sanctuary Island."

After a quick glance to the backseat, where Caitlin was snoring lightly, her head dropped onto her shoulder at a crazy angle, Andie launched herself across the gearshift. Sam speared his hands into her hair to tilt her head so he could kiss her smiling mouth. The kiss was salty with tears, and Sam was man enough to admit that a few of them might be his.

Andie drew back, gasping for air and sanity. "But, your job. The horse rescue operation, your business partner—"

"We'll work it out," Sam said. He had no idea how. It wouldn't be easy. He'd made a mess of things here, and it could all blow up in his face, but he had to try.

Sam smoothed his hand across her forehead and down her satiny cheek. Andie turned her face into his palm and pressed a burning kiss to the center.

"Come on," he murmured. "We're home. Let's get Caitlin inside and move this conversation to the bedroom."

"We're home," Andie breathed, delight and contentment shining from her eyes.

I'm home, Sam thought as he followed Andie into the house with Caitlin a warm, sleepy weight against his shoulder. *And I'm staying.*

* * *

When Andie blinked the sleep out of her eyes the next morning, she was alone in the bed. A quick pass of her hand over Sam's pillow showed his side of the bed was cool, but rumpled enough that she was sure he'd slept there for at least a while.

Struggling against her disappointment, she told herself this relationship had been two steps forward, one step back from the very beginning. Sam had opened up the night before in ways she hadn't truly expected yet; it made sense that he might have felt the need to pull back, to rebuild some of the walls that had crumbled between them.

I'll just have to get out my chisel and keep chipping away, Andie decided, swinging her legs out of bed and groping for her robe. *At least I'll see him at the graduation ceremony on Sunday.*

And he'd promised to stay on the island. To give them time to find out what this thing between them could be, how this love could grow if they nurtured it. That ought to be enough for now.

But the moment she stepped onto the hooked rug runner that lined the hallway, Andie heard Caitlin's high-pitched, rapid-fire babble interspersed with the deep rumble of Sam's voice. Grinning, she hustled down to the kitchen to find her granite countertops, the square table, and much of the floor liberally dusted with white powder.

"I'm making pancakes," Caitlin announced, holding up a wire whisk proudly, unaware that she was dripping bright yellow egg yolk all over her nightgown. "Sam is helping."

"I can see that," Andie said, biting the inside of her lip to keep from laughing. "And which one of us is going to help you clean up, I wonder?"

"That would be me," Sam volunteered with a

rueful twist to his mouth. "Sorry. We had a little too much fun with the flour sifter."

Andie had to kiss that wry smile. She used her thumb to wipe a slash of white from his cheek and said, "Thanks for staying. And for helping Caitlin make breakfast. This is the best morning I've had in a while."

Owen used to love pancakes. Sunday morning breakfasts were some of the few good times she remembered with her family—their father would make pancakes, they'd all go to church, then she and Owen would play touch football in the park until Dad called them inside.

Pulling her into his arms, Sam pressed a kiss to the top of her head. "Hey, I bet I've got something that will cheer you up."

"Sam!" Caitlin called from her perch on a kitchen chair by the counter to the right of the stove. "I scrambled the eggs. Help me pour the milk."

Eyes wide, Sam practically cleared the kitchen in single bound to stop Caitlin from lifting the heavy glass jug. "Gotcha! Here we go. Andie, your surprise is on the coffee table. Go take a look and I'll bring you a cup of coffee in a second."

Grateful for the chance to take a moment alone to get her emotions under control, Andie slipped out of the kitchen as Caitlin leaned precariously over her bowl of beaten eggs and dribbled the milk in with Sam's supporting hand under the heaviest part of the jug.

That sight did more to restore Andie's spirits than anything could . . . or so she thought, until she spotted the folded copy of today's *Sanctuary Gazette* lying on the coffee table.

SHERIFF SHEPARD SINGLEHANDEDLY
SAVES THE DAY!

Andie laughed out loud and settled on the sofa to read the rest of the article. By the time she looked up to see Sam holding out a deliciously fragrant mug full of milky coffee, she'd moved on to the announcement of today's town-wide celebration down at the pier to welcome friends and far-flung family to the island for tomorrow's graduation ceremony. The island got so few visitors, they tended to make a big deal of the few times a year that the ferry brought in big crowds. This afternoon would find almost the entire population of the town clustered down by the docks to greet the ferry. Andie was almost glad she was suspended—coordinating the details of the Graduation Ferry Party was a huge annual hassle.

"How did you like your latest appearance in the *Gazette*?" Sam wanted to know. "The reporter takes a slightly different tone with you this time."

"You have to give it to Wyatt Hawkins," she said cupping the mug thankfully and taking a blissful sip. "The man works tirelessly to make sure Sanctuary gets the scoop. He must have been up all night to get this into the morning paper."

"He sent this one out as a special bulletin, too, so everyone in town got an email alert about the story. I especially liked the way he described what happened when he called on the city council members to get their reactions."

She snickered into her mug. "Who would have guessed that Dabney Leeds wears basketball shorts and a white cotton undershirt to bed?"

"Or answers the door to his mansion himself," Sam agreed. "But maybe his butler is off duty at two in the morning."

"That actually makes me think a bit better of Leeds. The whole article is like that—I can't believe how many people were willing to go on record to praise the woman they'd all but drummed out of office mere days before."

"Last night reminded them what they have with you." Sam shrugged, satisfaction in every strong line of his body. "I wouldn't be surprised if you get a call from the council sometime today, letting you know their investigation is concluded and your suspension is over."

"Well, after the way Wyatt basically demanded it on behalf of the whole town. And look, there's a whole long section about you, too! I guess he finally dug a little deeper and found out about all the good you do for abused horses."

"I saw that." Sam seemed quietly pleased. "He even implied there must have been some injustice in my sentencing, since it didn't make sense that a man who'd been convicted of animal cruelty would dedicate his life to rescuing animals from cruelty."

"Which is exactly what I said at the time! But it's nice for all of Sanctuary Island to see your devotion to protecting animals written down here in black and white." Andie shook her head, bemused. "Yesterday, we were this close to being tarred and feathered. Today, we're heroes. This is why I'll never make a good politician. People are so fickle!"

"I prefer to think of it as them finally getting their heads out of their—" Sam broke off, a panicked look coming over his face. "Did you hear that? Just a minute."

"Hear what?" Andie asked, but he'd already dashed back into the kitchen. There was a loud clatter, as if someone had upended the silverware drawer and scattered forks and spoons across the floor.

"Nothing!" he shouted from behind the closed kitchen door. "Everything's cool. We've got it under control. Just . . . maybe don't come back in here for a few minutes."

Another bang surprised a laugh out of Andie. She immediately felt guilty for laughing and being even a little happy, when God only knew where her brother was and what might be happening to him, but one of her few memories of her mother shimmered through her mind.

The memory was scented lightly with the apples and cloves of the pies her mother had loved to bake. It was soft around the edges, like an old photograph that had been handled many times. "Be happy," her mother had said. "As much as you can for as long as you can. And be grateful for every scrap of happiness life gifts you with. Happiness is precious, don't squander it. You never know when you'll have it again."

Andie had clung to that after her mother died, without any real hope of ever feeling happy again. She'd tried, she really had. But it had taken Sanctuary Island, a surprise niece, and a handsome ex-con to get her there. And no matter what else life threw at her, she had to be grateful for Sam and Caitlin. To resist the happiness they brought wouldn't do anything except turn Andie bitter.

Happiness is precious, don't squander it.

"I won't, Mama. I promise," Andie whispered to the silent room.

With that vow fresh on her heart and a determined smile on her face, Andie rejoined the wonderful chaos of her kitchen. Her family.

When Sam's phone rang just as he was sliding the maple-syrup-smeared plates into the sink, Andie narrowed her eyes at him in mock anger.

"I didn't plan this, I swear," Sam chortled, backing away from the sink. One look at the caller's name was enough to turn humor into dread. "Leave them to soak if you want, I'll wash them later. But I have to take this."

Andie's brows went up in question, but he didn't give her time to voice it. Thumbing the answer button he said, "Brennan here."

"We've got a problem." Lucas's tension radiated through the phone connection.

"Hold on." Sam walked out of the kitchen as casually as he could, intensely aware of Andie's shrug at Caitlin and the sudden hush from the little girl who'd been chattering basically nonstop for two hours. Sam couldn't bear to hear whatever this bad news was while standing in the kitchen with the two of them.

Of course, as he let himself into Andie's bedroom and sat on the bed where they'd held each other all night long, he realized this might not be any easier.

"Okay, I'm alone," he told his business partner.

"There's good news and bad news," Lucas warned grimly. "Which do you want first?"

"Good news."

"The cops aren't doing much to find the lieutenant governor's missing horse."

Sam let out a breath. "That . . . does seem like good news. What's the bad?"

"The Lieutenant Governor hired a posse of thugs to track you down and question you. They're not constrained by having no jurisdiction in Sanctuary Island. They're on their way there now."

Sam's blood ran cold. Having the cops run him to ground here would have been bad, but as little as he cared for organized law enforcement, at least he could've counted on them not to drag anyone else into this mess. But a band of hired guns? There was no telling what they'd do to earn the bounty Lt. Gov. Wallace had put on Sam's head.

"Thanks for the warning," he managed to grind out through a locked jaw.

"Don't waste time thanking me," Lucas snapped. "Just get the hell out of Dodge, and take that poor horse with you. These guys aren't playing, Sam. Do not hang around waiting for them to find you."

"I'll do what I have to." Sam hung up the phone without another word, his mind racing down various paths, testing scenarios, looking for a way out. Anything that would keep him from breaking his promise to Andie less than twenty-four hours after making it.

But every path circled back to the same truth: when he'd stolen Queenie, he'd assumed responsibility for her welfare. If those men showed up on Sanctuary, they'd doubtless have pictures and identifying marks mapped out—they'd instantly recognize Queenie as the lieutenant governor's stolen property.

They'd be within their rights to go to the local authorities with their proof and demand that Sam give Queenie to them. And by the time they got here, Sanctuary Island's local authorities might well include Andie Shepard once more.

That's what ultimately decided him. He couldn't

do that to Andie now, when she was getting her life back on track.

If he was going down, he damn sure wasn't dragging Andie down with him.

Chapter Twenty-Two

Taylor scowled out her window at the sunshine and chirping birds. They were offensively cheery when all she wanted was to burrow deeper into her bed and sleep through the next forty-eight hours.

"Tay, get up," her father shouted up the staircase. "We're heading out to meet the ferry in less than an hour."

"I'm not going!" she yelled.

"You have to! Your Aunt Beatrice is coming."

"Aunt Bea will understand," Taylor protested, kicking back the covers and glaring at her bedroom door.

It was true. If there was anyone in this family who could relate to the pain of a broken heart, it was Aunt Beatrice. Of course, she'd done as much heart breaking as she had suffered being brokenhearted, but as she liked to say, that just meant she was well rounded.

"Aunt Beatrice might understand, but I don't." Harrison McNamara opened her door and stuck his head in with that characteristic paternal disregard for Taylor's privacy. "What's the matter, monkey?"

For some reason, the babyish nickname made something twist in Taylor's chest. Pressing her lips together, she pulled her pillow over her face and spoke through it. "Nothing. I'm fine. Have fun at the party. Wake me up after graduation."

She heard footsteps, but instead of retreating down the stairs they seemed to be coming closer. Her dad's "oof" as he tripped over the backpack she'd tossed by her desk confirmed it.

Throwing the pillow to the foot of the bed, Taylor sat up and regarded her father with annoyance. "Go away."

But years of dealing with Taylor and her teenage hormones and mood swings had apparently given her father a very thick skin. Nothing but concern showed on his distinguished face as he sat on the end of her bed and felt around the blankets until he could clasp her ankle through them. The touch was oddly comforting, but Taylor was no dummy. She knew it was partly intended to keep her still long enough for Dad to pry her feelings out into the open.

"Talk to me, monkey. Or I could go get Jo, if you'd rather."

Dad was trying to be totally understanding, but Taylor could tell it would hurt his feelings if she asked to speak to her stepmother instead. Besides . . . "I don't only talk to Jo," Taylor pointed out grumpily. "Maybe I used to, but you and I are doing better now, right?"

"You mean after spending your teenage years locked in a battle of wills, you're finally ready to talk to me . . . right when you're about to leave home?" At least Dad looked amused about it.

Taylor bunched her sheets over her tank-top-clad boobs and pinned them down with her arms so she could lean back against the headrest. "We didn't fight that much."

Dad gave her a look. "Right. And you never snuck out or missed curfew or trespassed and got arrested for underage drinking."

"We weren't charged," Taylor argued automatically. "My record is clean."

"Mmm. Thanks to Sheriff Shepard." Dad's gaze sharpened on her face, as if the mere mention of the night she and Matt had gotten in trouble had tipped him off. "Is this about Matt? Honey, are you upset about graduation? I know it's going to be an adjustment, spending next year at different colleges, but—"

"I can't wait to adjust, then," Taylor interrupted, wiggling her foot in her father's warm grasp. She had just the thing to distract him from this convo about Matt. "And I'm not going to college, Dad. At least, not next year. I want to take a year off and travel."

To her everlasting shock, instead of launching into the same argument they'd had every other time her post-graduation plans came up, Dad pressed his lips together tightly and nodded once. "I think that might be a good idea."

Taylor almost fell off the bed. "What? Dad, you hate this idea! What changed your mind?"

"It may have been pointed out to me that yours is a temperament that benefits from following your passions. And that you're unlikely to have a successful college experience if you don't want to be there . . . but that a year spent seeing the world might give you the perspective you need to come home and enjoy being a student again."

Sometimes, Taylor loved her stepmother so much,

she could hardly stand it. She lunged at her father and hugged him around the neck. "Daddy! Thank you!"

"Make sure you spend some time in County Clare, in Ireland," he said gruffly, holding her tight. "It's good to know where you come from."

"I already know where I come from," Taylor told him. "And I promise I'll stay safe and be smart and come home to you in a year."

"You'd better."

They sniffled together for a minute longer before Taylor sat back and pretended to have something in her eye. Dad had allergies too, so he totally got it.

Clearing his throat, Dad fixed her with a knowing stare. "Don't think this means you're getting out of going down to the ferry with us. Unless you want to cough up a good reason why you should stay in bed."

The concession about spending a year abroad made Taylor almost feel like she owed her dad something—wait. Giving him an impressed look, she said, "Man, you're good. I want to go to business school so I can learn how to out negotiate you."

"Good luck with that," Dad said. "Now spill."

"Oh, fine." Taylor fell back against her pillows. "Matt and I had a fight. Worst ever."

"That's too bad, but I'm sure you'll make up. It would be a shame to spend the summer fighting with your best friend."

Dad wasn't getting it. "No, I mean, we're not fighting. It's just . . . over."

"Your friendship? Surely you can make up."

Taylor smiled a little. "Thanks for not asking what I did, by the way. There was a time when you would've assumed this was all my fault."

Those bushy steel-gray brows drew together in a frown. "If I made you feel that way, I'm sorry, Taylor. In any case, I'd never assume that now. You've grown into a fine young woman, with a strong sense of who you are. You're smart and you work hard. You care about other people and you fight for what you want. I'm proud of you. And your mom would be proud too if she were here."

Dang it, this was the *worst* season for allergies. Taylor rubbed at her eyes and made an effort to keep her voice steady. "Sometimes maybe I fight too hard for what I want. I . . . told Matt I was in love with him."

Dad reared backwards like she'd slapped him. "And he didn't immediately tell you he loves you, too? The next time I see that little—"

"No, don't." Taylor took a deep breath and let it out on a shrug. "It is what it is. Matt has a right not to be in love with me."

"That's true. He has a right to be an irretrievable idiot who deserves to get stuck with the likes of Cora Coles' vapid, brainless daughter for the rest of his life."

"Dad!" Taylor couldn't help laughing. Suddenly, she felt like maybe she could handle going to the ferry party after all. Pushing her feet against her father's hip, she shoved him over a few inches. "Go on, get out of here so I can get dressed."

"You'll come with us?"

He looked so happy that Taylor felt bad that she'd made a fuss about it. "Aunt Bea would probably turn right around and get back on the ferry if I'm not there to greet her."

Dad paused at the doorway. "Are you sure? The whole town usually turns out for these things."

Matt would probably be there, was what he meant. But it was a small island and they were bound to run into each other at some point. Tomorrow at graduation, if not before. Taylor lifted her chin. "I'm sure. I have nothing to be ashamed of."

And for the first time since last night, she knew that was true. So she loved someone who didn't love her back. At least she'd told him. She fought for what she wanted. That wasn't such a bad way to be.

Taylor bounced off the bed and into her closet, sifting through the flannels and T-shirts to find something different. She wasn't ashamed . . . but that didn't mean she couldn't show up at the ferry party in something that would make Matt see what he was missing.

Caitlin had been quiet since Sam abruptly left the kitchen to take that phone call. To give Sam the time and privacy he obviously needed, Andie had put Caitlin in the bath and started getting her ready for the day. She smoothed the brush one last time through the finally untangled red waves of the little girl's hair before starting to braid it down her back.

"It's almost time to go down and see the ferry," Andie told her. "There's a big festival to welcome the visitors who are coming to town for graduation, with ice cream and balloons and—"

Caitlin slid off the chair, pulling the trailing ends of her braid from Andie's fingers. "Are you going to make me leave?"

"What? No!" Shocked, Andie hugged her niece, but Caitlin stayed stiff and unyielding in her arms. "Honey, why would you think that?"

"Because I'm bad," Caitlin whispered. The words

were muffled against the thin cotton of Andie's sweater, but they sent a chill down her spine.

"Look at me." Taking Caitlin by the shoulders, Andie moved her back far enough to be able to stare right into those eyes, Owen's exact shade of aquamarine—and every bit as shadowed as she remembered her brother's gaze. "You are not bad. And even if you do something bad, you're still my girl. Remember?"

It took a second, but eventually Caitlin nodded. Keeping her gaze on the ground, she asked, "If Sam did something bad, would you make him leave?"

Andie's stomach tightened. She hadn't talked to Caitlin much about the upheaval that had led to Andie being around more during the day. She hadn't thought Caitlin needed to know—but kids were more perceptive than they seemed, sometimes. Obviously, Caitlin had picked up on the tension surrounding Sam's criminal past and Andie's job.

But how to answer her question? "It's not exactly the same, sweetie. You're my family. It's my job to love you no matter what."

"But you love Sam, and he loves you. I heard him say it."

The memory filled Andie with light. "It's true. But love between grown-ups is different. There are things Sam could do to make me send him away—for instance, if he hurt you."

"He wouldn't," Caitlin said, so confidently that it made Andie smile.

"I know. I couldn't love a man who would, and I can't imagine Sam ever hurting anyone, least of all his favorite riding student—but I'm trying to explain that as much as I love Sam, I can't promise we'll be together forever, no matter what. Life is long and complicated—no one could make a promise like that and be sure of keeping it."

"Hmm." Caitlin made a dissatisfied face, then turned her back so that Andie could tie off her dangling braid. "What if I did something against the law? Would you have to arrest me?"

"I'm not the sheriff right now," Andie reminded her. "And if you did something illegal, I'd want to find out why. I'd want to understand why you felt you had to do it, and I'd help you any way I could."

The way Caitlin bent her head forward made the braid swing to the side, exposing the vulnerable nape of her pale neck. The sight of it awoke an all-consuming tenderness in Andie's chest.

"I stole something once," Caitlin said, fast, like ripping off a bandage.

Andie blinked at the back of Caitlin's head. "Oh." She had so many questions—What was it? Were you caught? But she settled on, "How old were you?"

Caitlin shrugged stiffly, still facing away from Andie. "I don't remember. It was a candy bar. I took it from the thing by the cash register at the grocery store by our house, where I lived with my mom."

Andie sucked in a silent breath. Caitlin never talked about her mother. Ever. "Did you get in trouble?"

"My mom didn't care. She laughed about it. But she told me if I was bad like that again, the police would come and take me away and I'd have to live at prison."

Every ounce of Andie's blood heated to boiling. That woman. If Caitlin's mom weren't dead already, Andie would be tempted to find her and slap the crap out of her. "That's not what would happen,"

Andie said now, striving for calm as she encouraged Caitlin to face her with a gentle hand on her shoulder. "You're still a minor, which means the police and the courts treat you differently. But stealing is illegal, and I know you know it's wrong. So why did you do it?"

Caitlin shrugged, mouth tight and lashes lowered. She looked like the girl who'd first arrived on Andie's doorstep weeks ago, silent and withdrawn. "I don't know. I was hungry, I guess."

So hungry that she'd resorted to stealing. Andie put that together with the other things Caitlin had let slip about her former life—the way Caitlin hesitated to trust women, the mother who forgot about her when a new boyfriend was in the picture and hadn't cared when her daughter was caught stealing . . .

Andie made an intuitive leap and hoped she wasn't about to screw this up. "Caitlin. Did your mom make you breakfast, lunch, and dinner? Or did she forget sometimes?"

Looking uncomfortable, Caitlin shrugged again. "There was usually cereal and stuff. I could reach it if I pulled a chair over to climb up on the counter."

Andie's heart squeezed tight. Cereal. That this child poured for herself, after risking breaking her neck by climbing around the kitchen cabinets like they were a jungle gym. "Caitlin."

The little girl's eyes sharpened, taking on that too-adult gleam she'd almost shed over the past few weeks. "My mother didn't want me. She never said it, but I'm not stupid."

"No, you're not stupid. Which means I know you can tell how much I *do* want you. No matter what you did in the past, and no matter what you might do in the future. You know you're my girl."

Caitlin's chin quivered, but she smiled, the shadows clearing from her eyes until they were the bright blue of a summer sky. "Yeah. I guess I do know that. Okay. Let's go find Sam."

"First, a hug. Nonnegotiable."

Caitlin sighed and rolled her eyes, but when Andie gathered the slight body into her arms, Caitlin clung hard for a long moment. Blinking back tears, Andie said roughly, "Come on. Let's go see if Sam's off the phone yet."

Parenting was full of conversations like this, she'd discovered. Like an endless pop quiz in a subject she hadn't signed up for, but somehow Andie felt as if she wasn't failing too horribly. If she kept repeating that she loved Caitlin, and tried to be honest with her, Andie thought she couldn't go all that wrong.

Ignoring the fact that there was currently a very important question Andie wasn't answering truthfully—*When is my dad coming home?*—she peered down the quiet hallway. Caitlin slipped past her to check the kitchen.

"Sam?"

No answer. He must still be on the phone in her room. But it was almost time to leave for the ferry, and Andie really didn't want Caitlin to miss her first big Sanctuary Island festival. Andie crossed the hall to knock quietly on her bedroom door. "Hey, sorry to bug you, but I need to get in there and grab some clothes from the dresser really fast. Sam? Can I come in?"

She listened, but there was nothing to hear. Turning the knob slowly, Andie cracked her door open then pushed it wide. Her bedroom was empty.

The whole house felt empty.

"Aunt Andie!" Caitlin cried from the living room.

Heart pounding, Andie ran down the hall to find her niece clutching a piece of paper, tears welling in her eyes. "What is it? Are you okay?"

"He left," Caitlin said, shoving the paper at her.

Andie felt the blood drain from her face. Her fingertips tingled then went numb as she took the paper from Caitlin. It was a note, written in Sam's dark, declarative scrawl.

Andie and Caitlin,

Please believe that I love you both with my whole heart. That's why I have to leave. I've done something that could endanger anyone near me, and if anything ever happened to either of you because of me I couldn't live with it. I know I'm breaking my promise, Andie, and I won't ask you to forgive me. But once I make everything right, I swear I'll come back so you can tell me off in person. Until then, take care of each other and remember,

I love you.
Sam

Andie had to read it twice before she could make any sense of it. Sam was gone. After he'd promised to stay. Anger, disbelief, betrayal, sorrow—emotions swirled up like a tornado trying to sweep Andie along, but her brain kicked in.

That conversation Caitlin had instigated, all about committing crimes and being sent away . . . and then this. It was too big a coincidence. And what she'd told Caitlin was true too—Sam would never hurt either of them deliberately. Andie knew that in her bones. So if he'd left, which he knew would hurt them both, he had to have a good reason. And Andie's instincts told her that Caitlin might have an idea of what that reason could be.

Her shaky hand steadied as she waved Sam's note at Caitlin. "Okay. We're going to fix this, but I need your help. What do you know about Sam that I don't?"

Caitlin bit her lip, obviously reluctant to snitch, and Andie ran a hand through her hair. "Sweetie, he says in his note that he might be in danger. I want to help him, but I can't help if I don't know what's going on."

Worry crumpled Caitlin's face. "Queenie isn't his," she said in a rush. "I mean, she is now, but he didn't buy her. He stole her and brought her here. Taylor and I heard him on the phone with someone talking about it. I think it was the same person who called him today."

Andie blew out a breath. She wasn't as staggered as she thought she'd be. Deep down, it was almost a relief to know that her instincts hadn't been wrong to send up red flags when Sam Brennan came back to town. So there it was . . . Sam was a horse thief.

If Taylor knew, that meant Jo Ellen Hollister was likely to know too. And if Sam was leaving the island to escape justice, he'd have to take the evidence with him.

"I know where he's going," Andie said, grabbing Caitlin's hand and snagging her cell phone from the table by the front door. "Come on, we've got some calls to make."

Chapter Twenty-Three

The ring of Taylor's phone startled her into nearly dropping the ice cream cone she'd bought from Miss Ruth's table in the town square. She tripped over the curb and back onto Main Street, which had been closed to traffic for the festival, juggling the phone with the cone and trying desperately not to drip homemade mint chip on her white linen sundress.

When she got the cone upright again and found shelter from the flow of pedestrians by climbing the steps to stand in front of the CLOSED sign on the Hackley's Hardware door, she looked at her phone.

The missed call was from Matt.

A drop of melting ice cream hit her hand while she stared at the phone. Taylor sighed, not sure she could enjoy her cone anymore.

"So you're screening my calls?"

She stiffened at the voice from out of the crowd below her. The river of townspeople parted, and there he was, in the same outfit he'd been wearing the night before but now the khakis and blue button-down were wrinkled, as if he'd slept in them. Although judging by the bruise-colored shadows under his eyes, Matt hadn't gotten a lot of sleep the night before.

Stomping on her instinctive urge to ask if he was all right, Taylor gathered as much dignity as she could while standing there with an ice cream cone slowly melting over her hand. "I didn't get to my phone in time. What did you need?"

"I wanted to find you."

"Well, you've found me." The ice cream situation was getting seriously messy. Taylor gave up and started licking to control the damage. Maybe it made her look like a five-year-old, but at least it kept her from having to meet Matt's gaze.

"We need to talk."

Taylor controlled her flinch by sitting in one of the rocking chairs usually occupied by the town gossips, two old guys who pretended to play checkers at the table set up between the chairs but who actually used their vantage point in front of the hardware store in the middle of Main Street to make note of every interesting happening in the town.

"I said what I needed to say last night," she told him, turning back to her ice cream cone. "I don't want to pretend it didn't happen, and go on like before watching you and Dakota ride off into the sunset together. So if that's what you're here to tell me—"

"It's not," Matt broke in. "And maybe you got to say what you needed to last night, but I didn't. So when I said 'we need to talk' I misspoke. I meant, I need to talk and you need to listen. Do you want a napkin?"

"Nope." Taylor met his stare and held it as she defiantly licked a dribble of green-tinged cream off her wrist before giving up and tossing the rest in the trashcan by the door.

She could see Matt's Adam's apple bob as he swallowed. "Okay then. Here's the deal. My dad is an asshole."

The raw disappointment in Matt's voice drilled through the walls Taylor had erected around her heart. Emotion started to trickle out, sympathy and love and the desire to hold Matt's hand and tell him everything would be all right, but Taylor plugged up the hole. She couldn't afford any leaks. "I know. I saw his rap sheet."

"He hit my mom," Matt said, sinking in the rocking chair across from Taylor. He stared out across the town square, but Taylor had a feeling he wasn't seeing the smiling people milling around buying cotton candy and getting their kids' faces painted. Matt was lost in a memory of his life before he came to Sanctuary Island—a life he was suddenly viewing from a new perspective. "She never told me why we had to leave Charlottesville and come here, or why she didn't like for me to talk to Dad . . . not that he made much of an effort to talk to me. Until I looked him up and told him exactly where to find us."

The urge to comfort overwhelmed Taylor's defenses. "Hey, I thought it was a good idea, too, remember? You couldn't have known what he was really like."

Matt turned his head far enough to catch Taylor's eyes, and the misery she saw in his face shook her. "He had a gun. In a bag hidden behind the cottage, he had a gun. He brought it with him. Here, to Sanctuary Island. To my house, where my mother lives. The house I told him how to find."

"Oh my—Matt." Taylor clenched her hands

around the rocker's arms to stop herself from reaching out to him. "But he didn't get a chance to use it. Everyone is safe. Nothing happened."

"Because of you."

Taylor felt her ears go hot with embarrassment at the way he was staring at her. "No, not really. I didn't do anything. Sheriff Shepard was the one who—"

"I know, and I'm going to thank her, too, but Taylor. You were the one who put it all together and had the guts to tell my mom what was happening. She said the restraining order was your idea."

"I wanted to keep him away from you," she admitted softly. "And it didn't work, anyway."

"But because of you, Sheriff Shepard knew who he was, and she stopped him before he could come inside and do . . . whatever he planned to do with that gun. So thank you."

A thank-you. That's what Matt wanted to say. And Taylor got it, she did—what happened last night changed everything Matt thought about his past, and if it had gone another way, it could have changed his future forever. It made sense that he'd be preoccupied with that, and not with her dumb, blurted out confession of love.

So Taylor pasted on a polite smile and stood up. "You're welcome. But I really didn't do anything. It was mostly Sheriff Shepard. Now, if that's all, I'd better go find my dad. I'm sure he's looking for me."

He wasn't. The ferry wasn't due to arrive for another hour, and that was when they'd agreed to meet up by the pier, but Matt didn't need to know that.

"That's not all," Matt protested, lunging out of his chair to block her path. "I wanted to tell you that Dakota broke up with me."

A tiny bomb exploded in Taylor's head. She blinked, dizzy for a second, but when the smoke cleared she narrowed her eyes on Matt's hopeful face. What did he think, that now he was single, Taylor would be happy to step in as replacement girlfriend? "I'm sorry," she said stiffly. "That sucks."

"No, it doesn't." Matt scrubbed both hands through his hair, blowing out a frustrated breath. "Man, I'm messing this all up. I knew she was going to when I called her this morning, because I told her I decided to go to Stanford instead of UVA."

"Oh." Taylor managed a genuine smile, even as her heart turned to stone. Stanford. Three thousand miles away. "I'm really happy for you. It's what you've wanted for a long time."

Matt laughed darkly, a manic light sparking in his eyes. "What I've wanted for a long time . . . Tay, you have to know that's *you*."

She stiffened all over in disbelief. "Dating someone else for the last year was a funny way of showing it."

"I didn't know you wanted me back," Matt protested. "That night we almost kissed, down at the cove—you told your dad we were just friends. And I thought, fine. I can do just friends. You're my *best* friend."

Taylor swallowed and crossed her arms over her chest. "Right. And Dakota was your girlfriend. Until she dumped you and now suddenly you're telling me you want me? How dumb and desperate do you think I am?"

"Tay, please. I don't think that at all. Look, Dakota was a mistake. I see that now, but I thought love was about making a commitment and sticking to it. The way I used to wish my parents had done."

He leaned his hands on the wrought-iron railing that bordered the hardware store's front stoop, his back a long, tensed line of unhappiness. The walls around Taylor's heart shook with the force of emotions trying to escape. At this point, the raging torrent was only held back by fear.

"And now?" she managed to ask.

Matt hung his head, and Taylor's fingers itched to brush through the short, bristly hairs at the nape of his neck. "Now . . . I think love is about putting the other person's needs before yours. Like when my mom let me blame her for the divorce so I wouldn't have to know how bad my dad is."

He turned to prop his hips on the railing and gave her a smile. "Or the way you encouraged me to follow my dreams," he said. "Even when you knew they'd take me away from you."

Taylor closed her eyes. She could feel the dam about to break, to drown her in the rising tide of feelings. "So what. Any decent friend would have done the same."

With a rueful laugh, Matt said, "That's probably true, and maybe I should've read the signs when Dakota did the opposite."

Taylor couldn't help but give him the side eye for that one. "Duh, you think?"

"I know, I know." Matt held up his hands, distracting her with the way his shirt sleeves were rolled to the elbow, exposing his strong, tanned forearms. "I've got a lot to learn about love. My point is . . ."

He cleared his throat. Then with a determined set to his mouth, he stepped away from the railing and clasped Taylor's ice-cream sticky fingers in his. "My point is, I want to learn about love with you. If we're together, we can figure it out. And . . ."

Taylor didn't give him a chance to say what else he wanted, because inside her the dam had finally broken. Love, longing, giddy happiness, and the culmination of a lot of daydreams came spilling out and all she could do was lean up on her toes and kiss him.

With a groan, Matt untangled their fingers and curved his arms around her back, pressing her close. His kiss was confident but still searching, as if he really did want to learn her by heart. Taylor melted faster than homemade ice cream on the first day of summer.

When the need for air finally pulled them apart, Matt gasped, "You didn't let me finish."

"There's more?" Taylor tucked her nose into his neck, right where it sloped into his broad, muscled shoulder. She'd had her eye on that spot for a long time.

"Yeah." She could hear him swallow. What could he be about to ask that he'd be uncertain of now? Curious, she tipped her head back to catch him licking his lips nervously. "I want to defer my Stanford admission for a year and go backpacking around the world with you. If you'll have me."

"Matt!" Taylor wasn't proud of the squeal she made just then, but it couldn't be helped. "Of course I'll have you! Every time I pictured the trip, even when I knew I'd be walking the streets of London or climbing the Spanish Steps in Rome alone, I always imagined you at my side."

He kissed her again and a wave of happiness washed over Taylor, nearly knocking her off her feet. Or maybe that was the way Matt weakened her knees by skimming his hands up the sides of her neck to cup the shape of her head in his hands so he could gaze down at her.

"And when we're done seeing the world," he said, "and we get our degrees, we'll come home to Sanctuary Island."

"This place will always be home to me," Taylor agreed, turning in Matt's arms to gaze out over the crowd walking, talking, laughing, living under the 'Welcome to Sanctuary' sign that stretched across Main Street. "No matter how far we travel, it will be here for us, waiting with open arms."

"You helped me learn to love it here," Matt said, pressing a kiss to her hair, right above her ear. "But I wouldn't be surprised to find out that no matter where we go, I'll feel at home—as long as I'm with you."

Taylor savored the feeling of pure happiness, like bubbles bursting in her chest, until the buzz of her phone distracted her. "Who's calling me now?" she wondered, frowning down at the screen.

Andie Shepard. Thumbing the answer button, Taylor said, "Hi Sheriff. What's up?"

The conversation lasted only a few minutes, but they were enough to widen Taylor's eyes and get her adrenaline jumping. When she clicked the phone off, she raised her eyebrows at Matt. "So. You wanted to thank Sheriff Shepard? I've got the perfect way."

Sam parked the truck he'd borrowed from Windy Corner as close to the pier as he could get it, which wasn't all that close since the festival in the town square was directly in his path. This would have to be good enough.

He ran around to the back to let Queenie out of the trailer, praying that she stayed calm through the walk down to the docks. His work with her over the last two months had definitely helped, but she was still skittish and easily startled. And, of course, being ripped away from her soul mate, Lucky, had already riled her up.

"I'm sorry, girl," Sam said, unlatching the trailer door. "But we have to leave now and Lucky's not ready to come with us."

If Sam left it any longer, he might not be able to force himself to go, and damn the consequences.

"I wouldn't do that, if I were you."

The steady voice from behind him made Sam lean his forehead against the cold metal of the trailer door for a brief moment. "Andie. You found my note."

"I did." Her hand appeared beside his head, gently relatching the trailer door and sliding the bolt home. "Talk to me, Sam. Where are you going and why are you taking Queenie?"

The ferry horn sounded again, closer this time, and panic shot into Sam's bloodstream. "Please, Andie, you've gotta let me go. I need to get Queenie away from here before—"

He stopped, the lie sitting on his tongue like a rock. He clenched his fists, unable to bring himself to lie any longer.

"Before her rightful owner arrives and finds her here," Andie finished, still in that calm, steady tone.

Sam's brain exploded. He gaped at her, probably looking like a landed fish gasping for oxygen, but honestly. "Well, damn. Is there anything you miss?"

"Plenty," Andie said, with a wry shrug. "For instance, the fact that you're a fugitive from justice."

Defeat wanted to drag him down, but Sam squared his shoulders under the burden of his own brutal choices. "I know you've got no reason to trust me, but I swear to you, I had to take her. In the eyes of the law, she's property—not a living, breathing creature with the ability to feel pain and fear. There is no justice for an animal like Queenie, not without my help."

The words ground out of him like shells crushed underfoot, but Andie only smiled. It was a sad smile that didn't reach her gorgeous eyes. "I've got the best reason in the world to trust you," she said slowly. "I love you, and I know you love me, too. And more than that, I know you. Queenie's legal owner abused her, didn't he?"

"Yes. He found out she has a heart murmur, which isn't life threatening but would make it almost impossible to sell her and recoup the hundreds of thousands he paid for her. She's insured for millions, though—worth more dead than alive, unless anyone finds out about the heart murmur. So he bought off the vet who did the exam, but thank God, the vet had second thoughts."

"And he came to you."

Sam nodded briskly, flooded with urgency to get away, get gone before the bounty hunters showed up and endangered everyone he held dear. "The vet told me about the heart murmur. And he also told me he'd filled a prescription for Queenie for a medication that would be deadly for a horse with her condition."

"Her owner was going to poison her for the insurance money."

"Gradually, bit by bit," Sam agreed, the sick cruelty of it twisting his guts. "He was killing her."

"Okay, I completely see why she needed to be removed from her owner's custody," Andie said, putting her hands on her hips. "But why not go to the authorities?"

Sam snorted. "You mean, like the ones who

trumped up charges and had me imprisoned for a crime I didn't commit?"

"That was a different situation," Andie argued. "A wealthy, connected family, corrupt police . . ."

Weariness weighed down Sam's soul. "Queenie's legal owner is Garry Wallace."

Andie froze. "The lieutenant governor of Virginia," she clarified weakly. "Well. Crap."

"Exactly." Sam pressed a hand against the closed trailer door. "I couldn't risk it. I know how these things go. It's hard enough going through proper channels to get an abused animal rescued—in most states, horses are still regarded as livestock. Their owners can basically do whatever they want to them. Even when the abuse is flagrant, it can take months to get the official wheels turning. Queenie didn't have months."

Andie nodded to herself, as if he'd confirmed something she already believed. "Okay, that's what I needed to know."

Stepping up close to Sam, Andie put her hand beside his where it rested on the latched door of the trailer, then banged it loudly, twice. With a rumble, the truck's engine roared to life. Startled, Sam darted around the side of the trailer only to see Jo Ellen give him a cheery salute through the open driver's window before she pulled the trailer away from the curb, taking Queenie with her.

Chapter Twenty-Four

"What the hell are you doing?" Sam snarled, his big body going tense.

"I'm proving to you that you don't have to go it alone anymore, since you obviously don't believe it yet."

"You mean . . ."

"I'm not confiscating Queenie to turn her over to the authorities." Andie faced him down, head held high and voice sure. "I'm helping you steal her."

Sam's jaw dropped, then clenched tightly as his eyes darkened with regret. "This is exactly why I tried to leave. Andie, don't do this. Don't let me ruin your life."

Some last bit of worry or doubt that had lain coiled in Andie's belly melted away. "You left to save us," she said, aware of the huskiness of her own voice and not even trying to hide it. "But Sam, we don't need to be rescued. I'm not an abused horse you have to save. I can make my own judgment calls and my own choices, and I'll stand by them."

The muscles of his shoulders bunched under his

faded black T-shirt. "This is a bad call," he said baldly. "You have Caitlin to think about—what if your brother never comes home? You're all she's got. You can't get involved in something like this, Andie."

Andie went toe-to-toe with Sam, poking a stiff finger into his chest. "Don't tell me what I can't do. You think I could look Caitlin in the face if I let the horse she loves get sent back to certain death? If I am going to be her only parental figure," she said, voice breaking, "I'm sure as hell going to try to show her how to be strong, to stand up for what she believes in, and to protect those who can't protect themselves."

Visibly conflicted, Sam frowned. "Where is Caitlin, anyway?"

"She's with Taylor and Matt."

The ferry horn blew again, piercingly loud. Sam looked around, apparently just now noticing that the town square had cleared out completely. Only a few stragglers remained, tidying up their booths and tables before hurrying down the hill to the docks.

Sam turned back to her, and from the grim determination hardening his jaw, Andie knew he was about to make one final appeal. "Please," he rasped. "Call Jo back. Let me take Queenie and get on the ferry, and get her out of here before the men who are looking for us make it to Sanctuary Island."

"It's too late for that, I'm afraid," Andie told him, aching to take his hand and squeeze it for reassurance. "I pulled in a few favors and got in touch with the ferryboat captain. Along with the crowd of graduation guests, most of whom are related to Sanctuary residents, there are three large gentlemen who don't appear to be part of the onboard graduation festivities. According to the ferry's records, there are three names I don't recognize as being connected to

Sanctuary Island in any way—but when I got Ivy to run them through the system, they popped up."

Sam shook his head as if dazed. "Oh my God, Andie. How many people are you dragging into this?"

"That's what I'm trying to tell you," she said, impatience snapping at her heels. "No one has to be dragged. People here care about you, and they care about keeping that horse safe. Once I explained the situation, no one thought twice about helping out."

He stared at her for a long moment. "I never expected any of this."

"I know." He looked so dumbfounded, Andie had to lean up and kiss his scratchy cheek. "Don't worry. You'll get used to it."

"To what?"

"Being loved." Andie gave him a smile that came from the bottom of her heart, then hooked her arm through his elbow and started pulling him toward the docks. Doing something bad for a very good reason was turning out to be as satisfying as upholding the letter of the law had ever been. "Come on, we need to get down there."

"What for?" Sam resisted, setting his weight against her, and Andie sighed. She'd never budge him if he didn't want to go. "Andie, stop. What's the plan? I mean, Jo can take Queenie back to Windy Corner, but they're bound to search the biggest stables on the island."

"Jo's not driving the trailer to Windy Corner," Andie started, but a loud cheer from down the hill distracted her. "Sam, please. We need to get down there and confront those men when they get off the ferry. Everything hinges on it."

"Andie—"

"Sam." She reached up to cup his face between her palms and stare into his beautiful, confused brown eyes. "Can you trust me?"

The fact that he didn't hesitate for even an instant warmed Andie all the way down to the soles of her feet. "I do trust you."

She rewarded him with a kiss, the brush of their lips settling something in her soul even as the rest of Andie geared up for a fight.

"Come on, then." She grabbed his hand and ran for the docks. "Let's give those thugs a big Sanctuary Island welcome."

Sam's mind was racing faster than his feet, trying to figure out what Andie was doing and how he could talk her out of it. Before he could come up with anything, they were pushing through the crowd of Sanctuary Island residents who'd packed the parking lot by the pier where the ferry had docked.

A warm slap on the back startled Sam. He looked around, but everyone in his vicinity was smiling at him, or nodding solemnly. A tiny, white-haired lady leaning on a cane winked at him.

"What's going on?" he muttered to Andie out of the corner of his mouth. "Why are they all looking at me like that?"

"I told you, they like you. Now stop flirting with Miss Ruth and look for the lieutenant governor's men!"

Passengers were already pouring out of the ferry, which had been decked out in streamers and balloons in green and white, Sanctuary High's school colors. All around them, teenagers and their parents shouted, waved over their visiting family. There were hugs and congratulations, enough noise to scare the flock of gulls who lived on the Summer Harbor boathouse into taking wing, adding their loud shrieks to the pandemonium.

And in the center of it all, Sam spotted three huge, hulking muscle men cutting through the happy townsfolk like sharks through a school of clownfish. People shrank from them as they passed, as if they gave off a palpable air of barely contained violence.

At his side, Andie tensed and her hand went to her belt where she usually wore her Taser. But she wasn't in uniform—because of him, Sam remembered with a stab of self-hatred—and she dropped her hand to her side.

Sam stepped in front of her, confronting the hired enforcers dead on. "Hello, boys. Looking for someone?"

The tallest one, a Teutonic bruiser with an almost colorless complexion and pale straw-colored hair, narrowed his light gray eyes. "Yeah. Sam Brennan. That you?"

"It is. Who's asking?"

"Lieutenant Governor Garry Wallace sent us." When the man smiled, a scar at the corner of his mouth pulled his lips into a snarl. "Come with us now, Mr. Brennan."

"He's not going anywhere with you, Mr. Struecher," Andie said, stepping up to Sam's side.

The way Struecher's pale eyes zeroed in on Andie made the hairs on the back of Sam's neck rise. "And who are you?"

"A friend of Sam's," she said, with a casual glance around the crowd that had gathered around this little confrontation. "Sam has a lot of friends on Sanctuary Island, as it happens."

The pair of guys behind Struecher looked around, seeming surprised at the serious nods, scowls, and crossed arms they saw in the crowd. Sam sympathized with them—he could hardly believe what he was seeing, either. Struecher never took his eyes off Andie, though.

"I wonder," he said. "Would Mr. Brennan have so many friends if they knew he'd stolen a horse from the lieutenant governor's own stables?"

"They might ask to see proof," said a querulous old voice from out of the crowd. "Rather than taking some muscle-bound hooligan's word for it."

Andie sucked in a breath beside him, and when Sam saw who'd spoken, he understood why. Dabney Leeds hobbled to the front of the crowd, rapping people's legs with his cane if they didn't get out of his way fast enough. Trailing behind him on a plaid leather leash was a white bulldog wearing a green and white dog-size varsity letterman's jacket and a long-suffering expression.

"Now, what's this all about, Sheriff?" Dabney asked, directing the question to Andie.

To her credit, she never missed a beat. With a cool tilt of her chin in the direction of Struecher and his guys, she said, "These gentlemen believe they have the right to come onto our island and remove someone without a warrant or any proof of wrongdoing. Unless—I'm sorry." Andie glanced back at Struecher. "*Do* you have a warrant?"

The furious way he clenched his jaw was answer enough. "Two months ago, Queen's Ransom, a very valuable Thoroughbred mare, disappeared from the lieutenant governor's barn. Our investigation shows that Sam Brennan arrived on this island with a mare two months ago. It's not proof, but here is Brennan. Where is the horse? One look at it will prove that it's the lieutenant governor's property."

Sam tensed. Struecher kept calling Queenie "it," as if she was an inanimate object. Out of sight of the thugs, Andie put a warning hand on the fist he didn't remember clenching.

"I have no idea where the lieutenant governor's horse is," Sam was able to say with complete honesty, meeting Struecher's assessing stare without flinching.

"Of course, he admits nothing," one of the thugs sneered, "but someone on this island must have witnessed his arrival."

"Hmmm," said Miss Ruth, the woman who'd made eyes at Sam earlier. "I don't remember a horse, and I definitely remember when Sam arrived. A woman takes note of a man like that."

"I'm not a woman," said a male voice behind Sam. "But I'm pretty observant. I think I'd know if a man who's been living in my house for two months were a criminal."

Sam turned in time to see his cousin Penny's rich, handsome husband step forward to stand at his back in a blatant show of support. Sam gave Dylan Harrington a short nod, more touched than he knew how to express. Gratitude dried his throat—not only for the support, but for the fact that Dylan appeared to be alone. Which meant he'd accomplished the impossible and convinced Penny to stay home and out of trouble, for once.

"What about the ferry captain? He will be our proof." Struecher was going to grind his molars to dust if he kept clamping his jaw like that.

"Well, bring him out," Dabney Leeds demanded

irritably. "Let's get this business over with, we have a graduation to celebrate."

Sam's heart sped up as the crowd parted to let the grizzled old captain through. Sam remembered him from the day he'd arrived, mostly because he was wearing the same neon-green bowling jersey in some shiny material that caught the light. His name, Buddy, was stitched over the right breast in hot-pink thread. "Yeah?"

"Do you have records of this man's arrival on Sanctuary Island two months ago?" Andie asked in her best official business voice.

Buddy spat a thoughtful stream of tobacco juice into the empty soda can he held. "Nope."

"No records?" Struecher insisted. "That's ridiculous. You must have a ship's manifesto of some kind, for insurance purposes. I demand that you produce it immediately."

"Can't."

Sam had to admire Buddy's economy with words. A strange sensation was gathering under his breastbone, hot and buoyant as if he'd swallowed a helium balloon. It took a minute, but he finally recognized it as hope.

Somehow, Andie seemed to have gotten the entire town in on her crazy scheme. He couldn't fathom how such a feat was even possible.

"Don't keep the logs for longer than a couple weeks," Buddy was explaining in a bored tone. "Ain't any kind of point to it."

"The point," Struecher ground out, "is that the lieutenant governor's stolen horse is on this island somewhere, and I intend to find it."

"Gosh," piped up a woman wearing a trim shirtwaist dress covered in polka dots, with her hair in sleek waves like she was on her way to a sock hop. "That sounds an awful lot like you want to conduct an illegal search of private property. Can they do that, Sheriff?"

"No, Ivy, I'm afraid not," Andie replied calmly, hooking her thumbs in her belt and staring at Struecher and his goons, implacable as the dawn. "If these men want to search any part of Sanctuary Island, they're going to need a proper warrant."

"Which I'm afraid may be difficult to acquire," Dabney Leeds announced with visible satisfaction. "Since everyone on this island is prepared to swear that when Sam Brennan arrived on that ferry two months ago, he was alone."

Sam glanced around the group of townsfolk. Lots of them were familiar faces—the woman who owned the hardware store where he'd picked up leather polish, the parents of Sam's favorite Windy Corner Therapeutic Riding client, Rachel, a ten-year-old girl with Down Syndrome . . . but there were plenty of people he'd never met or spoken to. Yet here they were, standing shoulder to shoulder in solidarity to protect a man they barely knew and a horse they were denying even existed.

It was like nothing Sam had ever experienced. He could only imagine that this was what having a family felt like.

"I may have been alone when I got here," he said, loudly enough for everyone to hear, "but I'm not alone anymore. So go on back to the lieutenant governor and tell him he's got the wrong idea about me."

Struecher opened his mouth to reply, but when he hesitated, Andie said softly, "Go on, Kurt. You did your best. There's nothing here for you, and if the lieutenant governor is smart, he'll cut his losses and move on."

"Yes," Dabney Leeds agreed, banging his cane on the ground. "Tell Garry from me that this is a fight he can't win. Much like his next election will be, without my contribution to his coffers. I'm not interested in giving money to animal abusers. I'd rather support those who fight for the cause of protecting animals. That makes Sam Brennan a hero in my book, not a criminal."

Struecher glanced from Leeds to Andie, scanning the determined faces of the gathered townspeople before landing on Sam again. His scarred mouth twitched, as if he was fighting a smile. "I'll convey your message to my employer. It's possible this business has become more trouble than it's worth to him."

With a sharp jerk of his head, he sent his silent pair of back-up goons hulking off toward the ferry. Sam started to let go of the breath he'd been holding, almost unable to believe everything that had happened in the last few minutes, but then Kurt Struecher turned back one last time.

"Good-bye, Mr. Brennan," he said, holding out his huge, battle-hardened hand. "It's rare, you know. This kind of loyalty. I hope you appreciate it."

"Believe me," Sam replied, shaking the man's hand with a surreal feeling of watching the whole scene from outside his body, "I do."

Struecher nodded as if satisfied before shaking Andie's hand too. "If you are ever in need of work," he told her, passing her a white card embossed with his name and number, "please call me."

"Excuse me," Dabney Leeds interrupted imperiously. "But Sheriff Shepard already has a job."

Trust Leeds to see which way the political wind was blowing and throw his weight behind the winner. Dabney Leeds never backed a loser.

Andie shrugged at Struecher. "Guess I'm unavailable for now. Thanks for the thought, though." And she pocketed the card, grinning when Leeds harrumphed in annoyance.

Struecher's gaze turned to the top of the hill leading up to the town square, the road bordered with maritime pines and the brilliant blue sky stretching overhead. "This is a nice place, your Sanctuary Island."

And with that, he turned on his heel with military precision and marched back to the ferry to join his men. Buddy spat another stream of tobacco juice and ambled after them to raise the gangplank and ready the ferry for the return trip to the mainland.

Sam watched them go, still in a daze, until Andie threw her arms around him.

"We did it," she said into his ear. "They're gone. You and Queenie are safe."

"Thank you," Sam said, just for her. Then, more loudly, "Thank you, everyone. This town is amazing. There's no place like it. I've never had a home, not really—but I can't imagine any place better to put down roots and start a new life than Sanctuary Island."

All around them, people cheered and clapped. Dylan shook him by the shoulder, and Miss Ruth tugged him away from Andie and pulled him down for a loud, smacking kiss right on the mouth. Lightheaded from the adrenaline crash, Sam reeled from well-wisher to well-wisher as it seemed like every person on the island wanted to hug and congratulate him.

"But how did you all even know what was going down?" Sam finally managed to ask Andie.

"I had Wyatt Hawkins send out one of his special bulletins," Andie answered. "We've really got to get you on the island email loop."

"And everyone read it," Sam said, still trying to piece it together. "And somehow, you got every person in town to agree to the same story?"

"This is Sanctuary Island, boy," Dabney Leeds declared, stooping creakily to pet his panting bulldog. "The answer is in the name. Since the town was first founded, this island has been a sanctuary for those with no place else to go—especially wild horses. We don't hold with cruelty to animals on this island. No sir."

"But still," Sam shook his head. "The lengths you all went to."

"Mmm," Andie agreed, shooting Leeds an arch look. "Including reinstating me as Sheriff on the spot. Does this mean you're withdrawing your grandson from the election?"

"Nash is an amazing young man," Leeds said, waving away the entire situation as if he hadn't plotted against Andie's campaign for weeks. "He'll find some other use for his many talents here on Sanctuary Island. We already have a sheriff."

Andie broke into a huge smile, and Sam couldn't resist the urge to sweep her up and twirl her around. Everything in him wanted to let go, to believe in this perfect happy ending, but he'd lived too many years one step ahead of disaster. It was tough not to look over his shoulder to see what was coming for him.

Letting Andie's toes touch the ground, Sam stared down into her relaxed, jubilant face. "They could still come back," he said, fear and worry like a barbed-wire cage around his heart. "If they get a warrant to search Jo's barn, they'll find her."

"No, they won't. Come on, let me show you." Andie stepped backwards, her eyes bright with excitement. She kept Sam's hand clasped in hers, and he followed her.

After this, Sam knew he would follow her anywhere.

Chapter Twenty-Five

"This is the road down to Heartbreak Cove," Sam said, staring out the SUV's windshield.

"Where you found Lucky." Andie steered carefully down the double-rutted, unpaved lane. The wax myrtles and groundsels were taking over again, slowly growing over the tracks made by vehicles. If she didn't find another couple of teenagers necking out here so she could assign them the community service of clearing back the plant life, pretty soon this lane would be impassable.

Maybe that was a good thing, she decided as the SUV rolled to a stop next to the Windy Corner horse trailer. *This place is meant to be wild and free. Maybe we should give it back to the wilderness.*

"What are we . . ."?

Sam's voice died out as he gazed out over the waving sea of cordgrass and spotted the horse trailer parked by the willow tree. "Andie. We're going to turn her loose."

"Not just her," Andie said, cutting the engine and opening her door.

Sam met her at the back of the SUV, beside the horse trailer's open back doors. He peered into it, seeming unsurprised to find Queenie still tied up inside. But next to her, nuzzling affectionately at Queenie's neck, was a gray-dappled wild colt.

"Jo drove the trailer back to Windy Corner where she picked up Lucky, and then I asked her to drop the horses off here. Taylor and Matt brought Caitlin along with them to let her say good-bye to Queenie, and then they drove Jo home." Andie was aware she was babbling, but she couldn't seem to stop. "So far, none of them have done anything they'd need to feel guilty about, and I wanted to keep it that way."

"You thought of everything." Sam's voice was neutral, his expression unreadable in profile as he studied the two horses he'd worked so hard to rehabilitate.

Andie noticed she was twisting her hands in her white cotton shirttails and tried to cut it out. "Well, the turning loose thing was Jo's idea, actually. She said you'd done it before, when you weren't able to get an abused horse to the point of trusting humans again."

Closing his eyes, Sam huffed out a laugh. "So she knew about that."

"I know Queenie isn't a hopeless case, and she was never mistreated in quite the same way as some of the horses you've rescued, but this land is protected. There are strict rules about who can and can't have contact with the wild horses, so even if Lieutenant governor Wallace tries to come back here with a warrant—"

"Queenie will be safe," Sam finished. He glanced down at Andie for the first time since he figured out her plan, and the wonder in his dark chocolate eyes brought a lump of emotion to Andie's throat. "Andie. I can't believe . . . You're amazing."

The praise disconcerted her. She tucked her hair behind her ears and gestured nervously at the pair of horses. "It makes sense. And I thought, if we release Lucky and Queenie together, they can start their own band."

"A second chance at love and family," Sam said quietly, reaching out slowly to slide his hands around her waist and pull her in tight. He dropped his forehead to rest it against hers. "I can hardly believe you're doing all of this. Andie Shepard, defender of the law."

Even though the teasing lilt in his tone was gentle, Andie pulled back. She wanted to make sure he understood. "I know the law says I should turn Queenie over to her rightful owner, but I can't believe that's the *right* thing to do. Being with you—loving you—has given me a new faith in my instincts, even when they don't agree with the letter of the law."

The corner of Sam's mouth kicked up in a wry half-grin. "I turned you into a rebel."

"Maybe," Andie said, shrugging. "But a rebel with a good cause. I believe in what you do, Sam. And I want to help."

"You already have," he told her, shaking his head. "More than you should. If anything blows back on you, or the town, because of this . . ."

Andie put her hand flat against his chest, feeling the steady thud of his heart vibrate through her palm. "Stop. I made my choice. We all did. Sanctuary Island is behind you, Sam. You're one of us now, part of the community, whether you like it or not."

"You too, Sheriff." Sam raised a pleased brow. "I guess neither of us is an outsider anymore."

Warmth and acceptance lit Andie up from the inside. "You're right. We're home."

Bending his head, Sam sealed it with a kiss that sent sharply pleasurable tingles cascading over Andie's whole body. When he lifted his head, he said, "Home. I like that."

A short whinny from inside the trailer reminded Andie that they weren't alone. "Are you ready to do this thing?"

Sam grinned, an eager light of anticipation gleaming in his eyes. "Ready as I'll ever be."

Together they set up the ramp and unhooked the horses, backing them carefully out of the trailer. Andie held Queenie's lead the way she'd learned during her volunteer hours at Windy Corner, and scratched her short fingernails along the line of the mare's coarse mane.

"Thank you for bringing him to me," she whispered into Queenie's long, sensitive ear while Sam cautiously wrangled the more-volatile wild colt down the ramp.

The mare craned her neck to nudge her nose into Andie's pockets, looking for a treat. With a sigh, Andie produced one last peppermint and stroked the side of Queenie's face as she crunched it. The mare gave her an expectant look from her deep liquid eyes, a long silent moment of communication that made Andie wonder just how much Queenie understood. Maybe it was crazy, but Andie almost felt as if the mare was thanking her, too.

"Okay," Sam said softly, even as the wild colt's ears pricked and his head lifted to scent the salty breeze. "Time to go home, Lucky."

With a deft move, Sam slipped the soft halter over Lucky's ears and turned him loose with a fond slap to the hindquarters. The colt immediately cantered away, down the sloping hill toward the beach, but when he realized he was alone, he stopped. Glancing back over his shoulder, neck arched and long, tangled mane blowing in the wind, Lucky trumpeted a call for his mate.

Queenie jerked her head once, the lead rope almost flying out of Andie's hands before she tightened her grip, startled. "I think she's ready to go with him."

Sam grabbed the sides of the halter with both hands and pressed a fast kiss to the white starburst on Queenie's black forehead. "Be safe and happy," he told her. "And live a good life."

Stepping back, Sam nodded to Andie, who felt her insides clench. She offered him the rope. "Do you want to do it?"

"This is your plan, sweetheart," Sam said with a quirked smile. "You do the honors. Unless you want plausible deniability."

"I think it's a bit late for that." With fingers that shook, Andie unbuckled the halter that had Queenie's name scrawled over a bit of masking tape on the side. It took her a second, but she got it off the mare in a jangle of hardware. Queenie shook her head, as if she enjoyed the freedom of movement.

Across the salt marsh, the wild colt called to her again, and Queenie whickered a response. She stepped closer to Sam, bumping him with her head hard enough to knock him back a pace, but Sam leaned into it and slung an arm over her withers. "Go on," he told her, choking on the words. "Get out of here."

With one last lip at Sam's caressing hand, Queenie trotted away, picking up speed until she met Lucky, who wheeled and paced her as she thundered across the beach. The horses' churning hooves kicked up sand and splashed through the foamy shallows, their tails streaming behind them like pennants caught in a gale.

Andie's heart swelled until it pressed at the confines of her ribs, a solid ache that felt strangely good. "We let them go, released them into the wild. It's strange, but *I'm* the one who feels free."

Sam's strong arms wrapped around her from behind, his broad chest against her back. "You gave them a new life," he murmured into her hair. "Together."

She hummed with pleasure as anticipation, hope, and joy welled up in her chest. Spinning in his arms, Andie crashed her mouth into his with reckless abandon. She felt everything at once, as if the entire universe were contained in a single kiss, in the wild freedom of her body against Sam's.

"Now it's our turn," she whispered against his lips before he deepened the kiss. Every touch was a promise, ever caress a vow for their future, and Andie gave herself up to it.

Amidst the near perfect joy of the moment, she winged a swift prayer of thanks up to the heavens—for the quirk of fate that had landed Sam Brennan, horse thief and ex-con, in the arms of the law of Sanctuary Island. For the family of her heart, the townspeople here, and for the family she'd created with Sam and Caitlin.

And even though no joy could be perfect for her until she could give her niece the knowledge of exactly what had happened to Owen, Andie seized the gift of this moment, and the gift of the man in her arms, and vowed never to let him go.

Epilogue

Landstuhl Regional Medical Center
Germany

Everything was darkness. Waves of pain crested and receded like the ocean. The soldier swam in that ocean, he didn't know how long. Time meant nothing. The words he heard in snatches from time to time meant nothing, either. If he got too close to the surface, to the patchy light drawing him up from the depths, the pain would wash over him and tumble him back under.

The soldier floated in the black depths and waited for the light to come back. It hurt—everything hurt—but beneath the need to escape the pain, a stronger need began to beat in time with the faint pulse of his heart.

Home.

Get home.

Home.

He didn't even know what that meant, couldn't picture "home" in his fractured, tormented mind, but he felt its draw like a hook in his chest. And every time the darkness threatened to drown him, the soldier kicked and flailed, lungs bursting and heart thundering, pushing himself closer to the surface where the pain waited. Because that was the way home. And he had to get there. Not just for himself, but for . . .

Loud beeping and frantic voices, hands pressing on his arms and legs, a burning rasp in his throat, and a hoarse voice shouting.

Owen Shepard, Sergeant First Class of the Army Rangers of the 3rd Battalion, 75th Rangers Regiment, woke up.

"Calm down," a German-accented voice said. "Sergeant, please. You must be calm."

Owen sucked in a shallow breath, and the shouting died away. He was the one who'd been shouting. The other voice leaned in nearer as the IV attached to Owen's left arm burned slightly. He couldn't see, everything was blurry white, and when he tried to lift his right hand to pull away the softness covering his face, nothing happened.

"You're in a military hospital," the voice said swiftly. "Med-evaced from Ramstein. You were in an explosion, but you are recovering."

The medic went on, detailing injuries, but it was all static in Owen's ears. He was messed up pretty bad. That was all he knew, and he'd known that even before he woke up.

Panic welled in Owen's chest as the dark ocean began to rise, sucking at his consciousness. Whatever the medic had injected in his IV worked fast. Before he slid under again, Owen gritted his teeth and forced his heavy right hand to move, grasping the medic's sleeve.

"Yes?" the German accent said. "What is it?"

Owen licked his dry, cracked lips. "Get me home for Christmas, Doc. My little girl is waiting for me."

Catch up on the Sanctuary Island series
by Lily Everett!

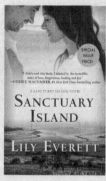

Available now from St. Martin's Paperbacks

Don't miss the Hero Project trilogy
by Lily Everett!

 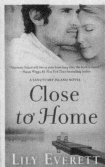 

Available now   Coming February 2017   Coming March 2017

from St. Martin's Paperbacks